ALWAYS A BROTHER

T0321578

ALWAYS A BROTHER

Michael Shenk

ELM HILL

A Division of
HarperCollins Christian Publishing

www.elmhillbooks.com

Always a Brother

Published in Nashville, Tennessee, by Elm Hill, an imprint of Thomas Nelson. Elm Hill and Thomas Nelson are registered trademarks of HarperCollins Christian Publishing, Inc.

Elm Hill titles may be purchased in bulk for educational, business, fund-raising, or sales promotional use. For information, please e-mail SpecialMarkets@ ThomasNelson.com.

Publisher's Note: This novel is a work of fiction. Names, characters, places, and incidents are either products of the author's imagination or used fictitiously. All characters are fictional, and any similarity to people living or dead is purely coincidental.

Scripture quotation is taken from the King James Version. Public domain.

Cover photography: Caroline Shenk

Library of Congress Cataloging-in-Publication Data

Library of Congress Control Number: 2019918917

ISBN 978-1-400327225 (Paperback)
ISBN 978-1-400327232 (Hardbound)
ISBN 978-1-400327249 (eBook)

DEDICATION

I dedicate this story to my wife, Jean
Devoted, talented, lovely, and gracious,
words that only begin to describe what I feel
when I see you. You've prayed Psalm 90:17 for
years – thank you for being the best partner ever.

Acknowledgement
and Thanks

Many thanks to Bill, Xandra, and Donavan for your guidance and advice. Thank you, Sharalyn, for the hours of editing and encouragement. Caroline, thank you for the cover photography and design ideas.

Thank you, Mom, for your shining example of how a person should live, and for reading me stories over and over and over. Dad, thanks for teaching me to read and for being a friend and brother as well as a father. Thanks to the best Mother-in-law ever, who has never stopped asking, "so when is that book coming out?" and to my late Father-in-law for inspiring me to try new things.

Thank you, Jean, Vincent, Stephen, Micaela and Caroline, for being the best family I could ever hope for and for the wonderful years we have already enjoyed together *(road trip!)*, and welcome Ashley, Jeff, Erika, and Davis – lucky us, lucky you – the best is yet to come! *Uno mas?*

Thank you to my grandparents; Grandpa Ron who expected the cutting edges of both men and steel to be sharp, and Grandpa Royden who lived his life like he plowed his fields – straight and true. Grandma Schweitzer made and served the finest popsicles in Idaho, I wish I could have another. Grandma Shenk, thanks for being an example of courage and for loving life, may your 96th year be the best one ever!

Finally, thank you to Mr. Lewis, Mr. Michener, Mr. Ludlum, Mr. Grisham, Mr. Smith, Mr. Burke, Mr. Peretti, Mr. Berton, and all the others who have enriched so many lives, including mine, something a good brother would do.

INTRODUCTION

Early Winter 1986 – Vanderhoof, British Columbia

The girl shivered. She slid her chair closer to the open oven. The electricity was on again, the hot stench of the dirty element pushed into the cold apartment. She wanted to go to the other room where the heater was running, but the crying made her sad, the noise was too much. A pink notebook was open, held to her leg by her elbow. It was snowing, and she wrote about it. She wrote about winter, and the apartment, and the fear. Her nose was running, and she wiped it on her sleeve. She wrote about being forced from her home. She wrote about the people who helped her. She wrote about being left by her family. She wrote about her boyfriend and being away from her unhappy home and how he made her feel.

She wrote more about him, and who she had thought he would be to her. She wrote about how happy she was until he left. She wrote how she was safe. Until he left. She wrote lines about being lonely.

She scooted her chair to the other side of the oven door and wondered who had turned on the electricity. She wrote about what it was like to not be noticed, or have nice clothes, or be pretty. She wrote about the old lady who brought her a box of food the day before Christmas.

She wrote about the nurses at the hospital. She wrote about her baby. She wrote that her father and stepmother were angry with her and how she let them down. She wrote about rules. She wrote about what her stepbrothers did to her, and how it made her feel and how she had no friends to talk to and how her mom called her a whore and her dad swore and told her it was her fault anyway and God hated her.

She cried.

She wrote about the chickadee that landed on her windowsill. She wondered if it was hungry. She wrote about being hungry. She wrote about two cans of tomato soup left on the shelf. She wrote about the nurse who visited her, and then came back with a pan of lasagna and baby clothes.

She wrote how she didn't know how to name her baby. Or how to feed him. Or what to do. She wrote that her sixteenth birthday was soon, and she had never had a birthday in town and had never had a birthday present. She wrote that her family had moved away. She wrote that she had nothing. She wrote about the man across the hall who had food. She wrote what she had to trade for food.

She went and looked at her baby. He was quiet now. The room was warmer.

She left the apartment and went across the hall and knocked on the door.

Early Summer, 1987 – Burnaby, British Columbia

He sighed and crossed his legs. According to his appointment book, the next client was a crier. He scanned his notes, deciding where to start. The door opened and she came in.

"Hello, Jan. I'm glad you came today." He rose from his desk, extending a welcome.

She sat, quiet, hands in her lap, waiting. She held tissues.

Later, he asked, "So, Jan, what are you thinking about work? Your time away is nearly complete, almost done."

She was still crying.

"I just don't know if I can go back!"

She fought to maintain composure, and mentally he shook his head, reviewing her background. She was an athlete, or had been, a track and soccer star in high school, had excelled in her studies of criminology, graduated high in her class, hailed from a prominent family in a major city. A real winner. But within her first three months as an RCMP officer, she had encountered a sorrow and pain so deep that he doubted she would recover. He waited, expression calm, deeply wishing for a cigarette; her time was almost up.

"It's just, I just feel … I feel so helpless!" She cried more.

"Jan, what are the segments, the pieces, that make you feel this way?" He spoke calmly, serene. Dying for a cigarette.

A flicker of anger, she tensed, shoulders hunching slightly. This was good.

"It's just not fair, and no one did anything about it!"

"Mmm-hmm." He nodded encouragingly, glasses hanging from his left hand.

"First, this girl was obviously struggling. A neighbour had reported that she thought maybe the girl was sleeping with men for food. We, I, didn't do anything!" She cried some more before speaking again.

"Then she disappeared, and I checked her apartment, and I didn't know she had a baby!" She was visibly angry, cheeks flushed now. "How was I supposed to know there was a baby in the box? There were no baby things, no crib, bottles."

She took a breath. "I know, I know, we've been over this before. It's not like it was my fault—but it *was!*"

He blew out his breath, a little too loudly, then coughed to cover his show of feelings. He lit a cigarette. Much better.

She ignored him and his flexing jaw, somehow deflating, the anger replaced by depression. "How can I be a police officer, supposedly *helping* people. I lived across the street from this girl. *Right across the street!* From a teenage girl who had a baby, no family, no food, no support, no one who even knew she needed help!"

"Do you want to talk about the diary, the one you found?" It irritated him that he continued to clarify his questions. He exhaled and pressed on.

He felt it might be painful but worth the risk if he could help her find a way to realize she was not to blame, not responsible for the horrendous neglect of a young girl. She was a victim herself, like two guys from his crew in Vietnam, still struggling today.

The rain traced lines on the filmed windows. Her crying steadied as he led her once again through the details she had found in the diary, and he took redundant notes.

Yes, she felt like the diary had been written for her. Yes, she knew the *Jan* written at the top of each page almost certainly stood for *January*. No, she was not the only person responsible for this girl.

He started a new paragraph, forcing his grip on the pen to relax.

Yes, when the girl had approached her shyly on the sidewalk, asking what to do when the heater and lights didn't work, and she told her to call her landlord, yes, that day she had told the girl her name.

He wrote on, smoke drifting from his second cigarette, wanting a drink.

No, she didn't think the girl even knew what a landlord was, and most likely moved in with a guy who had then moved away.

Yes, the girl had mentioned a boyfriend who had broken up with her, but probably had never had a boyfriend previously, and most likely didn't really understand what had happened. She hadn't appeared to be drinking or doing drugs, but seemed detached, distant, a ghost.

He was following the thought pattern but drifting somewhat. He nodded thoughtfully and absently, as she continued.

The diary had seemed to indicate that the girl's parents had withdrawn her from school when she was fourteen or fifteen because "she was stupid and didn't need school anyway," as she had written in one entry.

During a lull, he broke in quietly, "Jan, what do your senses tell us about the situation?"

"Well, I saw there was a problem …"

"And?"

"I should have done more about what I saw."

"Now Jan, let's not be negative here. Let's simply explore what your senses have to say."

"Well, yes, I saw there was a problem, and I did report it."

She tensed, ready to add the negative, which he forestalled smoothly "And then the next?"

This was familiar ground. "I felt something was wrong, and I did something about it."

"Mmm-hmm?" His mouth was dry, and he noticed he was flexing his jaw. He wanted a drink.

"I heard there was a problem and followed up on it." She stopped, blocking the negative comment that was to follow.

He was surprised when she looked up quietly, eyes hollow, locking on his. Her voice rose, and his neck tensed painfully with a sudden chill. He realized they were losing ground, and he may have been very, very unprepared for this session. He flinched when she shifted toward him in her chair. He looked up at her and stopped taking notes.

"The smell!" she stared at him, as if he should know. "It was terrible! All these empty soup cans, crammed in the cupboard under the sink, not rinsed. Lots of them, they smelled so bad! And the oven door was open. I thought something was burning, but it was only the oven, turned on 'high'. And then I went in the bathroom."

She stood abruptly, formidable, shifting from foot to foot. "In the bathroom, well, *the smell*. There were diapers on the floor behind the toilet, lots of diapers. But I still didn't know *she* had a baby!"

She was shrieking now. His receptionist would hear; she would know what to do.

"I still didn't know she had a *baby!* I ran down to the dumpster where I had carried the box of old, dirty clothes. I heard crying!"

She slammed her hands flat on his desk, leaning toward him. "I heard the baby crying in the box of clothes. The baby I dropped in the trash."

She collapsed to her knees, forehead on her forearms which were now flat on his desk, strident voice turning to a hollow whisper.

Between sobbing breaths, she forced out sentences. "I put a baby in the garbage. I only took him out just before the truck took it away, the garbage. I almost killed the baby."

This was a breakthrough. It hadn't been in the file or come up in earlier appointments. He was shocked, and then distracted further when the door burst open. The receptionist walked two steps into the office and stopped.

Rattled, he asked, "And how did this make you feel?"

The air seemed to leave the room. The words came from some deep and stupid place, a place to which he had never previously stooped.

The receptionist, large and grandmotherly, bustled forward and knelt beside the crying woman, hugging her to herself, turning the woman away from her therapist.

"There, there, my dear. Don't worry about how it made you feel. Let's just cry for a while." She turned slightly, glaring at her boss.

The woman cried, and then opened up, phrase after phrase.

"I feel so helpless to fix what I did. I wish I could go back and do everything over," she sobbed into a safe place. "We got the baby up to the hospital, and he was okay, later. He was so small and cold and sad."

She cried some more, and the receptionist moved her to the velour couch. She sat in the corner, pulling the young woman to lean against her, rocking her gently.

"The girl had been gone for two days, the people downstairs had heard the baby crying, but thought the girl was home. How could a baby cry for two days, alone, hungry and cold, and no one check? Why didn't they tell me there was a baby? How could I come and carry him down to the garbage with the other trash? I thought the box was full of dirty clothes and diapers! Who puts a baby in a cardboard box! Oh, God, how could this even happen?

The receptionist rocked and hugged and sent her boss to get hot chocolate.

"Sweetie, was the baby okay?"

"Yes, he was okay. I stayed at the hospital until he pulled through. Two big men, I think they were his uncles, maybe? Well, they came up to the hospital, and I told them what I knew."

She looked at the receptionist for the first time. "I was so scared of them; they were big and stern and so concerned. It was like they hadn't seen the baby before. Later I thought maybe they didn't know about him. I thought they would yell at me, but they just looked at me when I told them what happened. They only said a couple things. They asked about 'the mother'. We didn't even know at that point she had disappeared, like, for good."

She accepted a cup of hot chocolate from the counsellor and turned back to the receptionist.

"Then they asked what his name was. They didn't know the baby's name, and I didn't either. The nurse checked, and the mother hadn't named him yet."

She began to cry again, deep, wrenching sobs.

"The baby could have died without a name, no one would have known he was missing. He would have," she paused to breathe, words coming one at a time, *"he would have just been gone."*

The receptionist set the hot chocolate on the floor and rocked and hugged. The broken young woman cried.

"Do you think the baby would be safe with the big men?" the receptionist asked quietly.

The young woman got her breath, and straightened, the question penetrating her sorrow and sense of failure and certainty that life could never be the same.

"Yes." She opened her eyes, wiping tears, nodding, "Yes, he would be safe with them."

She sat very still then, leaning back on the grandmotherly shoulder, breathing steadily.

"Yes," she whispered, "he will be safe with them."

CHAPTER 1

May 2017 - Vanderhoof, British Columbia

Johnny Amund sat in his truck and realized Frank had scared him. He swore, reversing his empty logging truck into the narrow turnaround, dust lifting like heavy smoke from the powder blanketing the road. Yes, he had been scared, the feeling quickly turning to an anger which hung in the cab like the dust he could see in the rear-view mirror.

Through his anger, Johnny could smell summer. The distinctive odor of bruised tree bark and underbrush, and the heavy clay churned to mud by forestry equipment, pungent through the open windows of his cab. Though narrow, the access road was well constructed for the heavy logging trucks transporting valuable timber to the sawmill. He completed his turn with casual skill and parked his Peterbilt in the loading area.

The truck's frame rocked as the brakes locked, dust under the vehicle swirling. Frank skillfully lifted the trailer off Johnny's truck with the big track loader and, log by log, began building another balanced load. Johnny couldn't fault the loader operator's ability and held back from blustering defensively at the thought of their interaction earlier that day.

On the early trip, Frank had asked Johnny to move his truck forward a few meters in the loading area. Johnny had ignored Frank's terse request over the company radio channel as he was already settling in to complete his log book entry. Minutes later, Johnny had cursed Frank on the radio when the operator bumped the rear stakes due to the uneven ground by the trailer, startling Johnny.

Instead of keying his mic and replying, Frank had stopped his machine, climbed down from the high cab of his loader, and vaulted up smoothly to look in Johnny's open window. Something in Frank's manner made Johnny realize he should listen.

"Never speak to me like that. Move your truck forward, and I'll finish loading." A line had been drawn. Expectations were clear.

Something in the quiet way Frank spoke, and the ease with which he climbed back up into the loader, and the lack of response on the radio to Johnny's insult, seemed sinister, unlike anything in Johnny's previous experience. The others tuned to the Banks Mountain Contracting private radio channel would know something had happened, and Johnny could feel their silent presence.

The big rig shuddered on its axles each time logs were added. Johnny felt somehow diminished. He couldn't verbalize why, but knew inwardly he would not challenge Frank over the incident or try to make his life miserable in the coming days, as he normally did to coworkers who crossed him.

Johnny was a decent worker, but not as good as he could be, and he knew it. He hadn't set out to be a trucker, and certainly had no desire to own a logging truck himself and face the constant challenge of keeping it serviceable for the long hours and extreme conditions that could rip axles off frames. The quality of his work had dropped soon after high school, leveling off as adequate.

Work during the week, relax on weekends with friends and some-times with his wife, depending on how the relational winds were blowing. In short, Johnny worked for the paycheck, thought little about the future, and rationalized his lifestyle choices when his wife pointed out how other guys his age were building their careers, thinking about the future. Johnny Amund was a bystander, not a player; complacency was easier than challenge.

In Johnny's experience, the guys you worked with were part of the scenery. Like waitresses, or a cashier in a store, or a neighbour a few doors down—they were not part of his life, and he wasn't involved in theirs.

Friends are important. Johnny thought about this as he chose his track, truck and trailer bumping and swaying heavily on the narrow access lane, the slow part of the trip. Stopping in the pullout before entering the Forest Service Road, he checked his load and lights, and stamped the loaded logs with the heavy marking hammer. Returning the hammer to its blue bucket on the roadside, Johnny powered up his windows while waiting for several loaded trucks to pass. Swinging wide across the gravel road, dust still swirling from the passing trucks, Johnny shifted through the gears. The power of the big engine, and the challenge of putting that power to good use, never got old.

By habit he keyed his microphone and called his kilometers as required for safety on the Forest Service Road. As he acknowledged the passing trucks on the way back to the mill with a nod or raised hand, he realized for the first time that he was passing drivers, not trucks. There was a man who had looked old to Johnny ten years before; here was a woman he recognized from high school; next came an out-of-town contractor he didn't know. Not friends, but they were certainly part of his life, maybe even important.

The exchange earlier with Frank gnawed at his thoughts. It had been similar to a time years ago he had teased a girl while waiting for the school bus, stepping on her shoelaces, not really thinking. He had not thought of her older brother. The older boy defended his sister, kicking Johnny in the stomach and telling him to "grow up, loser." The kick had been mostly ineffectual, hadn't hurt for long, but Johnny understood his intention, and left the girl alone from that time on, even treating her with respect.

He shook his head and cursed, face flushed with embarrassment at both past and present. Was he doing the same thing as an adult? Johnny thought of himself as a good worker, and a capable man, but started to think about what it meant to be strong. He wore a reality television-inspired beard—though he would never admit it—and chose his work clothes intentionally. Brands were as important as function: this is how a trucker needs to look.

Johnny swore under his breath, and for the first time in his adult life, faced the fact that he was not as successful as he wanted to be. Was he a big, dumb bully? He wasn't a fighter but would react quickly when he didn't like something. At least he responded to a person's face, not behind their back. He had learned that from his uncles, a personal code he had not neglected. And being big helped.

Driving on, Johnny knew he could be proud of the good choices he made daily on the road. He liked being a log truck driver and understood that his job was important in the BC economy. So why was he frustrated? Why did he feel so hollow?

The day had started poorly.

"Johnny, your alarm is going. It's already after four o'clock, get up!" Mary's voice was strained, sleepy. "You want to be late again?"

Johnny's wife normally got up several hours after Johnny, before leaving for her job. When Johnny went to bed early, she normally spent several hours working with her horses, and planned for extra sleep in the morning.

"Seriously, Johnny, come on! She pushed herself out of bed, stretching. "I can't sleep when I know you might be late, and I don't need to get up yet." She opened the roller blind before heading to the kitchen in the small house Johnny had inherited.

The sun had not yet risen in the northeastern horizon, but the cool air was liquid, thick with gold and purple light filtered through the low line of cloud. Mary had hurried to make Johnny a lunch so he would not be late. She forced open the sticky aluminum-framed kitchen window to hear the robins and other songbirds as they insistently welcomed the day. The scent of new leaves and wild rose blooms in the cool air, clear and full of promise, had captured Mary's attention, softening her disappointment.

Johnny had expected harsh words when he appeared in the kitchen, but the only sounds came from the coffee pot dripping and snorting on the counter. He joined Mary, standing in the open door. Johnny inhaled the serenity, grateful when Mary slipped her arm around him for a moment, before returning to the kitchen to fill his thermos and lunch box in her efficient way.

Hours later, as Johnny set the brakes on the company's Peterbilt in the last pullout before the highway, stretching as he circled the truck to check his load, he was thinking of Mary standing on the porch with a cup of coffee when he left home that morning. She deserved more. Much more than he was giving.

She had left him briefly several years before but came back when he agreed to cut back on his antisocial behavior and solo drinking, basically begging her to come home. He was immensely relieved when she returned, although he couldn't express it.

"I know you mean well, Johnny, and I love you, but I don't want to be your *mother*. I want to know you can take care of me, too, and maybe be a good dad someday."

These words had been echoed in many conversations ever since.

Like traffic laws and fishing regulations, they seemed logical but vague, like there were more pages he couldn't read. He didn't want to push Mary away, even though he didn't feel like changing. He knew she was right; he enjoyed her attention, although he hated to think of it as mothering.

Yes, he did take advantage of Mary, and the way she couldn't stop herself from helping him. Her mother, a woman whose nagging Johnny had come to despise, called this "enabling." She said it like it was some sort of a special word, a word made to be used on guys like Johnny. Johnny often couldn't or didn't define his feelings, but he knew he hated hearing his mother-in-law's criticisms regarding his character—especially when he knew she was correct.

Nearing the sawmill, downshifting smoothly, Johnny was still thinking. Why had he mouthed off to Frank about a problem that he'd created himself? And Frank wasn't afraid to confront him. Frank was probably sick of his behavior. This was a new thought. Was he always rude to Frank? Did the other guys think so, too? Red-faced, alone in his cab, Johnny thought.

CHAPTER 2

Johnny Amund and the others at Banks Mountain Contracting worked steadily throughout the early summer, taking advantage of good conditions, watching the sawmill log yards begin to fill. The summer paychecks were welcome after six weeks of spring breakup when the truck was parked.

The radiator on his truck had needed replacing, and Johnny volunteered to help the mechanics, surprising everyone. Johnny had helped his uncles many hours on the farm and was secretly pleased when the mechanics appreciated his abilities. Old Pete had commented, "I knew there was still a farm boy in there somewhere," his vague statement taken as a compliment. Johnny spent a few more evenings in the shop, as well as a few Saturday mornings when the work piled up, helping the mechanics get more of a weekend.

July was hot and windy, and when the fire hazard increased, Banks Mountain Contracting and a dozen other logging shows were forced to stop active logging. The mechanics, glad for Johnny's help, quickly did any high-priority maintenance on equipment that was likely to be enlisted by the Ministry of Forests for firefighting.

Following an afternoon thunderstorm, a dozen wildfires were

soon raging in the Vanderhoof forest area, whipped up by the strong winds, devouring hectares of forest by the hundred. Johnny's truck was not needed for fire duty, and he had some free time on his hands.

When Mary suggested visiting her father for several days, Johnny didn't respond well. "But Johnny, it would be fun, and I can take a week off if I want! Dad has a house on the lake, and we've never been there, they would love if we came for a visit."

Johnny couldn't verbalize his reluctance of facing the unknown, and his angry and illogical response embarrassed him. He escaped by storming out in a childish huff to spend the rest of the day on a nearby lake with a six-pack of warm beer; the ice, worms, and other supplies forgotten in his haste to escape. He returned home later, sunburned and sheepish, with only two small trout for his trouble.

Mary had spent all day fuelling her anger, but the sight of her husband standing in their driveway by his dusty 4x4, staring down at the forgotten items, melted something inside her. She met him at the door and they both stumbled for words.

"Mary, I'm such a loser. I'm sorry I got so mad." He held his breath, blowing it out slowly.

She looked at him, hoping he would talk, and hoping she wouldn't.

"I was too pushy, I'm sorry. I know you don't want to go." She had walked with him to the pickup to unload his gear.

He stopped her, turning her to face him. "Mary, listen." He paused, absently rubbing his sunburned forearms. "I know you want to go visit your dad, and I want to go with you. I, ..." He stopped talking, unsure how to describe what he was feeling; the dread of meeting new people, of being in an unfamiliar place, the lack of preparation for the unknown. Was this fear? Was he actually afraid of going on a trip with Mary?

He had dragged the small aluminum boat to its rack behind the shed, while she brought his fishing pole and an empty potato chip bag from the bed of the truck.

"You must be starving! This is all you ate?"

He lifted the boat to its rack, grinning at her. "I could eat."

"Where is the motor?" The old outboard had not been in the truck. "*You didn't!*"

She looked up at him. Johnny had threatened to throw the ancient and unreliable relic overboard many times. Had he finally done it?

He grinned again, ruefully.

"I forgot to tighten the clamps when I put it on the boat. The second time I yanked the cord, well, over she went. Hey, where are the worms?"

They opened the cooler and shared the forgotten sandwiches at the picnic table behind the house, Mary laughing at Johnny's description of himself peering at the bubbles rising from the lost outboard, and Johnny relieved that Mary had released the worms into the flowerbed.

After the unfortunate beginning, they were surprised when they had a fantastic trip together, enjoying the time with Mary's dad, boating and fishing and soaking up some sun, extending their stay by a few days.

Al and his partner Joanne loved sharing their lake house, and though it took several days for Johnny to warm up to the evening barbeques and boating parties with guests coming and going, he soon began to enjoy himself. Mary was pleased when Johnny accepted Al's invitation to stay a few more days, and though he didn't comment, he didn't resist.

Johnny and Mary had not spent this much leisure time together in years. At home their time away from jobs did not usually coincide, and they usually spent their free time together working on the house and property, without meaningful communication. Arguments were common, and when Mary resorted to silence, Johnny responded by working longer hours.

Away from the normal routines and habits of home, Johnny watched Mary and found with growing dismay how terribly he had been taking her for granted. He saw how her father respected her, and how she quickly won Joanne's friendship.

Mary was beautiful and he appreciated the way she could light up a room and carry a conversation. Observing her now as she interacted with unfamiliar people, her bright personality and people skills were startling. Johnny realized that without Mary, he would not be making new friends or be enjoying the holiday so much. His feelings for her deepened, and she sensed the change, responding to his unpracticed compliments and the way his eyes followed her.

Mary was an honest person, and her feelings were usually easy to read, She didn't expect life to be free of pain or struggle, and intentionally practiced what she learned. While it was sometimes difficult to hold her tongue or keep from expressing disappointment in her husband, she had observed her own mother drive her father away and wanted desperately to avoid the same pattern. Johnny had been a strong teen, a quiet and responsible boy everyone looked up to. She had felt privileged to meet him, and thrilled when he asked her to marry him. But early in their relationship, circumstances beyond his control had changed him, compounding with earlier hurts she didn't fully understand.

Now, relaxing together away from the familiarity of home, the hope welling up inside her was almost more than she could bear. Mary was certain she could feel him changing, and the way he looked at her left her a little shaky. She loved her husband and welcomed Johnny's attention knowing it came from deep inside.

There was no doubt Johnny was changing, and she was responding. Even her father had commented on the fact that she was glowing. Al had grinned, "I think my little girl is in love."

At one evening party, Johnny and Al had come up from docking the boat, and he saw Mary standing with a group of people, lit by the glow of the low evening sun. Mary had looked away from the laughter-punctuated conversation, lifting her hand to shade her eyes with a graceful movement. Seeing Johnny, she smiled, excusing herself from the group. The evening light, stained red by forest fire smoke, smoldered in her dark hair, and painted her bare shoulders as she came lightly down the steps. Her arms were cool as she embraced him, momentarily leaning her upraised head against his chest, then led him up the steps by the hand.

The group had watched her leave, conversation stalling. Johnny felt as if something inside him would burst. The feeling of being singled out by a beautiful woman—the woman he loved—was breathtaking.

Hand in hand he followed her up the stairs, throat tight with emotion. He felt pride; both of his wife as a person, and that she was his. He felt shy—this was his own wife, and he didn't yet know her. He felt disappointment and regret for ignoring the love Mary had offered freely for years. He knew that he needed to give more, be more.

Johnny stopped their ascent on the landing just below the group, and lifted Mary, hugging her to himself. He turned them in a slow, easy circle; her hands cool on his cheeks, eyes glowing, looking into his. Setting her down smoothly, he leaned and whispered in her ear. Her dark eyes widened, bright with unshed tears, and she leaned into him. "I love you, too," she whispered back.

Then, taking his hand, she led him up the last steps to the terrace and introduced him to people he would later have no recollection of meeting.

Johnny was almost disappointed when he got the call that he would be back to work in several days – rain was in the forecast. Each minute with Mary seemed precious, and his reluctance to try new things was shrinking as a result.

"Johnny, Dad and Joanne are going to a Sunday service tomorrow morning, it's in a vineyard near here. Come with us?"

"Sure, sounds good to me." The simple words earned a quiet smile and a sigh, "Oh, Johnny, I am so happy."

The vineyard was hot, morning breeze scented with pine as well as unfamiliar desert smells. From the back of the crowd, Johnny enjoyed the music played by a live band, leaving his folding chair to look at the vines. Far below, boats left white wakes on the water, a contrast to the tan desert hills and their groves of dark coniferous trees across the lake.

The pastor was Joe, the guy with the wakeboard boat who had been at Al and Joanne's place a couple of times during the week. The sermon, if that what it was called outdoors, was short. Joe read a passage in the Bible about people being branches growing out from Jesus, and how the healthy branches grew more grapes. The simple explanation of growth and pruning made sense, but Johnny knew he didn't really understand the message, but felt connected to something solid.

At the end, they shared a communion service, like he had seen in movies. Johnny didn't participate, but he liked watching the solemn tradition from the background: the crusty loaf of bread on a heavy, pewter plate and dark bottles of wine standing in a row on a table, small glasses filled and accepted carefully, the bread and wine passed around soberly.

Mary was tanned, serene and lovely in her sundress. Johnny wondered if it was okay for Mary to look so good in church, smoking hot, actually. Her face was relaxed and smiling, athletic body strong from hours of riding and working her horses and glowing from the week of sun. So, this is how it felt to be happy.

Early Monday morning, with echoes of "Come again!" and "See you soon!" following them, Johnny grinned across the seat at Mary. She wiped her eyes and sighed, forcing her wind-blown hair into a ponytail. He was surprised at the sense of loss he experienced pulling away from Al's driveway, the extended hugs and goodbyes more poignant than he had expected. They *seemed* like family. She put her hand on his arm, waiting for his hand.

What could have been a nine-hour drive became a sixteen-hour honeymoon in itself. Brief stops in the sagebrush desert near Ashcroft, for ice cream in Cache Creek, antique stores in Clinton, pizza in Lac la Hache, and good coffee in Quesnel made the hours vanish. The familiar drive from Prince George to Vanderhoof was bittersweet in its normality, an hour to prepare for the predictability of routine.

Back at work, Johnny spent many hours behind the wheel listening to less comedy and more talk shows. He found himself interested in newfound advice about marriage, personal development, and financial planning. He began thinking of others and put it into practice.

"Johnny, I like how you've been helping the shop guys work on your truck," Mary said, sitting sideways to look at him as they drove into town to do some shopping on a Sunday morning.

Johnny busied himself checking his mirrors and fidgeting in his seat, deciding with an inner smile that he should also start calling the mechanics "the shop guys" whenever possible.

"It's like you," her voice trailed off. "Oh, I don't know, it's nice."

Johnny ignored her comment, and she reached over and tugged his beard.

"Hey! The beard's off limits," he growled, "even to pretty girls."

Mary laughed and steered the conversation to where they needed to shop, and the barbeque they had attended the previous evening.

Johnny was given a newer outfit to drive in the fall, when the Peterbilt was reconditioned to pull low-bed trailers. He took pride in his blue Kenworth tri-drive, and the new trailer rounded out the package perfectly. It was the first of a new series built by a local man-ufacturer – cutting-edge design and the best in the business, a status symbol.

Soon after the change, Johnny invited Mary to come along on a trip, and on her next day off, she met him at the scale yard. Pulling in to the scale, he saw Mary waiting by the scale shack, his oversized high-visibility jacket dwarfing her frame. She looked good, her dark ponytail spilling out the back of her baseball cap. The scale attendant gave him a thumbs-up as she crossed to his truck clutching the flap-ping jacket, hair blowing in a gust of wind, and Johnny found himself grinning back at the guy.

"Hello, Sexy," he said as she climbed in the passenger door and settled into the unfamiliar cab. She was even more attractive in her late twenties than she had been as a willowy, athletic teen.

"You talking to me or the lunch I packed?" she said, holding up a bulging brown bag resting on a box from a local bakery. She took the spare hard hat Johnny kept in the cab and pulled it over her ball cap, adjusting the fit deftly. She knew the sawmill safety rules and didn't comment, but Johnny knew the hard hat would be stowed as soon as the front wheels were back on the highway.

Between sandwiches, fresh coffee, and a healthy apple, Johnny explained the route and found himself going into the details of his job and forest practice he had never talked about. Clicking the lid shut on her coffee cup, she swivelled to face him. "Johnny. You're enjoying your job!" Mary looked surprised, and then began crying.

Johnny stared at her.

"I'm sorry, it just makes me so happy. I don't remember you ever actually *liking* your work. Or talking about it." She sniffed, and then just looked ahead as they turned off the pavement and began the two-hour drive up the Forest Service Road.

Johnny had no reply, but he knew Mary was right.

"Usually you don't say anything unless you are mad at someone, or had a breakdown, or whatever. Now you've got this nice truck to drive, and you've been helping fix things." She hesitated, unsure of her next words.

He flexed his fingers on the wheel, "Listen, I know I've been a real ..." he stopped and changed his words. "I want to be better. A better man, like, I don't know, like the good guy from a movie or something. I want to make you happy, I want to be someone we can both be proud of. I know you want kids, and if we do, I said *if* we do, I would want to be a good dad, you know?"

Mary unbuckled her seat belt, dropped the bakery box, knocked a hard hat flying, and Johnny struggled to keep the truck in his lane as she wrapped her arms around his neck and held him tight. For the first time in months, Johnny blew a shift, and was relieved when she returned to her seat. He watched her as she straightened up the objects scattered around the cab.

She smiled, a little shyly, and punched his shoulder.

"Hey, stop looking at me!"

He was smiling at her, watching.

"Stop it!"

She pulled an apple fritter from the box, tossing it to him. He caught it deftly, took a large bite, and smiled at her again.

"Mmm, I like it."

Her momentary embarrassment passed, and she started to enjoy the attention.

Mary filled their coffee cups, steam curling until she capped each cup. As they sipped, Mary asked questions, quietly at first, and then more intensely. She had grown up with a father who worked "in the bush," and was familiar with the strange hours, unexpected shutdowns due to dry or wet conditions, and the elusive "breakup season" that could last one month or three while the spring thaw took its course.

"Johnny, why do you only call on the radio at certain places on the road?"

He pointed out the many pullouts where the empty trucks going "up" the road pulled off to let the loaded trucks going "down" the right of way. He also explained that now there were speed limits, as opposed to years before when the speed was mostly unregulated on narrower roads with less traffic. Now with the volume of traffic, each road had a unique protocol to help keep the heavy traffic safe.

As Johnny brushed off and ate a donut Mary had retrieved, he chuckled. Never had he enjoyed a trip so much in almost ten years of driving.

"We've made it through the, um, partying," she said, then paused, leaving other struggles unsaid as they both thought about the tumultuous years. "We handled it okay when you lost your job, and now I have a good job, too."

"But we had to live with your mom," he interrupted, making a show of cringing.

Mary smiled ruefully.

She took a breath and faced him. She waited while he made his call, "Empty at 38," letting others nearby know he was starting up the steep, three-kilometer climb.

"Johnny, I think we can make it. I'm trying to not be so negative, and I know you have changed over the summer. You're more serious, or–" she brushed hair from her eyes, "I don't mean this as an insult, but it's like you are older, more grown up."

He looked at her directly, like he had when they were younger.

"I agree. I don't understand it, but it's like we sort of hit a 'reset' button. A new start in a way. I really started thinking about things this spring, and then the trip down to visit your dad and Joanne …"

She looked at him, eyes dark and questioning.

"I really enjoyed our trip this summer. It was almost like a honeymoon." He stopped, embarrassed. They had not been able to afford a honeymoon when they married, and simply spent a long weekend together making a trip to Chilliwack to buy a used pickup. This omission had been criticized by his mother-in-law for years, and sometimes by Mary as well, making it a subject Johnny avoided.

But Mary just smiled, and put her hand on his arm, giving it a gentle shake.

They were quiet for a few slow kilometers, giving each other room to think. As they crested the hill and passed several loaded trucks, they looked at each other.

Mary said, "So what now?"

CHAPTER 3

The summer had gone quickly, Mary thought. Johnny put in long hours driving and Mary was quick to pick up any overtime available. She wanted a baby, and her dream was as close to happening as it ever had been. Though she was a few years younger than Johnny, some of her friends already had kids starting elementary school.

The fallen aspen leaves were thick on the lawn surrounding their neat home. Mary was raking them, still crisp, onto a large tarp, and dragging them into the smaller corral. The clean, tannic smell reminded Mary of the heaps of leaves she had played in as a child. As she worked, more leaves fell; rich, golden coins on the green grass.

Johnny had inherited the house on ten acres from his Uncle Nelsson, and though it was small, both Johnny and Mary liked the house and location just out of town. Mary enjoyed yard work, and Johnny regularly used the well-equipped workshop that came with the house. They had not yet finished the empty basement but had built a spacious recreation room on one end.

Mary thought of the empty space in the other end of the basement, perfect for children's bedrooms. The thought of little jackets and rubber boots in a line next to theirs caused Mary to catch her breath. She could imagine children playing as she worked, maybe riding on the pile of leaves as she pulled the tarp across the grass.

She knew her children would be *impossibly* beautiful. Johnny's few photos from childhood had showed a nice-looking if serious boy and she had been a beautiful child, yes, their kids would be the best! She and Johnny could raise a good family, she *just knew.*

She and Johnny drifted together soon after she finished high school, no outstanding chemistry at first, but hanging out with the same group of friends at the lake, lots of partying. She had been attracted to his quiet, responsible but easygoing ways, and one night a ride home turned into spending the night at Johnny's place. This happened a few times, and when his roommate took a job on the oil patch, she moved in with Johnny.

Johnny had been employed at the tire shop where he worked diligently during afternoons and Saturdays through high school. The summer after graduation, he began to run the shop's small tow truck, which led to getting his certification to drive the larger tow truck several years later.

Soon after this promotion, Johnny had been at a New Year's party when his boss called, slurring his words, angrily insisting that Johnny take a late-night tow call. He wouldn't listen to Johnny's protest that he had been drinking as well. Stress and bad road conditions were factors several hours later when Johnny crashed on a slippery corner, wrecking the rig and losing his license due to his blood-alcohol level.

The tire shop owner, a loud and vulgar man losing his own messy battle with alcohol abuse, re-evaluated his life and decided several things needed to change. A happy life for him did not include operating tow trucks or providing employment for Johnny. Johnny spent several miserable months working short-term jobs where a driver's license was unnecessary and had not driven with alcohol in his system since.

Losing his license and job had been intensely humiliating to Johnny, as he knew better than to take that tow call and had only done so at the angry insistence of his threatening boss.

The moment of poor judgment overwhelmed Johnny's thoughts, and though his uncles understood and didn't criticize, their matter-of-fact acceptance of the situation did nothing to help Johnny recover.

Johnny didn't complain or slur his boss, but he began a descent into alcohol abuse fuelled by his bitterness. When his uncles were killed in an accident several months later, run off the road by a drunk driver while delivering hay, Johnny's depression deepened. The thought that Uncle Nelsson and Uncle Lars, the only family he had ever known, were killed by a person in the same condition as he when he ditched the tow truck seemed like a cruel punishment of fate. He began to believe the punishment was deserved. His dreams were terrifying, his thoughts during the day full of torment, experiences he shared with no one.

Several weeks after the funeral, Charlie had stopped by the farm with frozen meals from his restaurant. While loading the labeled cartons in the freezer together, he discovered the boy was truly alone. The Amund brothers, while not hermits, had not developed a network of friends.

He realized the boy wasn't talking to anyone and seated Johnny at the table while he whipped up breakfast. "Charlie, it could have been me. It's like I killed them! It isn't fair, I crashed a truck too, and wasn't even hurt. Uncle Nelsson used to say 'bad is called good when worse happens'; well I say worse just got worse. What am I going to do?" This went on as the breakfast cooled, and nothing Charlie suggested seemed to break through to the young man.

Charlie helped Johnny move to the house in town, found him a decent roommate and joined Johnny for several meetings with the executor. While Johnny expressed thanks, he didn't come for help and quietly pulled away.

Despite Charlie's efforts to provide support, the careful and responsible boy began a chaotic transformation into an angry and defensive young man. Though composed on the outside, Johnny was losing a mental battle. The fact that this had been his first and only serious mistake was no consolation.

When his license was reinstated, Johnny was hired by an out-of-town contractor too busy to do reference checks and had been driving trucks ever since.

Meeting Mary and eventually getting married was a definite bright spot in Johnny's life, but he couldn't truly give himself to Mary. She had been supportive but unable to help him escape his inner demons. Mary couldn't understand his struggle, as the big man she married was incapable of sharing the thoughts that were daily poisoning his emotional state.

Mary's mother, who was hard to get along with at the best of times, had alienated her unwanted son-in-law by referring to him as "The loser my daughter married," and generally tried to irritate him when they were forced to be in the same room. Mary had long since given up on having peace in the family, and until recently had been happy to pit the two of them against each other whenever it suited her convenience.

But Mary's father, on an infrequent visit on his way through town several years before, had planted a thought in her mind.

"You know, the big guy has some good things going for him. I was no great catch in my day, but when I got serious, I built a pretty good business." He scowled, "Good enough to keep your mother out of my hair while I enjoy my retirement." He had smiled when Mary rubbed his bald head, and said, "I'm sorry, I shouldn't speak that way about your mom."

"I know that the lifestyle I chose wrecked whatever chance at marriage we had. I know I wasn't a good husband, and I've apologized for that, and to you for being a lousy father."

He had shrugged and cleared his throat. "It seems I've been given a second chance, and I'm trying to do this one right, getting some good help, too.

"If Johnny decides to be somebody, he will make it happen. Lars and Nelsson were good men, and there is no reason why he can't turn out the same. I worked around them when I was young, and you couldn't ask for better guys. Not easy to get to know, but honest and hardworking every day of the week."

Mary's parents had separated while Mary was still in high school, and now her father was happy with his girlfriend of four years. While Al hadn't always been a good role model, she had loved him, and felt closer to him now that they were both older.

Several years ago, he had called Mary and apologized, and said he was working to make his life better and wanted to know if he could come visit. His apology was sincere, and the resulting discussion began to mend the hurts. In their first two-hour talk, they had come to realize Al's anger stemmed from Mary crossing a line, a line that even he did not fully understand, a line he was afraid of, and had never communicated to his daughter. Mary's hurt and angry reaction sprang from not understanding the inconsistency in her father's life - how he could be tolerant of, and even encourage, her underage drinking and partying, but be enraged when she came home stoned from a quiet evening at a friend's house?

They both agreed later that this discussion was the turning point in their relationship, and that the humility of Al's approach to reconciliation was far more powerful than the words spoken. Their relationship had rallied quickly, and they had each thanked each other repeatedly, the father amazed at the woman his little girl had become, and the daughter in the realization that her father was interested in her life, and she was interested in his.

Thinking about her father's opinion of Johnny, Mary pulled up his contact info on her phone and pushed the call icon.

"Hey, Kid!"

She smiled at the expected greeting from the gravelly voice. "Hi, Dad. How are you?"

"I'm fine, what's up?"

"Dad, I was thinking about what you said a couple of years ago about Johnny, that he could be a pretty good man if he tried." She paused. "Do you remember that?"

"Yes, I do. Is everything okay?"

After she assured him things were very good, he cleared his throat. "Do you know I met Johnny's father before he went to prison?"

"No, I never even thought about it." Mary was surprised. "Did you know him?"

"He was my cousin's bud, so I didn't know him well. He was a different sort, a cool customer. He looked like he stepped out of a cigarette ad on the back of an outdoor magazine, good-looking, looked real tough or maybe aloof. Seemed to have it together, drove a nice car, didn't lack for money, you know. Johnny was born after Svend moved away."

"But?" Mary prompted.

"Well, when we heard he was in jail, we were surprised, and figured things must have gone wrong somehow. He had moved out east somewhere, and I remember the talk going around when we found out. It was funny, eh … here we had known this guy who later killed someone, and he just seemed like anybody else, a pretty normal guy, really."

"Dad, do you know what actually happened? Johnny says he has never seen his father, and never plans to. All Johnny has said is that when his dad was selling property a deal went bad and he was accused of killing someone. In fact, that's all I've heard from anyone. No one even talks about it, like no one even really cares."

"I don't think anyone from here really did care at the time, so why would they now? Svend only lived here briefly, and then moved, and not many people knew him, although we knew his older brothers. He must have got into real estate when he moved east, because here he did some sort of work for the Department of Highways. I think he operated equipment or something."

Mary sighed. "Johnny never talks about him, only mentioned him once or twice, and clams up when I ask questions."

"Well, you called to ask what I had said about Johnny. Yes, I remember. One thing I know for sure about Johnny is that his uncles were good guys, but were much older than Svend, maybe twenty years, give or take. Svend was born in Canada or maybe the USA, I think. No accent or anything like his brothers."

Mary heard him walking, feet crunching in fall leaves.

"You know, I can remember it like it was last month. Time sure flies. Right after Johnny wrecked the tow truck, some guys were drinking coffee and talking at Charlie's one morning. I was on the way through town and stopped to say 'hey' to some friends. I guess your mother had spouted off to one of them about Johnny being a loser, not good enough to be dating you, and his uncles had heard about it. The boys were kidding Johnny's Uncle Nelsson, that if he would have straightened out as soon as they figured Johnny was going to, that he would own more land than his brother and wouldn't be running an insurance office. You know, just guys, kidding each other in the coffee shop.

"The other uncle, Lars, you know the one that owned land north of town, just shook his head and said, 'If I had to bet on anyone becoming a good man, I would bet on Johnny,' only he pronounced it 'Yonny' and we all laughed. While we were laughing, Lars finished his sentence. I think what he said was, 'He will be okay.' I thought I heard something about a brother, too, but the guys were so loud I may have been mistaken.

"I never forgot that, though, and I think you made a good choice on the big guy—always have, he'll come around. Look at all the crap he had to go through as a kid, never knowing his mother, or anything about his father. Anyone would have had trouble. I mean, heck, his uncles both died shortly after this conversation I'm referring to, the only family he knew."

Mary held her breath, hoping her father would go on.

"Lars also said, although the other guys were talking about insurance stuff with Nelsson, 'Yonny just needs a break. We all need a break in order to get started. This can be a hard country.' I think he meant it was not easy for a young man to get going, to start something on his own.

"Charlie was refilling our coffees, and he agreed with Lars. He stopped pouring and looked me straight in the eye and told me Johnny was going to be okay."

After she hung up, Mary noticed tears sliding down her cheeks, and she wondered if she could help Johnny find his break.

CHAPTER 4

J ohnny sat on the edge of the bed, quiet, aware of wind in the trees
outside the window. The bedroom was cool, and he eased up carefully and made his way to the kitchen. Mary's indifferent cat was
rounding its back outside on the porch, visible in the headlights of
Johnny's pickup when he activated the remote start.

The temperature on the digital display said negative 6°Celsius,
good weather. Roads should be freezing, tightening up. It was mid-November, usually a good time to haul logs, although the roads could get
rough when the snow arrived in the higher elevations.

Johnny made coffee and filled his thermos flask with hot water
to preheat. He needed socks and while checking the dryer, heard his
phone vibrating on the counter.

"Who's calling at four in the morning?" he mumbled, looking for
the call display. The maintenance shop number was displayed, and he
quickly answered.

"Johnny!" The voice was young, panicked. "He's just lying there, I
don't know what to do!"

The voice belonged to Jason, the apprentice who worked with the
heavy-duty mechanics.

"Who's lying there, where?" Johnny stopped. "Where are you? Who is there?"

"It's Pete. He's by the toolboxes. I'm in the shop!"

"Jason, is he breathing?" Johnny slowed down his questions, as he struggled to get some understanding of the situation. "Do you see blood?"

"I don't know, man, he is just lying here. Yeah, he is breathing."

The phone scraped on something and Johnny heard Jason talking, "Dude, what's going on, wake up, man, wake up!"

"Jason! Jason!" Johnny spoke intently into the phone, trying to get his attention. "Listen to me. What do you see in the shop? Look around you."

"I don't know, man, it's dark except by the bench here."

"Jason, go turn on the lights. I need to know what to do."

Johnny finished lacing his boots, turned off the coffee pot, and ran for his Chevy, phone connecting to the stereo, audible over the loud diesel motor.

Jason's strained voice came through the speakers as Johnny backed down the drive and accelerated up the road.

"There's tools all over the floor, man, and a puddle by the big box." He paused. "Oh, not good, there's a broken bottle here. Looks like whiskey."

"Jason, check Pete again!"

Johnny pulled onto the highway, the heavy pickup accelerating like a muscle car.

"Oh, man ..." Jason was crying now. "His head is all bloody!"

The apprentice was heaving and choking.

"Jason, listen to me. Go to your vehicle and drive out to the highway! Do it now!"

Johnny ended the call and punched in 911.

You've reached 911, go ahead.

Johnny broke in: "I would like to report an injury at the Banks Mountain Contracting shop." He gave the location. "This is John Amund. I work for Banks Mountain. Our apprentice just found Pete Macdonald, a mechanic, lying on the floor, and called me. I'm on my way to the shop right now."

The truck's heater fan was roaring, and Johnny turned it down, checking the back seat for his spare coat. He reached for his coffee, nope, he hadn't brought it along.

"Sir, it sounds like you're driving. Please slow down and wait for emergency personnel."

Johnny pressed END and called the boss.

"Mrs. B, this is Johnny."

"Go ahead." Her tone was flat, but intense. Johnny wondered briefly how that worked.

"Jason just called me and said that Pete's lying on the floor in the shop, tools all over the floor, and there's blood on his head. I told Jason to drive to the highway, and I called 911. Where's Mr. B, uh, Chet?"

"He's up north with the low-bed, left last night to move a skidder from the North Road to the Francis."

Johnny stopped. "Okay, I'm almost at the shop. I'll meet the cops and ambulance and do what I can."

"Okay, Johnny. I'll call one of the guys and let them know you won't take your first run today."

Johnny swore inwardly. Mrs. Banks was sharp; he hadn't thought of that yet.

Speeding through town, Johnny was thinking carefully now. He wanted to arrive at the scene first. Was Pete drunk? He didn't know if he was a partier. The man was older than Johnny with grown kids, but they had never known each other socially.

Had he been clubbed? Why would someone attack a mechanic early in the morning, or did it happen last night?

He didn't know Jason well, although when Jason had begun his apprenticeship, Mary had insisted they invite the young guy for Hockey Night. New to town, he seemed to like Johnny and though shy, enjoyed talking with Mary.

Several minutes later, Johnny slowed to exit Highway 16, flashing lights visible in his mirror. Turning, his headlights lit the cab of Jason's rusty Toyota, a frightened face momentarily visible in the stationary vehicle.

Turning into the wide lane leading into the huge yard, Johnny parked near the shop. He left the Chevy running and flipped the switch for the light bar, flooding the yard beside the big building with white light. Grabbing a jacket from the back seat, he ran across and entered the open door to look for Pete.

Pete's service truck was parked in the normal spot to the right of the shop near the side door. The hood was cool, windows frosted, apparently parked overnight.

The sirens were loud now, and Johnny hoped Jason would just stay put for a while; he needed to concentrate.

Jason had left the side door wide open in his hurry to leave. The furnace fan was roaring, and the only truck in the cavernous building was dry, a damp area on the floor underneath showing where snow and ice had recently melted.

As Johnny rushed to Pete, lying on the floor as Jason described, several emergency vehicles raced into the yard. Their flashing lights reflected on the trees surrounding the yard.

Pete indeed had a gash in his head, and Johnny stepped back when two paramedics pushed past him.

A Royal Canadian Mounted Police officer Johnny did not recognize checked his ID and name on his company high-visibility jacket, introducing himself as Constable Barton.

CHAPTER 5

Johnny opened one of the bay doors so the EMTs could back the ambulance into the building. He didn't understand all they were saying about Pete's condition, but he could see for himself that Pete would need stitches, and probably had a concussion. The unconscious mechanic was loaded efficiently and quickly and was soon in the ambulance on the way to the hospital.

The shop seemed empty with the EMTs and ambulance gone. Several cruisers pulled into the yard, and more RCMP officers entered the building. One handed Johnny and Barton each a paper cup of coffee and tossed the fibre tray in a nearby trash can.

Johnny had been looking around and his mind began to work.

"Look at this. Why would someone dump all these sockets on the floor?"

The officer with a camera was taking shots from all angles and straightened up to look at Johnny.

"What do you mean?"

"Nobody carries a whole tray of sockets around. You grab the ones you need and come back for more if you need another one," he paused, "and these are all regular sockets, ones you use with a ratchet, not an airgun. And they're small, no big ones."

He looked in several toolboxes. Pete's blue box didn't seem to be missing tools, but the other boxes, and a spare under the bench, had several drawers left open, largest sockets missing.

"That's really weird," Johnny said. "Pete didn't drop those sockets. The only truck in here looks like it's been here for a while. That one has been hauling on the Francis, and they've got snow up there, a lot of snow. It's all dry under the truck, even with the furnace going and the heated floor, there would still be some puddles if it came in late last night. It's been here for at least ten hours, I'm guessing. Whatever it needs probably wouldn't call for a bucket full of sockets."

They all turned, looking at the huge rig. Chunks of dirt and wood debris were on the floor, still damp from where snow and ice had melted and fallen from the frame.

Johnny swore. He was staring at the passenger door of the cab.

Barton followed his gaze, then turned to Johnny, face tense. "Stay here, Sir."

Barton and the other male officer walked toward the truck, Barton pulling his handgun from its holster. The officer with the camera stood by Johnny, camera aimed at the truck.

The cab had a small window at the bottom of the passenger door. The sole of a boot was pressed to the window. A yellow manufacturer tag was visible through the slight haze of road grime on the glass.

Johnny touched his chest pocket, vaguely aware of his phone vibrating in his jacket. He had not turned the ringer on.

Both officers now had their guns drawn. Barton nodded and was quickly up on the step without hesitation, while the other officer yanked the door open. Barton froze, then slowly holstered his weapon.

The second officer climbed up and motioned for the officer with the camera to join them.

Johnny ignored his buzzing phone, and with a sense of dread, he approached the truck.

The officer stood on the step, slowly sweeping the camera left then right across the inside of the cab. She then descended, taking care not to catch items on her belt on the aluminum step. She pulled a pair of latex gloves from her pocket and handed them to Johnny, snapping her gum, eyes level.

"Mr. Amund, take a look and see if this means anything to you," she said, skin stiff on her face.

Johnny gripped the chrome grab bar and with a short exhale, pulled himself up to look with morbid fascination at a set of clothes laid out across the floor of the truck. Small boots on the passenger side, Carhartt pants and a black hooded jacket across the middle, hard hat pressed against the driver's door. A greasy work glove was shoved down on top of the shift lever, middle finger extended, other fingers folded down. The familiar scent of the pine air freshener seemed out of place.

"Oh, man!" Johnny got out of the truck and reached for his phone.

There were four missed calls, all from Mrs. Banks.

As he hit redial, he noted the number on the side of the truck, 327.

"Yep, talk to me, Johnny."

"Who was driving 327? I know it was up the Francis." He waited, imagining Melissa Banks running her finger down the list she kept next to her wall calendar in the alcove where she coordinated company operations.

"Mrs. B, I'm in the shop, I'm going to put you on speaker."

"Johnny, it was Terry, Terry Mason."

Her voice was clear through the speaker.

"Started last week, just moved here from Alberta. How's Pete?"

"Ma'am, this is Officer Barton. Is Terry a practical joker? What do you know about him?" Barton asked.

"I don't know, just met *her* last week, just a little gal, but has some experience and good references from Alberta. What I want to know is how's Pete? She barked, "Is he on the way to the hospital?"

"The ambulance left a few minutes ago, Ma'am," Barton said. "How many employees do you have working today? Are you expecting more to be working in this shop?"

"Well, yeah, we're running a logging show here. There's probably twenty-five guys working today!" She was winding up, but Barton interrupted.

"Ma'am, please listen. We are going to need your help to secure this area. I'll be calling a crime scene unit from Prince George. There are some strange details here we need to take care of. We're going to need your employee, John, to help us out for a few hours, and we will need to talk to the apprentice who called him," he turned to face Johnny, "Jason, is it? The shop and property is now a crime scene, so please let your employees know not to come here."

The officers and Johnny turned in unison, startled, as the south bay door began to open and Mrs. Banks drove her SUV into the shop, front end dipping as she braked hard.

She launched out of her vehicle, holding her remote for the overhead door. "What is going on here!" She addressed Johnny, ignoring the RCMP officers. She slammed her door, marching over to the four in a cluster near the open passenger door on truck 327.

"Excuse me, Ma'am!"

Mrs. Banks stepped around Barton's outstretched arm and faced

Johnny directly. "Pete's been with us for years. I want to know what happened to him and how he's doing right now." Her eyes were snapping, anger covering her concern.

Her eyes darted to Johnny's left, noticing the tools on the floor and the broken bottle and whiskey on the concrete floor.

"Pete doesn't even drink. What's the booze doing in here, and why's it such a mess?" Their eyes followed hers, noting the neat rows of tools on the pegboard, the toolboxes lined up neatly, a stark contrast to the tools scattered on the floor.

Johnny's phone was vibrating again. "Who's on the phone?" Mrs. Banks snapped, "Maybe it's the hospital."

It was Mary. "Johnny, what's going on? You didn't take your coffee and your coat is on the couch. Where are you? The cat woke me up. It must have sneaked in when you left. Why is Jason's 4x4 parked at the end of our driveway?"

"Jason? I told him to wait by the highway! He was there when I came in, hang on." He put the phone on speaker, and quickly told the officers and Mrs. Banks what Mary had reported. He could hear the sound of Mary walking on the gravel drive.

"Johnny, I'm almost to his truck. It smells hot, like oil burning."

The officer with the camera leaned toward the phone. "Miss, go back to the house and lock the door!" She faced the others. "That Toyota that was by the highway when we came in?"

Johnny nodded.

"That's the guy who called you?"

He nodded again.

They all looked at his phone, and then they heard Mary scream. The call ended.

CHAPTER 6

The other police officer broke the stunned silence.

"Where is your house, Sir? Who is there besides your wife?" He sprinted for the door. "Give the info to Barton and he'll pass it on!"

They heard a powerful motor accelerating, frozen gravel spraying up on the undercarriage. A siren began to wail as the cruiser surged onto the road.

Jason? Could *Jason* have done this? And now he was at his house?

Johnny felt sick as he gave his address to Barton, who punched it into his phone, then spoke into his handheld radio, explaining the situation.

Johnny stared at his phone as it rang again. He saw Mary's name on the screen.

"Mary, what's going on? Are you okay?"

"Well, yeah. Why is Jason here?"

"There's been an accident at the shop. Pete was hurt. The police are here."

"Oh! I was worried you were hurt or something. What happened to Pete? He's the mechanic you've been helping out, right?" He could hear her tone changing from surprise to anger to about-to-cry.

"Is Jason there? What is he doing?" Johnny remembered the officer now racing toward his home, "Oh, the RCMP are on the way. We thought, we thought something bad was happening, maybe."

"Jason was sick, throwing up in the ditch. It scared me, sounded like an animal."

"Mary, take Jason in the house and calm him down. The police are going to come, and they'll be asking a lot of questions. We don't really know what's going on yet. It looks like someone hit Pete on the head, and one of the trucks is here, parked, when it should be out west." He stopped. "I will call you when I know more."

But Mary had something to do and told him she would call later. Before she ended the call, he heard her instructions to Jason to "get his skinny butt up to the house for some breakfast". Mary was tough He wouldn't worry about her. He knew she would take care of Jason, too.

His thoughts turned back to the situation at hand. Barton was on the radio, apprising his coworker of the situation.

Why were the clothes on the floor of the truck? Did they belong to Terry? He had never met her, or even heard her name. He was aware several new truckers had been hired over the previous weekend for the busy winter.

Was Terry playing a joke? Had she been assaulted? Were those her clothes? The workwear was smeared with the normal mud and grease accumulated during a day of winter trucking.

Good clothes, but definitely had seen some use before being laid out on the floor of the cab. The boots were a lot smaller than his size thirteens.

Both officers were back up on the truck's steps, looking through the cab and taking pictures. The one with the camera was now on the driver's side, and he heard her talking into her radio.

"Yes, I'll check.".

From the passenger side, Johnny was able to see through the wide-open door as she pulled a pen from her pocket and used it to carefully lift first the waist of the pants, then the waist of the shirt. When she lifted the hoody's waist band, Johnny recognized the yellow logo on a bunched-up green T-shirt and could see the pink and black lines of underwear.

Slowly returning the pen to her pocket, the police officer said, "Yes, all the clothes are here, underwear, yep," she listened, "yeah, socks are stuffed in the boots."

She looked down at the hard hat she had placed on the driver's seat. "Yes, there's some hair, blonde, stuck around the head band in the hard hat."

She climbed down, her conversation muted by the furnace blower.

Constable Barton climbed down, rounding the big rig to stand with Mrs. Banks. Johnny joined them. "John, this looks like a serious problem here. There will be an investigation team here in about an hour, and they are going to need to talk at length with the two of you," he nodded toward Melissa Banks and Johnny, "as well as Jason, and anyone else who was here at the shop recently."

The officer sighed. "I sure hope Mr. Macdonald is okay, and when he is able to talk, he may have all the information needed. We will have to wait until the hospital contacts us. We have an officer who should have arrived at the hospital by now." He glanced at the big clock on the wall and then confirmed by checking his watch.

"Why don't the two of you go get some breakfast and make a list of your employees and their phone numbers. Keep trying to contact your husband, Ma'am. He may know some details as well." He nodded toward Johnny. "Your foreman here, well, I'm assuming he's your fore-man, is steady. You're lucky to have him."

He handed them each a card, shaking hands with Mrs. Banks, then Johnny. "If you think of anything, call me. I'll be in touch soon. We will need to take statements, and the interviews with the investigation team may take some time. Get a good breakfast. It's early. This could be a long day."

He adjusted his equipment belt, his short frame looking as trim as was possible in the bulky vest. "I just hope your driver is okay, and this is some sort of joke. Okay, I expect to be calling you fairly soon."

"My house is the first one further down the road, the first left." Mrs. Banks was calm. "We will be there."

With a curt nod, Barton rejoined his fellow officer who was still on the phone.

CHAPTER 7

Johnny followed Mrs. Banks to her large house and parked beside her Escalade. In the house, she poured him a cup of coffee, and handed him a list of employees with their phone numbers.

"You start with everyone on the North Road where you're working, and I'll take the ones on the Francis." She was already making a racket in the kitchen, opening the refrigerator, leaving cupboard doors wide open. "I don't think everyone will answer their cell phones, but the ones who do can get on the radio and contact whoever is close to them." She turned, "And get Chet to call me. He needs to be here for this."

The Banks worked together running their business, and Chet was usually the human relations half of the team. Melissa Banks got things done, making sure safety practices were followed with all the necessary training, and that everyone was paid on time. Her husband was the "good cop" in the partnership.

"Hello, Jim? Yeah, were you at the shop yesterday? Did you see Pete?" Her voice was forceful, getting quieter as she went into another room. Johnny couldn't think, so he picked up one of the safety folders, a pad of paper from a stack of several on the desk, and a pen, and went into the living room, sitting in a leather chair with wide arms. He turned on the table lamp and wrote a few questions on the pad of paper. He wanted to ask the same questions to each of the people he called, all men on his route.

Were you at the shop yesterday? Did you see Pete yesterday or last night? Do you know Terry?

He opened the safety folder to the employee list and noticed two names written in blue ink below the printed list of names.

Terry Mason. Caleb Gray.

He finished writing her name and thought of what else to ask. He was shocked by the suddenness of the events. One minute he was getting ready for work; half an hour later there were all these new problems to sort and process. Inwardly he swore, thinking of Pete. Would he be okay?

The guy's name wasn't even Pete, Johnny had found out several years ago. His last name was Macdonald, and for many years had answered to "Mac". He had driven a Mack truck years ago, and when he upgraded to a long-nosed Peterbilt, everyone started calling him "Pete". He had laughingly told Johnny that when he got tired of his current name, all he had to do was buy a Kenworth, and he could be "Ken" for the rest of his life! Johnny hadn't thought to ask what his real name was.

Isaac La Crosse, the other full-time mechanic, spent much of his time servicing the logging equipment and trucks out in the bush. He had a well-equipped service truck, and according to Mrs. Banks had been several hours north replacing broken hydraulic lines on a feller-buncher, a large, tracked machine with boom-mounted grapples and saw head. This configuration allowed the operator to hold the tree while cutting it low to the ground, and then place the tree with others in a 'bunch'. The skidder operator would then drag the trees to the roadside where the processor operator would cut the logs to length and deck them for loading.

Johnny guessed Isaac was due back later today. There was a sleeper cab on the service truck, and often Isaac chose to spend the night in the bush, saving hours of driving on rough and busy roads. Like Pete, Isaac was resourceful and savvy, able to troubleshoot problems, and willing to work outdoors in the miserably cold winter conditions, the mud and mosquitos of spring, and the dust, heat and blackflies of summer.

Isaac answered on the second ring. "Hello, Clown 15, this is not the Complaint Department, but the Department of What's-Your-Problem-Now?" Normally, Johnny enjoyed Isaac's sarcastic wit on the phone, but not today.

"Isaac, when did you leave the shop yesterday?"

"Yesterday? I wish! I passed you on your last trip Tuesday. You may remember my courteous gesture of greeting?"

"Oh, yeah. Hey, Isaac, we've got a real problem here. We need to talk for a few minutes, so cut the crap."

Isaac went quiet, there was the muffled sound of a door slamming, then, "Okay, I'm in the buncher cab, up on a ridge. Good reception. Go ahead."

"Listen, sometime last night Pete got knocked unconscious in the shop. We don't know what happened exactly, or who did it, or if he just fell. He's in the hospital. I haven't heard how he's doing. Jason found him early this morning. I guess they were taking the smaller service truck somewhere, I don't know. Jason called me, I called 911, and they took Pete to the hospital. The cops came out, and then we found something really weird in the shop."

Isaac was silent, so Johnny went on.

"327 was parked in the shop, looked like it had been there for a while, eh, all dry underneath. That new driver, Terry Mason, had been driving it this week. She was gone, but her clothes were on the floor of the cab. They were set up like" he paused, "well, like she was wearing them, underwear and everything."

Isaac swore. "Oh, that sounds bad." He swore again, then said, "I met her at the shop on Sunday and showed her the rig she was starting in, and where things were, made sure she knew how to install chains, all that. She seemed decent, you know, she knew what she was doing, only asked a few questions. Didn't ask about satellite radio like the rest of you clowns always do first."

Johnny asked, "Any ideas? You heard of anything like this before?"

"Negative." Isaac said, "Halloween was only a few weeks ago. Sounds like something out of a horror movie, I don't know. What are the cops doing?"

"They closed the shop, bringing out a team to investigate. This is going to be a pain this week, no place to service our rigs. Chet is up there somewhere, moving a skidder, I think. Can you get him to call as soon as he can?"

Johnny explained about calling everyone to find out who had been around the shop or had last seen Pete.

Isaac had a better idea. "Listen, Johnny. Let me call the guys on this route. I'll get a hold of the boss-man, too, eh. He can take the service truck and boogie back down the hill right away. I'll finish the move and bring the low-bed later. Got a few things to finish, but I won't need the service truck if I don't get the parts Pete was bringing up for me. Right now, I was just double-checking this buncher over before Hoser here starts his shift."

Johnny grinned in the empty room; some things never stopped

being funny. Isaac called all the machine operators "Hoser" and the truckers "Clown." In Isaac's phone, Johnny knew he showed up as "Clown 15."

Several years earlier, an equipment operator had complained to Isaac, feeling the younger man should be respectful, and call him by name. Isaac had peered around the hydraulic hose he was wrestling into the bundle on the head of a feller buncher. His acidic reply, overheard by a government safety inspector, had become legendary. "You go the rest of the winter without destroying another hose, and I will never call you "Hoser" again, Hoser." Isaac's accent, the whiny nature of the recipient, and the seven uses of the f word in the short sentence combined to make the story a coffee-shop favorite.

Isaac's continual use of the "f-word" had gotten him in trouble on the radio, and in other situations. At his sister's church wedding, she finally told him in exasperation, "Just shut up, you dumb cluck!" He analyzed the issue and began to substitute the word "cluck," although with his accent it came out as "clock." This provided some head-shaking and many laughs on the open radio channels where coarse language was prohibited.

A pointed memo from the sawmill had targeted "the use of vulgar words on company radio channels, including substitutions for those considered most vulgar ..." soon after Isaac's change of vocabulary. The fact that the memo was issued from a fussy executive, who over the years had irritated many, turned the reproof into an instant sensation, actually lifting morale during the exhausting winter season. Isaac proudly taped a copy of the memo on the ceiling of his service truck and on the lid of his toolbox.

For all his irreverent ways, Isaac was intelligent, and several times had been invited to factories to critique new designs. He had proved to be a diagnostic genius and other mechanics frequently called Isaac for advice. He was also a certified first aid attendant, good in emergencies. Isaac was well liked by many, even if he was quick to call you out if you made a stupid mistake, neglected maintenance, or God forbid, borrowed his tools.

They agreed that Isaac would call back when he had contacted everyone he could, and that Johnny would try to get an update on Pete, so the employees heard straight from their company, rather than a second-hand, embellished account. From previous experience with highway or logging accidents, they knew how quickly information was spread by gossips on social media, bringing confusion to a situation already overloaded with stress.

CHAPTER 8

Johnny had just checked in with Mary but put her on hold when another call came through. It was Constable Barton, who asked Johnny to meet him and the investigation team at the Banks Mountain shop when the team arrived. When he got back on the line with Mary, she told him the police were interviewing Jason. He heard her pouring coffee and taking a cautious sip.

"Before the police came in, Jason told me about finding Pete. He said he was going to meet Pete early, and they were taking the service truck out to fix something and were going to meet Isaac La Crosse somewhere to drop off some parts." She sipped again. "Jason calmed down after he ate. I made him drink some water, too

"He was so irrational at first. I mean, has he never seen a fight? How bad did Pete look? Was there blood all over?"

"No, there wasn't that much blood. Maybe just finding Pete lying there, the shop lights were off, he couldn't see what the deal was. I think the suspense or surprise got to him, it was pretty creepy."

Johnny explained what he and Melissa Banks were doing, and how Isaac was helping as well.

"I'll call you later, or better yet, you call me on your break. Maybe we can meet for lunch today."

Johnny was surprised at how calm he was. Finishing some of the contact work made him feel good. He got up to go to connect with Mrs. Banks, picking up the binder and his scrawled notes.

Phone pressed to her ear, Mrs. Banks pointed Johnny to the table, placing a sizzling pan of scrambled eggs on a metal trivet. She nodded toward the toaster on the counter and then poured a glass of orange juice, putting the pitcher back in the refrigerator. Turning back to the counter, she wrote something on her notepad, and then ended her call.

"Well?"

Johnny cleared his throat, "Isaac is calling the guys on the North Road. He will swap the service truck for the low-bed and haul the skidder across the connector so Chet can come straight back. He will call when he gets through to everybody."

Johnny's phone pinged. He looked down, speaking as he read the message. "It's Isaac. Somebody is driving up to where Chet is going to be unloading. They will let him know what's going on."

Mrs. Banks had information of her own. "I was able to reach five of the truckers, and they will pass the info on to the bush crews. Whenever they have cell service, they'll text, and let me know if they hear any information we need."

Melissa, Isaac, and Johnny were serving as the company's safety team and had made a plan the previous spring that it seemed to be working well. Contacting several dozen workers, most of whom were out of cell range, was not easy but essential. Forest fires were a huge and worrisome issue in the summers, and careful management of hot machines was mandatory.

Mrs. Banks's phone rang. It was a trucker informing her he would be out of cell range any time but would be contacting the boss in less than fifteen minutes.

Melissa Banks looked at Johnny, seeing him in a different light. He was a tall, bulky young man. When they hired him, he was no great catch, but recently had been really pulling his weight, and both Pete and Isaac had commented that he had been helping in the shop. In Pete's words, "He's been a real decent guy to work with lately, real decent."

She liked Johnny's wife. Mary looked a little rough around the edges. No, that wasn't quite fair, Melissa thought. She wouldn't describe Mary as hard... no, but she didn't smile as much as a pretty young woman should. She wasn't afraid to confront a demanding customer at the grocery store. Melissa had heard several times that Mary handled the younger employees well, and despite not putting up with any of their lame excuses, lateness, or substance abuse, had earned their love and respect, and was invited to graduations and sports events of the teens she supervised.

Several years earlier, Melissa had asked her youngest son the required, "So how was school?" and was surprised when he answered with words other than "fine" or "okay". Mary Amund had been a guest speaker at Career Day, and he had enjoyed the direct and humorous stories from her experience with young workers, laughing as he explained.

As Melissa put the dishes away, she considered the fact that Johnny had been very calm, made good decisions, and had been excellent working with the police officers earlier. She was happy she had insisted Johnny take first aid training and serve on the company's safety committee. Her gut feeling a year ago was that Johnny was growing up.

She felt she had been correct, and she decided to watch him closely as events unfolded.

Johnny turned toward her. "Mrs. B, tell me about Terry Mason. I know nothing about her. Could she be …" his voice trailed off.

Johnny's phone rang, and she hurried across to the table.

"It's Barton," he mouthed, listening, nodding his head. "Oh, that's just excellent." He gave her a thumbs-up. "Pete seems to be okay," he whispered. "Okay, we'll be right there."

Hanging up, Johnny said Pete was awake, had a concussion, but was coherent. The RCMP wanted Johnny to come there right away, in case he could make sense out of what Pete might say.

They rushed outside, crunched across the bare and frozen driveway, and headed for the hospital in the SUV. Their conversation on the trip to the hospital was centered around the missing trucker, Mrs. Banks giving Johnny her impression of Terry, and the information she remembered from the young woman's resume.

As the SUV bumped into the hospital parking lot, Johnny had the image of a petite blonde woman in her thirties, energetic, and skilled at her job. During the walk into the hospital, Johnny noticed several women who perfectly fit the description.

CHAPTER 9

B arton met them in the small lobby and introduced them to a short man in khakis and a blue parka. "This is Sergeant Jacobs." he said. "He's our lead investigator. He'll go with us to talk with Pete, and then we'll go out to the shop and wait for the rest of the team who are still on the road."

They shook hands and each introduced themselves. Following Barton, they walked through the wide hallway, past a bustling nurses' station, and navigated around several food carts.

Turning a corner and continuing down another hallway, the group entered the room Barton indicated as he held the door politely then closed it behind himself and followed them inside.

Pete was in a hospital bed, adjusted to a sitting position. There was a bandage on a shaved portion of his head above his right ear. Pulling the linens up to cover his flimsy gown, he peered at them, looking nervous and embarrassed.

A nurse who had been standing on the other side of the bed gave some quick instructions. "The doctor says that besides a concussion, Mr. Macdonald is fine. He needed eight stitches and a little cleaning up, but it's okay if you ask a few questions. Mr. Macdonald needs to rest and shouldn't talk for too long." She smiled and left the room.

"So, I got knocked on the head, they tell me." He gingerly touched his forehead.

Melissa spoke. "Pete, I'm so sorry this happened. I'm glad you're okay." She leaned down and patted his arm, then straightened. "Is your head sore?"

He grimaced. "Yeah, you could say I've got a headache, not too bad though." Without the bulky work clothing he usually wore, Pete appeared diminutive in the bed, and looked as if his headache might be more than bad.

Melissa introduced the officers and explained they needed information on what happened. She didn't say anything about Terry Mason being missing.

"So," he looked at the half circle of people around the bed, "Terry, the new trucker, brought her truck in before dark. She had stopped at the truck wash and blew off most of the crud, pretty messy on the Francis. Didn't know we have our own pressure washer out back I guess, but that's neither here nor there. She had been partway up the Francis, eh, on her second trip when she called me and said she got a real bad driveline vibration ..." His voice trailed off at Johnny's shrug and raised eyebrows. "Okay, maybe you better ask me questions. I might ramble some."

Jacobs leaned forward a bit. "No, that's good, Mr. Macdonald. Just keep telling us what happened the rest of the afternoon."

"Well, I'd sent Jason out to the yard to change a trailer tire, eh, one that came down earlier, and he said it didn't look bad, and took it down to the tire shop. I told him after he got it fixed and put it on to go ahead and go home, 'cause we were going to leave early this morning for something or other."

Pete's battered hands looked large and strong and out of place on the sheets and were still greasy, nails half-mooned with shop grime. He studied them, turning his palms up, seeming to notice how filthy they were.

Mrs. Banks pulled a travel package of shop wipes from her coat pocket. Officer Barton winked at Johnny as she handed them to Pete. Pete scrubbed his hands with the moist cloth, the room filling with the pungent and familiar citrus scent of hand cleaner and continued.

"Jason texted me, eh, saying some guy waved him down when he was leaving the shop driveway, and asked if Terry Mason worked here. Jason said he didn't think so. That's 'cause he never met Terry yet. I told him she'd just started on the weekend, and she owns the brown Dodge parked in back."

Pete finished scrubbing his hands, and Melissa retrieved the used wipes, dropping them in the waste basket.

"He wanted to know if he should try to find them, but I told him to get the tire done and don't worry about it."

Jacobs looked up from his notes and said, "Mr. Macdonald, did Jason say anything about the people who asked about Ms. Mason?"

Pete said, "Well, yeah, he said 'the guys in the new car.'"

"Mmm-hmm?" Jacobs murmured, encouraging Pete to elaborate.

"The guys in the new car, eh, the ones that asked about Tracey, I mean, Terry."

"Did you see Jason when he came back from the tire shop?"

"Nope. I never seen him. I had told him to fix the tire and go home. We were leaving early in the morning."

Pete was fading. "But then that little gal, Terry, brought her truck in. She had stopped at the truck wash, eh, cause the truck was mostly clean, and I seen there was water frozen on it, drops of water," he paused, "but did I already say that?"

"That's okay, Mr. Macdonald, just tell us what happened next."

"Well, I was out by the service truck, loading some tools when I heard this terrible racket coming down the road, something grinding real bad, eh. I seen 327 coming, so went in and opened the door so she knew which bay to drive in." He rotated his head on his shoulders carefully, movements stiff.

"Once she stopped, I went for the control."

Jacobs looked at Johnny, eyebrows raised.

"The remote control for the overhead crane." Johnny whispered quickly as Pete continued without noticing.

"And then I heard a noise behind me. I put my hand on the bench to turn around, eh, and boom, something hit me pretty hard. I bumped into the wheel table, where I had parts and stuff to load in the service truck." He smiled ruefully. "I think I knocked some stuff on the floor."

"Did you knock over a container of sockets?" Officer Barton asked.

Pete squinted, wrinkles deepening. "Sockets, why would I have sockets? Got a big set in the service truck." He paused. "Last thing I remember was glass breaking." Again, his mouth twitched in a wry smile. "Sorry, Melissa, but I had a bottle of whiskey I was taking up for someone, must have knocked it down."

He went on. "I'm sure glad we have a heated floor. I was lying there all night I guess, knocked clean out. I woke up a couple of times, maybe, must've gone back to sleep. Someone had turned off the main lights."

Johnny had a question, "Pete, did you talk to Terry?"

"No, you think *she* slugged me?!" He looked alarmed. "At first, I figured maybe I'd caught the big one, eh, stroke or something. Now they tell me I was whacked on the head."

Barton assured him that it was unlikely Terry had been the one who hit him.

"Did you close the door?" Johnny wondered if Pete had closed the door before he was struck, or if someone else had closed the door and tidied up the scene.

"No, I was going for the crane when she was still pulling in, never even seen her get out of the truck. The door was wide open."

Melissa Banks could sense Pete was fading and took charge.

"Look, guys," she said, facing the men. "Let's give Pete some rest now." Turning back to Pete, she asked, "Is your daughter coming soon?"

"Yep, the nurse called her. She'll be here this morning, driving down from the Fort."

"Fort St. James." Johnny whispered to the officer.

As they trooped out of the room, Melissa said, "You let me know if you need anything, Pete."

He grinned weakly. "Okay. My daughter is bringing some smokes, eh, should be fine."

CHAPTER 10

Terry was having a bad day. It had started as normally as any day on a new job but had rapidly turned into a nightmare. She had been heading west on her second run when something went wrong with her truck's drive axles. Her mechanical trouble seemed very, very minor now, and she briefly wondered if the truck hadn't broken down, would this be happening?

Arriving finally back at the yard, she had driven the big rig toward the shop, turning sharply at the last minute when the huge door on her left began to open, and limped the truck inside. She saw the older mechanic by the toolboxes raise a hand and turn toward the bench. As she set the brakes, she noticed a movement in her mirror, assuming it was the door closing. Before shutting the big engine down, she rechecked the gauges, which all looked fine. As she reached down between the seats for her log book, someone was opening the driver's door, which surprised her.

Now, Terry groggily remembered being yanked out of the seat by a strong hand, and the last thing she could remember clearly was trying to land on her feet. There had been a strong chemical smell, maybe ether. As she began to regain consciousness, she noticed the smell of a new car, and the feel of stiff carpet. She was very cold, a feeling soon joined by a raging headache. Music was playing, painfully loud. She was lying in the trunk of a car under the rear speakers, road noise thrumming, blemishes in the road surface transmitting harshly.

She fought down panic, trying to focus. *I drove in the shop, fell out of the truck?* No, she had been pulled out. *Someone put me out with ether? Will I have brain damage? No, I wouldn't wonder that if I had brain damage.* Her thoughts were coming quicker and quicker.

Terry knew she should not call attention to herself. Faint light was coming from one side. She squinted and found she could see through a section of the back seat of a moving car. It smelled new, the scent making her feel nauseous. Her head was pounding, and she fought the urge to vomit. She could move her arms freely, but her whole body ached, and her stomach heaved when she moved.

"Okay, there is some heat coming through the back seat. I'm not hypothermic, just really cold." Then Terry noticed with horror that she could feel the carpet, that her bare skin was in contact with the floor. She was naked.

Her tears were hot on her cheek. Now she was feeling rage, and fear, too. She had left Alberta because she had a hunch it was unsafe, and less than a week of being in British Columbia, something more terrible than she had imagined was happening. *Think, Terry!* She willed herself.

She began flexing her muscles, encouraging blood to flow and warm her up. She began to hyperventilate, and fought to breathe steadily, head throbbing.

The road noise changed, new pavement. No thumps from the patches and crack sealing common to older asphalt roads. She heard the familiar click of the turn indicators as the driver changed lanes and turning to the back of the closed space, she could see a glow-in-the-dark emergency escape pull tab. *No, I can't just bail out on the highway.* Her thoughts were tangled but gaining clarity by the minute.

She reached around for her clothing and could feel nothing. The trunk was empty, besides what felt like several backpacks by her feet. *Okay, this must be a rental car.* She felt around some more, the nearest car rental was probably in Prince George, and from the feeling of the new road, and the amount of traffic they were passing, she guessed they were traveling in that direction. *When we get to the city, I need to be ready to get out. What do I do?*

Moving slowly through waves of nausea, Terry turned herself around in the trunk, for once thankful she was not tall. She kept back from the opening into the back seat, not wanting to be observed.

Light flashed through the dark interior every time a vehicle went by, but it was when the rental accelerated in a passing lane and spent several seconds passing a tractor trailer rig with a long string of marker lights, that Terry could get a good look at the profile of the passenger. What she saw only added to the horror. She shrank back from the rear seat.

Terry had chosen to leave a secure job in Alberta where she was well-liked by her employer. Following the abrupt and turbulent end to a long-term relationship, she had been happy to throw herself into work, not minding the long hours and transient living conditions. She hauled cargo from Calgary, Edmonton, Saskatoon, or other distribution centers, delivering it to the oil patch in northern Alberta.

Her living arrangements had varied. A bare and usually vacant apartment in Red Deer and countless hotels on the road had been the new normal, and not having children, or dependent family members, made this comparatively easy. And the money was terrific. Even after the oil boom began its decline, solid and dependable workers like Terry continued to make salaries that far exceeded the country's average.

Things changed when Terry met Joseph while eating a late meal at a local steakhouse in the northern city. He walked over from his table when the rest of his party left and asked if he could join her. He had been with a decent-looking group, and she nodded, her mouth full.

She learned his name, that he was from Toronto, had worked in the oil industry for a number of years, currently in the Fort MacMurray warehouse where she delivered cargo. Joseph said "eh" more than any person she had ever met.

He didn't seem to be hitting on her, referring to a girlfriend in Calgary, but was charming nonetheless. Over coffee and cherry cheese-cake, she found herself enjoying Joseph's company.

Growing up with brothers and a handful of male cousins in rural Saskatchewan, Terry was comfortable around men and enjoyed watching the hockey or football games in the sports bars along her route. She proudly wore her Calgary Flames jersey to hockey games and cheered for the Saskatchewan Roughriders from her home province during football season.

Over the next few months, Terry often bumped into Joseph during layovers in Fort Mac, joining him and his friends to watch a game in a sports bar, enjoying the conversation after so many hours spent alone on the road.

On one such occasion, Joseph gave Terry tickets to the Calgary Stampede, and though she had been unable to use them, she passed them on to grateful friends from Red Deer.

Months later Joseph had approached Terry in the warehouse, telling her he had been hunting, and had some frozen venison he needed to send down to his "bro" in Calgary, who was going to make it into sausage. He asked if she would haul for him, sort of a trade for the Stampede Tickets. He had told her that shipping was too expensive when his bro could just pick it up in Calgary, faster too.

This seemed out of character. Why would Joseph, who regularly picked up the group's tab following an evening watching a game in a local bar, think shipping a box of meat "too expensive"? Also, in their dozen or so times they had hung out, Joseph had never mentioned hunting.

She was annoyed, but she told him to go ahead and throw it in and didn't think much of it until Joseph's "bro" showed up to take the cooler. Joseph was slim and dark; this man couldn't possibly be his brother. He was stocky and blond, florid face reddened by the cold October wind. He said hello, not introducing himself by name, but handed her a cooler identical to the one filled with frozen meat and asked her to take some wild geese up to Joseph. Opening the weighty cooler, he showed her two large, frozen birds, shrink-wrapped in clear plastic bags, labeled with the information of a meat processing shop.

A day later, Joseph was first to meet her rig when she backed up to a loading ramp lit with a green light, the loose, dry snow blowing in strange snakes and sheets across the pavement of the plowed and frozen yard. She was tired and irritated by the delay at the end of her run. While Joseph was employed at the warehouse, he was in some management position, and she had never before seen him at the loading docks.

Joseph was delighted to receive the geese. Zipping his expensive parka, smeared with dust from his trip through the warehouse, he carried the cooler across the lot to his Jeep, the blacked-out windows shiny against the concrete wall of the last bay in the loading dock.

Although the SUV was four ramps over, Terry turned her head as she climbed the steps to the man door and saw what appeared to be an identical cooler, briefly lit before he closed the hatch.

This had taken place less than a month ago. And, on the drive back to southern Alberta, Terry had called her boss and resigned her position, citing personal reasons. Whatever Joseph was doing set off alarm bells in her mind, and she decided to simply remove herself from the situation. Terry wanted nothing to do with the illegal substances wreaking havoc on lives in the oil patch, never mind the danger of being an accidental courier.

Leaving a good job was nothing in the big picture. She could afford to take a few weeks to find work in another part of the country.

Now, in the trunk of the car, Terry recognized the profile of the passenger as Blake, a quiet man she had seen with Joseph many times. He and Joseph hadn't talked much while with a group, but she had seen them many times arriving at the bar or restaurant together, their mannerisms and quiet camaraderie suggesting they were close friends, or maybe even relatives. He was polite enough, and had a great smile, but seemed off somehow, maybe even sinister.

CHAPTER 11

H eading for the nearest men's room, Johnny quickly went over the facts, building a mental list as he did when troubleshooting a problem with his truck. He scrubbed and dried his hands carefully. He wanted to take nothing with him when leaving the hospital; the unfamiliar smell of disinfectant was bad enough.

It was still early morning when he joined Melissa Banks and Sergeant Jacobs near the nursing station. "Mr. Amund, let's go back to your garage—no, your shop."

Jacobs had a disarming smile, "I'm new to the north, well, to central BC. I transferred here from Regina, spent some time working at Depot." He was referring to the Royal Canadian Mounted Police training center, where recruits that could handle the intense training were turned into members of one of the best police forces worldwide.

"This will be the first investigation I lead up here. I will need your help, as I am not familiar with all the details of," he paused, looking at them both in turn, "a logging operation?" At their nods he continued, "I would like you both to come back to the shop, and as we take a good look at the scene, give us suggestions of things to look for, or items that are out of place."

He motioned with his head and led them down the hall toward the parking lot, asking a few questions about the town, location of the shop, and how many people the Banks employed.

The mid-November morning was chilly, and the first snow was falling in tiny flakes, swirling in the light breeze. Jacobs didn't seem to notice the cold, parka unzipped, hands bare as he walked toward his unmarked vehicle. Mrs. B, on the other hand, shivered and zipped her jacket to the very top, the collar looking uncomfortable and stiff.

Johnny brushed the light snow from the windows with his hand. Snow was snow; he had been dealing with it for weeks in the higher elevations where he was driving and was looking forward to getting the snowmobiles ready for some winter fun. This made him think of Mary, who was usually game for a weekend ride when her work rotation allowed. He brushed the snow off the rear window of the Cadillac, yanking his hand off the glass when Mrs. B turned on the rear wiper. He turned, Jacobs was watching him from the open window of his vehicle.

"I'll follow you to the shop," he called, reversing to give Mrs. Banks room to exit the lot.

As Mrs. Banks accelerated onto the street, heater fan blasting, Johnny sent a quick text to Mary to let her know they shouldn't plan to meet for lunch. Mrs. Banks turned on her radio, clicking on the Bluetooth and pushing the contact that read *HunnyBunny*. "Let's see if Chet is in cell range."

"HunnyBunny?!" Johnny was delighted. "Has Isaac ever seen that?" He chuckled, the unexpected humor feeling good.

You have reached... The familiar recording began, and she ended the call.

Johnny was still smiling, question in his eyes. Melissa could tell he did not want to be disrespectful.

"Yep, Isaac helped me figure out this whole stereo system, or whatever you call it. He is really good with electronic and computer equipment. He programs all the radios and stuff."

Johnny was suddenly alarmed. "Hey, am I in there, too?"

Mrs. Banks caught on. "There are no 'clowns' or 'hosers' in my contacts, just real names."

They shared a laugh as she scrolled up, his name jumping out at him. "There you are, 'J. Amund.'"

She looked across, sobering. "I am really worried about Terry. You know, I liked her right away. She seemed like she wanted the job, and was happy to work, you know. Kind of like you, John."

She stopped for a red light at the intersection of Highway 16, snow swirling from several eastbound chip trucks heavy with wood fiber, en route to the pulp mills in Prince George. The light changed, and she turned right, aiming the warming vehicle west of town.

"You know, Johnny, Chet and I have been talking about you. For the last few months, we have been really impressed by your responsibility, and how nice it is to work with you. Some of the guys have noticed, too, you know. Pete said you were decent to work with, and coming from him, that means a lot. Then, a couple weeks ago, Isaac was telling Chet how you are really keeping on top of your new truck, and how your preventative measures are saving time and money." She patted his arm. "This means a lot to us, Johnny. You've been with our company a bunch of years, and you actually feel like family, you know, like a big kid who has grown up. And we like Mary, too. She's good people." She popped him on the shoulder, hoping to take the embarrassment from the personal nature of her words.

She was quiet, giving Johnny space.

"Mrs. B, this summer I realized I wasn't the guy I wanted to be. So, I did some thinking– Well, I'm still trying to think it through. Mary and I have been talking about what we want out of life." He paused.

"Well, not just what we want, but what we can do, and how we can be part of something. You know, a lot of the kids that work at the grocery store just love Mary, and I guess it's because they look up to her. I want people to look up to me, too, so I need to change some stuff.

"I guess it's time to grow up. And when I started thinking about this, I found out I really like my job and the guys I work with."

He stopped speaking, red-faced in the cool, winter light.

"That's fine, Johnny, I know what you mean," she looked at him, "and don't worry, this is between you and me.

"And Johnny, now I am going to be a little vulnerable. Chet and I are not churchgoers, but my sister is, and at her church they have something called a 'prayer chain.'" She looked across to see if this was familiar to Johnny, but he just shrugged, shaking his head.

"When someone is sick, has an emergency, whatever, they have a bunch of people who pray for the person. I guess they call each other, and then pray. Well, I am calling my sister, and asking her if she will put Terry on their prayer chain. This is when we need all the help we can get. I don't know what I'm going to do if Terry gets hurt."

Johnny and Mary were not churchgoers either, even though he knew many people that were. They seemed the same as everyone else, except when they came to his door, all dressed up, with handouts and stuff, making him feel embarrassed, like he didn't know a lot of things.

He knew some churches in town were involved with the soup kitchen, and every Christmas he and Mary liked to donate a box of food. Last Christmas, when he helped Mary deliver a pickup load of food, collected in boxes set up by the checkout lanes at the grocery store, he had been a little shaken up to see two of his childhood buddies in the food line. These were the same friends with whom he had spent countless summer hours fishing and roaming the leased land his uncles farmed which bordered the reserve, taking their catch to an auntie's house, where she might prepare it for them, or joining his uncles for a simple hot meal of potatoes and meat, and of course, macaroni and cheese. Food that tasted just fine to starving young boys who had been running wild for hours.

His uncles usually took time to cook and eat their lunch in the small cabin on the leased property. They always gave a stern admonition to "not steal anything" when his friends left, making them laugh, as the uncles had nothing a boy would want to steal, and the food in the unlocked cabin was generously shared and free to be used at any time. Out of earshot, one of his friends would point at a farm implement or tractor and, imitating the uncles' accent and phrases, would solemnly announce a made-up plan to come steal, "dat darn-good-John-Deere-tractor so I can go do-a-good-day-work-in-the-fields and buy more mac-and-cheese," sparking laughter from a group of kids that wanted nothing to do with wearisome labor on the farm.

It was depressing to see some of these same friends in their current condition.

His thoughts returned to the present. Johnny had no problem if Mrs. Banks wanted to ask people to pray for this woman and thought it may even be a good idea. He wondered if the church his father-in-law attended had a prayer chain, too.

CHAPTER 12

Terry was gaining strength in the trunk. Her nausea was also growing. The ether was still strong on her skin, it smelled like starting fluid to her. No wonder she felt so sick. She willed herself to be okay.

She thought of Blake, in the front seat, and knew her instinct to leave Alberta was correct, but she had badly miscalculated the response from Joseph, and whoever else was involved. They had to be smuggling drugs, or something, and frozen meat seemed like a way to do it. With the thousands of trucks on Canadian highways, how could any policing agency stop the movement of prohibited items?

What was around her neck? Something cold that rattled when she moved, not a chain; her hands moved swiftly in the dark, touching, feeling. With horror she pulled at the macabre necklace of sockets, the weight impeding her movements. Working with shaking fingers, she untied the rope and freed herself from the heavy coils, the sockets rattling slightly in her desperate grip.

She carefully turned, and struggling onto her stomach, vomited into the corner of the trunk, her feet tangled in the backpacks. Weakly she turned on her side. Feeling no better, she turned her head and vomited again, shivering, almost losing consciousness.

She shook her head, pain exploding behind her eyes. Summoning her strength, she turned, her movement rocking the car slightly. The radio went silent and she froze, the car slowed somewhat. It resumed its speed, and the radio came back on, tuning to a hockey game. Head pounding, Terry reached for the greenish glow from the emergency trunk release. Getting a firm hold, she pulled. The trunk released, bouncing up slightly, the slipstream holding it down but not preventing the cold air from rushing in.

This time there was a shout from the front, and the driver slammed on the brakes. Terry rolled forward to slam into the seat back, unable to resist her momentum.

When the car stopped abruptly, the trunk lid rising on its springs, she struggled toward the opening, but before she could get over the edge, the two men had bolted out of the front seat. Pushing her harshly down, they slammed the lid, narrowly missing her right hand.

There was some heated conversation, and then the trunk opened again. Terry scrambled forward, but her legs were pinned together at the ankles with some sort of tape. A fist glanced off the side of her head, and she collapsed back into the trunk, pain soaring into lights and sounds and then blackness.

Terry was not unconscious, but thinking was difficult with the pain behind her eyes. The hockey game was turned up loud, or so it seemed under the rear speakers, and it was dark. Her thoughts were coming clearly now, the cold air and fear cutting through the sluggishness.

Terry accepted the danger she faced, she needed to act swiftly. From the advertisements on the radio, she knew she was near Prince George.

Okay, when we get to a town, I'll climb out of this trunk and fall on the road, she thought. *Getting run over in traffic is a much better risk that whatever these guys have planned.*

Her heart sank when the car slowed, crunching to a skidding stop on the gravel shoulder, then reversed hard. As Terry tried to stabilize herself, the driver roughly shifted back into drive and accelerated into a right turn off the highway. The vehicle bumped onto a side road, then slowed to a more cautious pace.

Terry made a new plan: when they stopped again, she would try to get into the back seat through the narrow opening. Maybe they'd leave the car running and might not be expecting this. She worked furiously on the thin tape holding her ankles together, head reeling, the hot, awful nausea sapping her strength.

It was shipping tape, probably from the partial roll that had been lying behind the seat in her truck cab. She had used it to hold her new BC license plate inside the front window of her Dodge pickup until she could mount it properly.

The tape was easy to cut with something sharp. Checking her fingernails, which she had painted bright red several days ago, she found a nail broken in her struggle to escape and began to work. She was able to puncture the tape and tear it. Then she turned her attention to the trunk lid, carefully trying to write with the red nail polish using the edges of her short nails, breaking off her efforts when she thought to search the backpacks for clothing. She found a folded T-shirt in the bottom of the first backpack, and awkwardly pulled it on, revelling in the feeling of being covered. Feeling deeper in the bag, she came out with a set of swim trunks with a drawstring and tied them on with a strong double knot.

No more than a few minutes had passed since turning off the road, and Terry was interrupted in her search for more clothing. She discarded the backpack when the vehicle slowed, accelerated, and then slammed to an abrupt stop, sliding briefly on the sealcoating, then skidding a few feet on a downhill gravel slope. The jerky movements caused her to vomit again.

There were curses and shouting from the front of the car. She tried to think– What was going on now? Where was she? *I want to live!* she screamed inside her head. Someone scored in the hockey game, horns blaring, the announcer's voice rising.

The car rocked, interior light coming on as the doors opened, and when the men got out of the car, Terry squeezed through the opening, pulling her feet into the warm interior just as the trunk opened. There was more shouting, and Terry couldn't understand the language.

She screamed, hoping someone was nearby. She reached frantically for the door locks, but the rear door on the passenger side was yanked open, and Joseph's friend Blake slid in, covering her mouth with his hands, his eyes wide and frightened under the dome light.

She struggled, and he twisted her head around. She was in an awkward position, and stopped fighting, hoping he wouldn't break her neck. He shook her head in both hands as she gripped his wrists, and told her to shut up, pulling her roughly to a sitting position. Her ankles scraped painfully on a heavy object with rough edges in the foot well behind the driver's seat.

Dogs began barking, and Blake swore in English, then switched to another language. In Blake's grip, Terry could see forward out of one eye. The view in the headlights' glare was terrifying. The car was parked by a lake, glassy with new ice. Her feet were touching a heavy cement block; a roll of duct tape was cradled in the otherwise empty front console. The conclusion was obvious. *They are going to drown me—I must escape.*

Terry was small, but a fighter and now had nothing to lose. The fear in Blake's eyes was worse than anger; something was going very wrong.

The driver slammed the trunk, and as he rushed to the open front door, lights came on in a house that had been unseen through fifty meters of bare trees, several dogs barking aggressively. With any luck they were waking the neighbourhood, if there was one.

Terry began to fight, but Blake put her in a headlock, choking her. Head throbbing, she stopped squirming, arms going slack by her sides.

The driver screamed at Blake and reversed up the road, slamming the car into a sliding J-turn and botching it, ramming from reverse to drive and back until he turned the car on the narrow road.

"You idiot! *You stupid idiot!* "Curses followed. "The lake is frozen. How can we throw someone in a lake that's frozen?" Blake was silent.

The car slid back onto the highway and accelerated east. Terry could see the compass reading on the digital display, could see the destination punched into the GPS, could see the name of the rental car company, could see the distance to their destination, could see that her kidnappers, or whatever they were, were making many mistakes.

"You idiot!" the driver shouted again, his voice too loud in the car. He thumbed open a phone. *A flip phone?* Terry thought.

He dialed a number as the car wandered across the center line. He jerked the car back, putting the phone to his ear, and spoke quietly in the language Terry couldn't understand.

The car slowed to speed limit, the driver taking deep breaths, visibly calming himself. Terry was shivering violently. She hardly noticed her lack of real clothing – survival was much more important. She wanted to say something, but her head hurt too badly.

The driver angrily snapped the phone closed and addressed Blake.

Look, idiot," he snarled, "I think someone saw us. Now we have to dump this car, get another vehicle, and *drive* back to Alberta. We'll, uh, lose her on the way." He turned back, fat neck creasing. "I will never work with you again, idiot, and they are going to give me your share of the job."

She felt Blake tense, but again, he made no reply. She held still, hoping they would not notice she was hearing everything, hoping the stress they were under would continue to cloud their judgment, giving her a chance to escape.

The driver tapped the brake, cancelling the cruise control. *Idiot yourself,* Terry thought, *driving with the cruise control on winter roads.* The professional driver in her recognized the inferior skill of an amateur; she began looking for a way to exploit it.

The situation changed much sooner than she expected as the car slowed, pulling up behind a flat deck work truck. A large, slow-moving man with long, gray hair and beard wearing a torn plaid insulated shirt and dirty pants was hefting a tire onto the flat deck, then bending down to retrieve a jack and tools. The angry driver parked and glared menacingly at the two in the rear seat. He exhaled, and got out of the car, shutting his door. He swaggered up to the man, hand raised in friendly greeting, the interior light of the rental car slowly dimming.

Blake tightened his grip on Terry, forcing her head down. She fought the impulse to struggle, waiting for a chance …

Then, Blake grabbed her wrists, yanked open the door, and dragged her from the car, bruising her knees as they bumped over the door sill onto the cold gravel. She slid and stumbled, her feet sliding over the edge of the road. It was a very steep slope. Terry racked her mind, searching for details of the still unfamiliar stretch of Highway 16.

She heard an angry bellow and then swearing from below the

embankment. The man from the work truck had been pushed over the edge. She hoped he had not been hurt. She tried to throw herself over the side, flailing her arms, trying to escape Blake's grip, but he simply forced one arm behind her back, flinging her forward into the hard, metal deck. She gasped, holding her bruised ribs, falling back and down, head slamming into the frozen ground.

She was vaguely aware of being pushed into the cab and gears grinding as the driver struggled with the unfamiliar vehicle. Then Terry lapsed back into unconsciousness.

CHAPTER 13

The investigative team consisted of Jacobs and two other officers who went through the known details with Johnny and Melissa Banks. Johnny was impressed with the quick and professional way the three investigators questioned them and searched the shop carefully.

They dusted for fingerprints, used some sort of tape to pick up samples on the floor, taking samples from the overalls hanging on the coat rack as well, "To rule out fibers intrinsic to the environment," Jacobs explained.

They had sent information to RCMP highway patrol in BC and Alberta, informing of a person presumed missing with Terry's description and the few details available. These were basic: An employee struck with an unidentified object, male, recovering in hospital. Another employee, blonde, female, late thirties, location still unknown. Eyewitness report of a clean car, rental maybe? With two men asking for the woman by the name of Terry Mason; confirmed name of women presumed missing.

As the morning went on, reports came in from Isaac and the other employees, and they found that no one besides Pete and Jason had been at the shop the previous afternoon, except for two drivers on

Johnny's shift who had driven around the shop to park their trucks for the night, and then left early in the morning before Jason had arrived. Neither man had entered the shop when parking their trucks or leaving in the morning.

Then, within the span of twenty minutes, the RCMP received several tips. A caller the Prince George dispatcher knew by name due to regular complaints, reported a disturbance at the public boat launch next to his property.

"It happened last night! The dogs were barking, eh, so I couldn't hear everything, but someone was having a party, that's for dang sure! There was a woman screaming, some yelling, nothing made sense?" His sentence sounded more like a question. "I am sick and tired of the partying that goes on all summer, and now in the fall! When are you going to do something about it, eh?" The dispatcher politely took notes during a lecture on the value of taxpayer's dollars, having several minutes to fill before coffee break.

The next call, which came to the Vanderhoof detachment, was more helpful.

This caller reported a car parked in the woods at the head of an ATV trail. She had noticed it while walking her dog early that morning. While listening to the radio on the half-hour drive to work, she began to wonder why a new car would be left on an ATV trail. None of the locals would park there; the kids, and some of their dads - she had smiled thinking of her husband on his ATV- came through that section of trail way too fast. Someone could get hurt. Due to the rash of thefts in the cottage community east of Vanderhoof, people took care of their toys, and vehicles especially.

When the dispatcher asked what color the car was, the woman

thought it was gray, or maybe blue, but for sure was clean, a newer model.

The next call was to the 911 call center. An angry young man reported that the previous evening, his father's one-ton had been boosted, the thieves pushing his dad over the embankment and driving off, the taillights of their car following the stolen Ford east on Highway 16.

The caller had finished his graveyard shift in a Vanderhoof sawmill, met some buds for breakfast, and then drove the twenty-five minutes to his dad's home in the lakeside community between Vanderhoof and Prince George.

"My welder's on that truck!" The young man was outraged and didn't care who knew it. "The old man didn't call in because he'd been drinking! My welder, actually, my welder *and* a boat-load of my tools are on that truck!" He wasn't much more help, but the 911 operator learned the older man had walked five kilometers to a friend's house where he drank beer and finished watching a hockey game before his friend drove him to his home, less than eight kilometres from where he changed his flat tire and lost his truck. The Canucks had won, making the lost truck seem like a minor issue at the time.

Chet Banks blew in with the service truck around noon, announcing he had been to see Pete, who was doing well, and demanded to know what they'd found about his newest trucker gone missing.

His arrival was timely, and Johnny guessed Mrs. B needed to go home and cry, and let her husband shoulder the responsibility. Chet was brash but likeable, and like his wife, got things done. He was a little intimidating. *No,* Johnny thought, *he's very intimidating.* But though Chet was quick to express displeasure over a mistake to an employee, or anyone else, for that matter, he apologized quickly if he was wrong, and expected others to do the same. The job was more important than anyone's feelings. He was a fair and generous boss, but not someone you wanted to disappoint.

It was obvious Jacobs and the other investigators liked him and took some time to ask him similar questions to the ones they had asked Johnny.

One of the facts that bothered them all was the collection of sockets littering the floor. Chet Banks squatted down, careful to avoid the areas marked off by ribbons, and surveyed the scene. He didn't comment on the whiskey, but Johnny knew he noticed.

Standing, he said, "Sockets are made of metal, have a hole in them, are expensive, easy to find, heavy." He straightened his knee, the pop making Johnny wince. "They are also hard to identify. Who has the time to scribe their name on sockets? We lose them by the handful in the bush, especially in the winter. Always buying new ones. Whatever the case, they didn't get these. Dropped them and left." He looked around. "I know it's snowing, but have you looked around outside?"

Jacobs nodded toward the door. "Let's go out there. I'm guessing you spend more time here than Johnny. Maybe you will see something we missed."

Johnny led the way out, taking time to grab a long-handled spade from the rack by the door.

They entered the covered lean-to where tires, dunnage, oil containers, and other paraphernalia would collect until the mechanics went on a rampage and cleaned it out. The space was organized, only a few months since a major clean-up.

Using the flashlight on his phone, Chet approached the wall of the shop. "Look at this. These aren't work boot tracks, they're some sort of shoe." They looked where he indicated, noting the set of footprints in the clay dust that led further back into the lean-to, and then back out toward the front of the shop, the to-and-fro tracks distinct from the many other prints of sharp-treaded work boots.

"Look," Jacobs said, holding up his foot. "I wear a size ten. These are a similar shape and size to the prints my boots are making." He looked at Johnny's feet, encased in expensive, heavy, and much larger work boots, then at Chet's footwear. "What size are yours?" he said, pointing at Chet's boots.

"Ten and a half," Chet said, stepping down beside a print Jacobs made. The work boot track was definitely bigger than the track made by the investigator's light boot, larger than the unique track near the wall. "Okay."

Chet continued into the gloom of the lean-to, using his phone light to look for details, careful to keep his feet clear of the tracks near the wall.

Next to a pile of wood dunnage was a neat stack of large concrete blocks. One was obviously missing from the stack. The blocks were covered with yard dust, and the outline of the missing one showed cleanly on the block now exposed.

Johnny pointed the shovel at a gleam in the shadow of a stack of used tires. Several dozen large sockets had been threaded on a cheap polyethylene rope, the bright yellow of the rope and the rounded sockets now standing out in the beams of light from Chet's phone and Jacobs's flashlight.

Chet turned away, shaking his head. "Not good, not good." His voice was flat but rose in volume. "Would you just look at that! They found the blocks and dumped the sockets and rope." He glared at the group. "Looks to me like they want to sink something."

With a curse he turned and walked back into the shop, avoiding the two officers taking photos of the tracks. Entering the shop, Jacobs and Johnny close behind, Chet dialed a number, then lowered his phone and turned off the flash light.

"Yeah, hello, Bob. You been fishing lately?"

They heard a hearty, "Well, hello to you, too, Chet. I'm just fine, thanks."

Johnny smiled briefly, recognizing the voice of Chet's buddy, a local pilot and avid fisherman. Bob had delivered parts several times to remote logging locations, a very uneconomical but quick delivery system, dropping expensive parts from several hundred feet, wrapped in bubble wrap with a long streamer trailing behind.

The legend was that once, a nonplussed mechanic had found the streamer Bob duct-taped to the box of parts was actually a crimson satin bathrobe, embossed with the stitched monogram "Amy," the name of Bob's now ex-wife.

"Bob, listen. Are the lakes still open? What have you seen from the air the last few days?" Chet asked, turning the speaker on without warning Bob.

"Well, the smaller lakes are frozen, and some of the bays on the bigger lakes, probably couldn't launch a boat now, but most launches are closed anyway. Hey," he chuckled into the phone, "I ever tell you about the time ..."

Chet cut him off. "Are you in town? If I needed a flight this afternoon, you available?"

"I'm twenty minutes out, coming back from the mine. Yeah, I could take you up later, what's up?"

"Okay, I'll call you soon." Chet abruptly hung up and turned to Jacobs. "Listen, who takes a person, leaves their clothes, grabs a *brick* on the way out, leaving a mess of sockets behind? I think we should be checking the local lakes, and we had better get on it. About four hours until it gets too dark to see. I hate to be judgmental, but we really have no idea who Terry is, and what she may be involved in. All the same, we need to figure this out now. I think she's in danger."

He paused as his phone rang, holding it at far enough away to see. "Hmph," he grunted, "unlisted number."

CHAPTER 14

Terry woke up again, disappointed and angry. She was lying in borrowed clothing on the floor in the back of a filthy bush truck. She was cold in the T-shirt and nylon shorts. The idiots who grabbed her had used plastic ties on her wrists that were now cutting into her skin. Her contacts were killing her. She was extremely thirsty, and her mouth tasted of vomit. She flexed her legs, now her ankles were securely taped. She needed to pee.

But Terry was feeling better, her headache not debilitating, and her mind clear. The vehicle was an older Ford crew cab, nearly identical to the one her dad drove when she was a teenager. She was on the floor. No, she was lying on fast food wrappers, tools, cords and straps, a phone book. Wow. The amount of clutter was amazing, and in it she saw her chance to escape.

Like her dad's old truck, the bolts holding the front seat to the floor were exposed, and she quickly broke the cheap plastic ties holding her wrists by sawing them on the sharp edges, noise from the engine and heavy tires masking any sound she was making.

The tape on her ankles was tougher, but she found a box knife among the scattered items. *Idiots!* she thought, and she stealthily sliced through the tape. Next, she quietly cleared the rubble away from the heat ducts under the front seat, allowing the warm air to flow.

She relaxed, that felt better. Turning slightly, she looked for clothing, blankets, anything to lessen the cold if she escaped. The rear seat was folded upright and had a woven cover, but there was no chance of removing it.

Searching quietly through the clutter, her hand closed on a cold metal object with a rough, knurled section at one end. *A torque wrench!* She slowly pulled it out, wincing when it caught, wiggling carefully, and sliding it awkwardly over her torso in the tight space, shivering as the cold metal rasped over her body.

Okay, Terry, time for shock and awe! She repeatedly flexed her muscles, then took a deep breath, and rising from the floor, she screamed, expelling all the sound she could muster. Holding the heavy wrench in both hands, she rammed the ratcheting end into the side of the driver's head as he turned, mouth open. The wrench made a sickening sound over the loud diesel engine, and he slumped forward, his foot thrusting down on the pedal, the heavy vehicle beginning to accelerate.

"Hey!" Blake swore as he reached for the wheel and knocked the shifter into neutral, the motor booming harshly, cutting in and out as the rev limiter kicked in.

Blake's head was in the middle of the truck and she punched at it but missed as he ducked. He was busy trying to get the driver's inert body off the accelerator pedal and steering wheel, and to knock the shifter back into gear without using the clutch, gears grinding. The truck was slowing rapidly, coasting uphill in neutral. She could see the Rocky Mountains ahead. It was broad daylight.

This time she swung the heavy tool left-handed at Blake's head, and he yelled in pain. Blood gushed from a deep cut above his left eye, effectively blinding him on the left side, and the truck continued to slow.

Terry ripped the door open on the familiar vehicle and turned, grabbing a reflective vest and a first aid kit from the seat. She stumbled to the ground and saw Blake struggling with the driver, dragging him into the passenger side. The truck was stopped now, and she heard the emergency brake engage, diesel engine rumbling. She dropped everything but the torque wrench and smashed at the driver's mirror. In several swings it was hanging from the heater wire, and she turned toward the window. She missed the driver's window as the truck lurched ahead, grinding and jerking in granny low, but connected with the rear passenger window, glass flying into the cab. Blake had gotten himself into the driver's seat, gears grinding as he forced the transmission into second gear.

Terry watched as the vehicle lurched up the hill picking up speed, then black smoke poured from the lugging engine as the driver shifted into third gear too early.

Terry dropped the wrench on the ground and quickly put on the vest. Ripping open the first aid kit, which was nearly as greasy and disgusting as the vest she had wrapped around herself, she pulled out rounds of gauze and tan stretchy wrap.

Scanning up and down the hill, she gathered her things and carefully walked down into the ditch and out of direct sight of traffic. Her bare feet were going numb as she skidded and slid down the frozen gravel shoulder, avoiding patches of dirty snow. She needed a ride but didn't want Blake seeing her if he came back.

The shiny emergency blanket was just large enough to make a flimsy skirt. With trembling fingers, she taped it carefully.

Now, she wrapped each foot in the ugly tan sports wrap, fastening it with the strips of duct tape that had been clinging to one leg, knowing better than to use the unreliable metal clips.

And there was a container of aspirin. She quickly chewed some of the bitter tablets, grateful for the sharp tang that negated the sour, sick taste of vomit.

The outfit was warmer than the T-shirt and shorts alone. Several vehicles had passed, traveling west down the hill. Now, hearing a high-powered engine approaching, she climbed back onto the road, standing next to the torque wrench, knowing better than to pick it up—she already looked crazy enough, dirty reflective vest clenched over her ill-dressed body.

The vehicle speeding up the hill was a Toyota pickup, flashing lights on top, WIDE LOAD emblazoned on a six-foot sign buffeting in the wind. The nose of the pilot car dipped as the driver hit the brakes, and from seventy-five meters Terry could see the driver lift a mic to her mouth.

Terry stood quietly as the pickup slowed, the passenger window silently rolling down. The concerned woman in the driver's seat was still, mouth formed in an "o." She slammed the truck into park and, with one last burst of words, dropped the handset and hurried around to Terry as a Western Star rushed by in the passing lane.

"Oh, my dear, what happened to you?" The woman put an arm around Terry, steadying her. She walked Terry to the passenger door, tossing a clipboard and some neatly stacked paperwork into the rear bench. Settling Terry in the seat, she reached across, cranking the heater to the highest setting, selecting the "vent" option that blew hot air directly onto Terry. She switched the heated seat control to the maximum.

"Dear, are you in trouble?" Her face was concerned, waiting for Terry's response.

"I don't think so. Two guys. I think I hurt one of them bad." The heavy smell of the woman's perfume and the blast of warm air on her face and body were such a relief that Terry began to sob.

"They're driving a flat deck Ford crew cab, it's blue. The driver's mirror is hanging off, and the rear driver-side window is broken."

"I see." Standing at Terry's open door, the woman said, "Okay. I'm Freda. I'm piloting for my husband." She indicated the wide load that had passed them and continued up the hill. "Right now, we are going to get some warm clothes on you, and some hot coffee inside, okay?"

Reaching across for the radio, Freda called her husband and gave a quick explanation.

Freda opened the rear door, and Terry heard the sound of a heavy zipper, three distinct "zips" from what she assumed was a suitcase being opened. The familiar scent of clothes fresh with fabric softener circulated through the vehicle.

The woman handed Terry some wet wipes, "Here you are, you need to clean your face. When she pulled down the visor and adjusted the mirror Terry was surprised to see blood dried on her face and on her arms as well. When her face and arms were clean, Freda helped Terry remove her vest and makeshift skirt. She quickly helped her pull on a thick, baby-blue sweatshirt with "World's Best Grandma" in large, loopy script across the front. Then a pair of underlayer leggings, new from a box. They were loose on Terry, but so warm. Finally came a set of stiff, freshly washed, blue coveralls. Terry had relieved herself before returning to the road and was finally feeling warm and somewhat comfortable.

The normality of sipping coffee from a thermos lid, and the smell of the clean clothing, touched her deeply. She continued to sob silently, shaking with relief, mind and body reeling from the ordeal. It was over. *No, it isn't,* she thought.

"Just a minute."

Freda, standing at her open door, stepped back as Terry, her feet still wrapped in the ACE bandages, got out. She walked several yards up the road to retrieve the torque wrench from the shoulder.

Freda had a pair of thick socks ready when she returned and helped her ease them on her bruised feet. Looking down, the sandy folds of dirty bandage and the greasy and bloodstained wrench were a stark contrast to the clean carpet and molded mats.

Terry concentrated on what to do next as Freda aggressively steered the pickup back onto the road and followed the direction in which her husband had disappeared several minutes earlier, the wind whistling over the light bar and WIDE LOAD sign as the speed increased.

Freda checked her phone and told Terry there was no reception, but they would catch her husband at the next pullout, hear Terry's story, and make the calls they needed to make.

Back in the Banks Mountain Contracting shop, Johnny listened with interest to half of Chet's conversation, and then to half of Jacobs's conversation when his phone rang as well. Jacobs ended his call, and Chet put his hand over his phone, muting it.

Jacobs started first. "That was ...," but Chet Banks cut him off.

"Terry is okay," he blurted, talking even more quickly than his normal rapid-fire. "She got picked up by a pilot car, the woman driving stopped for her, and now they're close to Jasper. She wants to know if she should call the cops?"

Jacobs asked to talk to Terry, and they could hear much of what she was saying, her volume rising as she went on.

Johnny's sense of relief shocked him, he was suddenly too hot, and removed his jacket. Having never met Terry, he was surprised how protective he felt, but hey, he was a loyal guy. "Riding for the brand" was a concept he understood and respected.

Jacobs told her he would call her right back and to go ahead and ride into Jasper with the couple. He would notify the Jasper RCMP. He hung up and faced them.

Jacobs said he would need to talk with Chet about moving forward. Chet nodded, holding up his phone. "Melissa says you two need to come to the house for lunch."

They did. Melissa Banks's authority was not to be questioned.

CHAPTER 15

The previous night his partner had demanded that Blake use the fuel tank on the back of the truck. He had parked behind a closed carwash, and Blake filled the fuel tank of the filthy vehicle by pumping fuel from the rounded, red tank on the back deck. He had dragged the grimy hose over the side in the dark, smearing his jacket, cold metal burning his unaccustomed hands. On trips to northern Alberta, he had heard workers talking about the difficulty of starting an engine that ran out of diesel, and he didn't want this to happen on the unplanned trip back to Alberta. He had never used a manual fuel pump, but it seemed to work fine, and he cranked the handle, until the reeking fuel erupted out of the filler neck, splashing his shoes.

Now, as he learned to shift the crude transmission in the work truck, he checked the fuel gauge. His partner of several days was slumped on the passenger seat, blood leaking from the wound in his head. He seemed to be unconscious, but breathing steadily, heavy body in danger of slipping onto the floor.

His own head was still bleeding slightly, the bundle of blue shop towel stopping the flow. The cut was long, right into the eyebrow, just like those he'd seen in a few MMA matches. This chick had hit him with a metal bar of some sort. He found himself swallowing repeatedly to avoid being sick, the rapid swelling causing the long gash to gape at least a centimeter wide when he removed the towelling. Several passing drivers had glanced in his direction, noticing the broken window, if not his bleeding head.

He swivelled the dusty sun visor to his side window. It drooped perfectly to cover the upper half of his head and face. He checked the heater – wide open. Litter from the back seat was swirling forward in the cab as the cold mountain air gusted in. There were chunks of glass in his hair and down his shirt.

It had been the worst twenty-four hours of Blake's life. He had been confident they could pick up the woman easily. He had planned to explain he was driving through, and since he heard she was in the area, to suggest they have dinner, and then let things play out, the trunk of the rental car an easy place to hold a captive until they got rid of her. It had been his idea to dispose of the woman in a lake; after all, once it froze over in the winter, how would anyone find her there? On Google Maps a big lake showed up close to the highway not far east of Vanderhoof, and he had assured Joseph it would be no problem to dump the body there. He had never done this type of work before, but how hard could it be? Blake assumed he would be in charge, but right away he recognized the heavy, dark haired man Joseph had assigned as his partner to be difficult. He realized now that his own arrogance had been his undoing; wanting to impress Joseph, he had committed to a job he couldn't finish.

They had waited near the shop on the side road and when he recognized the woman as she passed them in the truck, they simply followed her into the yard, got out of the car, and walked after the big rig into the cavernous and brightly-lit shop. His unfamiliar partner had surprised Blake. Surging forward, he picked up a fire axe from a steel table and smashed the thick hardwood handle down on a man in blue coveralls. The man's hat had flown off his head as he dropped to the concrete, bouncing off the workbench he had been leaning over. Then, his partner crossed in front of the truck, with Blake following uselessly behind, and yanked the woman out of her truck and pulled her to the floor, stunned. Grabbing a can of starting fluid from a box on a shelf, he sprayed a shop rag from the same shelf and knocked her back down. With one knee on her stomach, he held the reeking cloth over the woman's face, easily stifling her struggles. Blake had recoiled from the eyewatering stench. Dropping the can and rag, the partner stripped the woman of her clothing and effortlessly picked her up. Blake gaped, unable to look away from the woman's nakedness. The sudden violence was shocking; they had been in the shop less than a minute. The heavy man carried the woman to the car, snapping at Blake to bring the ether and rag. The trunk was ajar. Blake hadn't noticed the man click it open. With surprising care and efficiency, he had placed her in the trunk, then snapped at Blake again, like he was a kid, to come back in the shop and find the light switch. The man said he needed to leave a calling card, and while Blake turned off four light switches by the side door, his partner was up on the steps, leaning into in the cab of the truck. He emerged, nodding his head, mouth turned down into a satisfied expression. He yanked the rag from Blake's hand and wiped the handle of the axe, placing it back on the table and, flipped the grease rag to Blake who was still holding the can of starting fluid. Yelling for help, the heavy man began collecting sockets, assigning Blake to string them on a rope. He disappeared and soon came back carrying a concrete block. They had bolted for the car with the assortment of weights, leaving a mess behind. No one had seen them.

Blake had to admit the guy had seemed competent enough but was so abusive when Blake hadn't known what to do. Why be so aggressive and critical after they found out the lake was frozen, hammering away on how stupid Blake was? He hadn't considered the possibility of early ice either.

The man did have some good ideas. After they ditched the rented car and were Alberta bound in the stolen flat deck, his partner called the rental company and reported excitedly that the car had been "stolen from a rest area in southern BC, near Hope! No, I got a ride. Yes, I called the police. No, I don't know what the rest area is called!" and a whole string of lies delivered rapid-fire to a sleepy, unconcerned agent at the rental call center.

Ignoring the beauty of Jasper National Park, Blake sighed with relief when his phone pinged. Cell service was momentarily available as he crested a hill, nearing the tourist town of Jasper. Several missed calls were showing, but he opened the text from Joseph and instantly felt much better. "Parked at hotel in Jasper by pine trees, back lot. All good, exit door is fixed."

He recognized the location and understood with relief that Joseph had transportation arranged; they could abandon the truck and get back to home base.

Several hours later, Blake and his snoring partner were riding in a shipping container secured on a flat deck trailer. The exit plan Joseph had devised was genius, Blake thought. He leaned back in the comfortable seat of a side-by-side ATV, the soft suspension smoothing the trailer's rough ride, wrapped warmly in blankets taken from a hotel room. His forehead was throbbing but neatly bandaged, cooler of food and drinks in the seat next to him, and groggy from the pain medication Joseph had given him, Blake began to relax. His injured partner was sleeping noisily on a mattress on the floor, also covered with blankets.

They had parked in the lot behind the hotel as planned, the rear of the stolen flat deck similar to dozens like it in town. Trees obscured the front of the Ford from the street. A dozen parking slots over, positioned with clear passage to the exit, was a dump truck hitched to a trailer. Two young guys were smoking by the open door of the shipping container that was strapped on the equipment trailer, admiring a side-by-side ATV a third man was loading. They were talking too loudly, posturing, ribbing the guy as he swung the container doors closed, working hard to set the latches. "You paid too much, dude! It's a piece of junk!"

The young guy slammed the ramps into their slot, his grinning reply causing the watchers to swing away, covering their mouths. Blake watched in disgust. He still didn't understand Canadians. So much opportunity all around them, but so eager to spend all their time and energy and wages on noisy toys designed for use in the cold. The three men, arguing over their lunch destination, climbed into a rusty, lifted 4x4, two gaudy snowmobiles crouching like mutant insects on a deck above the cargo area, exaggerated tracks protruding far over the rear bumper. The noisy conversation was instantly muted when the engine roared to life.

Joseph had been listening attentively to the earlier conversation, but from his position on the other side of the vehicle, Blake had only heard fragments, something about delivering the trailer somewhere. Joseph nodded and motioned with his head at the closed storage container; "There's your ride, eh. Help me get your partner in there." Feeling competent, Blake moved the flat deck truck next to the container. Together, and none too gently, they helped the heavy man, now awake, into the container. There was a stack of used mattresses leaning next to a nearby dumpster, and obscured by parked vehicles, Joseph had quickly dragged a twin mattress into the container.

Before he closed the door, Joseph had appeared relieved, but was very clear in his instructions. "The trip will take at least five hours, eh. The cops are looking for you guys, roadblocks and all. Whatever you do, keep quiet when the truck stops!" He was taping Blake's cut as he spoke. "The driver won't know you're in the container, eh, so don't make any noise when he unhooks the trailer, or when he leaves. He'll park the container off in a safe place, and when he's gone, we'll get you out. His boss is cool with it, owes me one, eh." He looked at Blake, and Blake just nodded. Joseph seemed satisfied, so he was, too.

He pointed to the restaurant take-out bags and bottled drinks standing in an open cooler next to their backpacks. "You've got lots of food and water, so just hang tight, until the driver unhooks and is long gone. We will have to wait until it's all clear. You just hang in there, eh?"

He paused as he closed the container door and assured Blake, "Hey, man, don't worry. You made some mistakes, no big deal. I'll tell them that he screwed it up, not you, eh?" He inclined his head toward the sleeping man on the mattress. "And don't worry, I'll take care of the woman."

The truck stopped a few times, and as instructed, Blake made no sound. Five hours into the trip they were bumping slowly on a rough road, the tools, fuel drums, bundles of fence posts and pallets of wire bundles making ominous sounds in the dark. The meagre light coming through the welded vents near the roofline had ceased completely.

The driver took his time positioning the trailer, and Blake could hear him whistling as he unhooked. He felt a fondness toward the man who had unknowingly helped him escape. He wished he could thank him.

Twenty minutes later, the driver passed through a gate, set the brakes on the truck, and got out, stretching his back as he dialed a familiar number.

"Hey, Dad, how's it going?"

He fumbled to light a cigarette, listening.

"Yeah, uh-uh. Yep."

He listened some more.

"You betcha. I just dropped it all off, just in time, too. The road's still dry but it's going to snow any time. Yes, the supplies will be safe, it's a brand-new shipping container! You can't get in one of those unless you got some dynamite or a cutting torch! Yep, the Polaris is in there, too, all tuned up and ready to go."

The man swung the gate closed, wrapping the heavy chain around the metal posts, clicking the padlock into place.

"No, the container isn't locked, but I parked it with the rear doors tight against the other one. No one can get in unless they bring a truck to pull the trailer ahead, but who's going way the heck back there? Ain't no one going to be there 'til we start the fencing contract next spring, and I'm locking the gate as we speak!"

He was still whistling as he left the property and checked the dash clock. With some luck he could be back to the main drag in an hour flat, a few more to drop off the dump truck, and then home in time to watch the last half of the hockey game. Life was good, eh?

CHAPTER 16

Details were shared in the Banks's warm kitchen, where Johnny was being fed for the second time in one day.

Melissa Banks expressed her relief by digging several frozen homemade pies out of the freezer and putting then into the oven. "No reason we can't have a late dessert, the officers still working in the shop would like some, and the whole crew will be stopping in, not going to be getting much work done this afternoon."

It felt good, being included in the conversation and investigation. Today was a day for Johnny to listen and learn. His mind was working, analyzing: *Bad things happen quick. The people I work with matter. The Banks respect their employees and take care of them. Jacobs and Barton were decent cops. Terry is safe.*

He was, for once, anticipating Mary's "so how was work today, Honey?"

The investigation would now be focused on finding the people who had assaulted Pete and abducted Terry. Clues were being gathered in the shop, the abandoned rental car, and the stolen Ford flat deck found burning behind a hotel in Jasper by some shocked tourists whose many photos documented the demise of truck, welder, and tools.

Jacobs pushed back from the table. "A few more details for you. The officer in Jasper was impressed with Terry's work on the bad guys. Even though the cab was burned up, the driver's mirror was hanging by a wire, and the rear window on the driver's side was shattered." He grinned. "You said she's not that big? Might want to look over her resume, could be unexpected credentials in there."

He seemed to be enjoying the moment of levity. He looked over at Johnny, "From the description by my fellow officer, this lady sounds pretty tough! Even as big as you are, friend, I'd be careful to stay on her good side. He paused, grin fading. "Terry kept the wrench she used to disable the driver and wound the other guy. Smart of her to keep it for evidence, but something to think about.

"Folks, I am glad this turned out so well. It appears Pete will be fine, and Terry wasn't hurt badly." He paused. The suspense and danger hadn't dissipated. "Now our job is to find out who did this, and it appears that Terry will be able to identify the men when we track them down. You have been a big help, and I think we'll be finished in your shop very soon; should be usable in a few hours."

Jacobs's phone rang. He walked out on the porch, closing the door behind him. He returned shortly, saying the team needed a few minutes of his time and then he would be driving back to Prince George. He would interview Terry in Prince George in the morning, as she was riding back to the northern capital with the woman who had helped her near Jasper.

With Jacobs gone, Johnny looked to Chet, preparing to ask for directions for the remainder of the day. The snow had been falling steadily, the change in the landscape startling as it was each year. Melissa was leaving for the hospital with a plate of food for Pete, with strict instructions to Chet to remove the pies from the oven. Johnny recalled the boss had worked all night, and instead of waiting for instructions, he took some initiative.

"Hey, Boss, how about I get the yard plowed, and then see if I can figure out what's wrong with Terry's truck?" From the blank look, he realized Chet Banks didn't know about the trouble with the truck. He explained quickly, and then volunteered to remove the pies from the oven as well. "Get some sleep, Boss, you look tired. I will take care of stuff in the shop." Setting a reminder, Johnny left the warm kitchen and kicked through the new snow to his pickup for the short drive back to the shop to get the plow.

In the skid-steer, Johnny followed his tracks back to the Banks's house to clear their lane and parking area first. The timer vibrated before the driveway was finished, and as he dutifully headed toward to the house, Mrs. B drove back into the yard. Johnny, relieved to be off 'pie duty' told her he would be in the shop the rest of the day. "I don't have time for a trip now, and with Pete gone for a few days, I told Mr. B that I'll start on 327 as soon as the RCMP are gone."

"Johnny, thanks for the help today. Chet needs some sleep alright, he's been up a long time."

As he was walking away, she called after him, "I'll bring dessert to the shop soon, don't let the guys leave!"

Finishing the driveway, Johnny returned to the shop, and leaving the skid-steer idling outside, went in to check on the progress. Jacobs was gone, but the other two officers said he was welcome to work on the truck, as they had collected all the evidence they needed. They also suggested he collect Terry's clothes, as she didn't need to see how they were arranged. He passed on the message about dessert and figured he would let Mrs. B deal with the clothing when she arrived.

He finished plowing the several acres of gravelled yard around the shop. When several trucks came in just before dark, he was glad he had cleared the parking area out back first.

As he was shutting down the skid-steer in the lean-to, two truckers walked over, demanding to know what was going on and how Pete was doing. There was a lot of bluster, but they were truly concerned. Johnny gave them a quick update and told them to come to the shop for pie when they had finished with their trucks, heading out to fuel up the skid steer.

Melissa Banks had a brightly striped beach towel, of all things, covering the lunch-room table. Now the table held three large pies, steaming in the cool air of the shop. A bucket of ice cream sat next to paper plates. The two RCMP officers were smiling over gigantic slabs of Saskatoon pie and ice-cream. Mrs. B took orders, dished out more for the newcomers, and the questions and answers became shorter as they all dug in.

When the RCMP officers left, she followed. Johnny and the other truckers waited respectfully until the taillights of the vehicles turned out of the yard, and then each helped themselves to another large slice of pie. They agreed there should be some left for Isaac La Crosse, but leaving one of the pies completely untouched was a bad idea, as, in Johnny's words, "Isaac may feel uncomfortable about cutting into a new pie." They agreed, and as one of them said, "Helping ol' Isaac by each eating a piece of this untouched rhubarb pie was the only decent thing we can do."

Jason showed up then, and though he was still pale and strained, he quickly polished off the Saskatoon pie. Shaking the crumbs out into the garbage can, he stacked the empty pie tin under the rhubarb pie, "Isaac will never notice."

The boy was learning, but Johnny knew Isaac would, indeed, notice.

After a chuckle, Johnny told the truckers about the trouble with 327, and they were happy to help diagnose the problem. The one who started the truck was startled by the clothing Johnny had forgotten to remove. Respectfully, they stacked the clothing on the passenger seat.

They worked quietly, thoughts for the most part guarded. It seemed a bond had formed that was not there before. Johnny had worked with the men for several years, but now they seemed more like friends than coworkers.

An hour later, using supplies Isaac kept stocked in the parts room, the problem was fixed, three truckers and an apprentice pitching in to do a job their mechanic was unable to do, on a truck that would have no driver for several days. Jason surprised them with his knowledge and ability, relaxing as he worked.

As Johnny parked the repaired truck next to the others in the yard, the falling snow melting before freezing on the shop-warm vehicle, he considered the hour spent working together; certainly not a waste of time.

CHAPTER 17

O n Friday morning Johnny left the house early following a quick breakfast and coffee with Mary. The big rig, which he brought home the previous evening, was idling in the drive, cab cleared of snow, ready for the day that would add another 600 kilometers on the odometer. Johnny backed out of the driveway, window open, subconsciously listening for irregular rattles or squeaks. Johnny inhaled the fresh air moving off the ridge from the northeast as it purged the valley of the industrial haze that sometimes hovered over town. Mary would be curled on the couch near the glowing wood-pellet stove, TV set low, catching another hour or so of sleep before caring for her horses and leaving for work.

It was unbelievable, Johnny thought, how different this morning was from yesterday. Normal. Regular. Not full of unknown danger. He knew Terry was still dealing with her own experience and would be in Prince George with the RCMP. Nothing was normal for her yet, and how could it be? She had only started her job on Monday, and today was Friday. Johnny hoped she would stay with the company, though he figured it would depend on the resolution of the situation.

Over toast and eggs, Mary had not been so patient, returning to the train of thought she had expressed eloquently the previous evening. She thought "this Terry person" should keep right on travelling, for her own sake, and that of Banks Mountain. If Pete's injury was a result of something stupid Terry had done or been involved with, she would have some things to say!

"Why does she get so wound up?" he said aloud.

He passed the hobby farm where Isaac lived. A light shone through the window in one of the ramshackle garages, and there were snowmobile tracks everywhere. Johnny grinned. The first six inches of snow was not enough for a very smooth ride. Isaac must have been busy working on an old snowmobile when he got home last night, and now he was already up and around, a typical mechanic, always making something better. Maybe this winter he and Mary could invite Isaac to join them for a weekend of riding.

Johnny's first trip took much longer than usual, as the other Banks Mountain truckers were eager to hear the story. Each time Johnny's truck was loaded, or while he waited to unload at the mill, people seemed to be waiting for a conversation. It had snowed well over a foot, and traffic was slower today, trucks waiting for space to chain up in the pullouts, drivers climbing up to talk through Johnny's window.

Chet was out on the grader, clearing snow from the roads which provided access to the area Banks Mountain was harvesting. For Chet, grading was serious business; he had no time to shoot the breeze until the road was clear, tersely redirecting questions to Johnny. So, while installing chains for the hills, or taking them off for longer flat stretches of road, Johnny found himself to be the company spokesman.

On his second trip, the snow started falling again just north of the valley. The main Forest Service Road was busy, slippery, uphill grades rough from tire-spin. Waiting in a chain-up area while a service truck blocked the road and pulled two pickups from the ditch, Johnny spent ten minutes talking to several truckers from his crew and an out-of-town subcontractor working for one of the big companies.

The out-of-towner was from a more mountainous region of Southern BC, and though the terrain did not impress him, the amount of traffic did. A fair comedian who enjoyed attention, their laughter following his colorful description of "double parking to chain up", spurred him on, and he continued, rapid-fire, ending with the quip, "Well looks like the boys is okay, yes sir! What doesn't kill ya makes ya slower!"

They paused as the first pickup to be extricated parked in the pull-out near them, the sweating, red-faced driver using a shovel to hack the packed snow out of his front wheel wells so he could safely drive back to town. Glancing over, he raised a hand sheepishly at the watchers. The other pickup was soon on the road as well, its driver limping back to probe the ditch with a long metal pry-bar. He came out with a chainsaw and held it up in their direction, grinning, before tossing it casually in the back of his pickup.

No one was criticizing anybody else today as the two pickups each departed in their respective directions; the tracks had been clear, both drivers had displayed the skill earned from many years on slippery bush roads as they safely avoided each other on a bad corner, and no real harm was done. Johnny realized that just last winter he might have been complaining to the other drivers, the ten-minute delay more important at the time than the safety of the men or equipment.

Back on the road and way behind schedule, he mulled this over, worrying the concept like a raven on a frozen carcass he had passed earlier. He shook his head, ashamed. Johnny knew that until recently, the delay would have been foremost in his mind. He knew he would have cursed and complained, not considering the guys in the ditch.

What had the trucker said, "What doesn't kill you makes you *slower*?" Normally Johnny enjoyed sarcasm, but today it seemed foolish. He didn't want to be slower, he wanted to be *stronger*, he wanted to grow.

He enjoyed spending more time with Mary, she was even getting up early so they could eat breakfast together. He pounded the steering wheel. "*I will get stronger, I will be a better man.*"

He continued speaking aloud in the empty cab, ignoring the radio chatter. "It's not Mary changing, I'm actually the one who's changing. Now she wants to be with me more." No, that wasn't right. He tried again. "Mary has always been the same. It's me who is changing. I thought she was always nagging and pushy, and she was, but it was my fault."

He smacked the steering wheel, then his leg. He cursed unconsciously, using a phrase his uncles had reserved for the most shocking occasions.

Johnny Amund rolled up the North Road in an empty logging truck, a loose tire chain clashing rhythmically. His thoughts were coming in waves. He drove, letting them wash through his mind.

"So yesterday, I helped around the shop all day, might not even get paid because my job is to drive. And I don't even care, never even thought about it until now!"

He stopped speaking aloud, thoughts running on.

Rubbing his eyes, he remembered a recent Sunday afternoon spent with Mary replacing the top rail around the breaking corral and then raking leaves onto a big tarp and dragging them into the smaller corral. He smiled at the thought, Mary had jumped on the pile of leaves on the sliding tarp, her sudden weight ripping the tarp from his grip. The horses had leaned over the fence, bobbing their heads as their master and the big one rolled around in a pile of leaves, laughing. That had been a good day, he wanted more like it.

He was still thinking while he removed the dripping chains and hung them, scoured shiny by snow, on their rack. His thoughts were focused now on Mary, on doing things for Mary, the simple changes he had made. These changes or corrections were helping him become a stronger man.

Though simple, he could see the choices he was making were actually responsible for the difference in their life together. He was asking himself daily what his uncles would've advised, trying to eliminate the habits they would have considered to have no worth. They were big on independence but had also made it clear that the world judged a man by what it saw him do, how it saw him live. *Choose how you want to live, Yonny, but live with the consequences of your choices.*

"Yonny, the important thing is what you *start* doing, more than what you *stop* doing." Uncle Nelsson had said one fall evening, grimy in his coveralls, tired from a long day discing.

Johnny had been frustrated, working to finish a school assignment, unhappy he had not been able to help his uncle in the fields. The way Uncle Nelsson spoke, standing calmly by the counter, had impressed the boy. The older man poured fresh coffee from the pot Johnny had brewed when he heard the John Deere coming in from the north field.

He lifted the mug in a salute of thanks, savoring the first sip of the strong brew.

"I could tell you to stop complaining, but you know I don't do that." He paused for another sip.

"And already you have figured out what I will tell you." His quick grin showed strong white teeth.

"What you need to do is think of all you have to be thankful for. When you start doing this, then there won't be anything to complain about. You will be happy."

He grinned again, stretching the kinks from his tired back. "Just like it makes me happy when there is always mysteriously a fresh pot of coffee waiting when I come in from the work."

The memory was crystal clear, as if Uncle Nelsson was riding with him. He missed the old man fiercely, had probably never grieved the loss of his uncles. Johnny wished he could tell them once again how much he appreciated all they had done for him, for providing a home and good training.

Johnny felt younger, like he had when his uncles were still alive. This was a good thing. He knew it had been a long time coming. He had enjoyed pleasing his uncles and other adults he admired. And they had been proud of him, they had said so several times. He remembered this clearly, memories he had treasured as a boy, forgotten in the bitter years since.

Uncle Nelsson had said that "starting" was more important than "stopping". And he had started.

He could talk with Mary. He had earned some trust, and she would be excited to try and figure it out together and if he could start something, well, Mary could help him keep going.

CHAPTER 18

F riday evening, Melissa Banks sent out a group text, splattered with emojis, to all the Banks Mountain employees.

Hello everybody. Bad things happened this week, but good things happened too. We're happy Pete is okay and Terry is back in town today and is fine. Chet and I would like to invite you all to a BBQ in the shop tomorrow night. If you already have plans, that's okay, more steak and lobster for us, that's right, steak and lobster! After we eat, we are going to have a quick meeting. Kids and partners welcome of course. Lots of room and food for all. Text me tonight if you can come. If you get the text later, come anyway. Bring lawn chairs. And warm clothes. PS Big thanks to Johnny for all the help yesterday!

She also called Johnny at home and asked if he and Mary would come early and help set up the shop. They told her they would be happy to help.

Mary was ecstatic. She had grown up with a father who threw

many memorable parties. Johnny was a little more reserved, but who could say no to Mrs. B? He was a little nervous to meet Terry.

Saturday morning, they slept in, padding around the kitchen in old sweats at 8:30 AM, enjoying good conversation while drinking coffee and eating pancakes. This led to activities that were a lot more fun, which meant they were back in the kitchen later for burnt coffee and floppy pancakes crisped in the toaster.

Johnny changed the oil in Mary's car while she prepared a salad. Soon finished, he fired up the snowmobiles, and took each for a quick lap of the yard. From the window Mary could see her quarter horses racing Johnny on the opposite side of the fence. Leaving her salad in the refrigerator, she grabbed a jacket on the way to join the fun.

The afternoon was busier than planned. Chet was absent, moving a machine for his brother. Johnny was sent to haul tables from a rental company, and when he returned was surprised to find the furnace roaring, and hot air billowing through the normally cool building. Mary was pressure washing the floor, and Jason was moving much faster than normal, snapping to attention each time Melissa gave a new order.

Johnny looked around grinning. Pete and Isaac kept a clean shop, but this was looking like one of the reality TV shows they sometimes watched in the lunchroom.

Jason was sent on a grocery run, excited to drive Melissa's Escalade. He blushed furiously when Melissa yelled across the shop, "And Jason, call that cutie I saw you with the other day, invite her to go shopping with you and to come to the party. That's an order!"

Johnny found himself pressed into duty when Jason left, and tried not to jump when Melissa snapped out a request. With tables set up on the drying floor, he went outside.

Isaac pulled in while Johnny was downing a beer from one of the large coolers standing lids-open to chill outside the large doors.

"What's the matter with you, Clown?"

Tossing him a beer, Johnny shook his head, pointing with his beard at the building. "Hurricane Melissa warning, hope you're not planning to work in there!"

Beer in hand, Isaac reached in the box of his beater truck, coming out with some broken parts from a snowmobile suspension. He headed toward the door, taking a long pull from his beer.

He opened the door, then shut it in his own face, dropping his parts in the snow. "Well…" He froze, his exclamation cut short as the door opened in front of him and Mrs. Banks appeared.

"I thought it was you!" She pointed a finger in Isaac's face, glancing at the parts in the snow. "Don't even think about welding in here today, Mr. La Crosse! Now help Johnny shovel the coolers full of snow, clean snow, and then…" her instructions were cut short when she closed the door.

Rattled, he turned to look for a shovel with which to help Johnny fill the coolers with snow, and tripped on his forgotten project, spilling his beer, and attempted to glare at Johnny whose laugh filled the yard.

If the party was as much fun as the preparation, it was going to be historic. Johnny and Isaac found the coolers quite heavy and too full to add enough snow. Lightening the load the only logical way, "it's five-o'clock somewhere!", they were busted when trying to balance a pyramid of empty cans on the first cooler they carried into the shop.

Mary joined Melissa in the tongue lashing that ensued, and Johnny and Isaac were quickly fed most of a salad and a pot of coffee. The boys ate with relish and howls of laughter, slapping each other on the back and repeating over and over in terrible accents, "I'll be back!" as they devoured the three-bean salad.

The ladies relaxed as the food and coffee, and a dose of embarrassment, helped the men calm down over the next hour, and when Chet stomped into the shop, tracking mud and snow onto the clean floor, he did a double take.

"Now that's what I call clean!" Shooting Isaac with a finger pistol, he slowly drawled some advice for future shop organization, which made even the exasperated women laugh.

Chet enjoyed the recap of the afternoon events. Mary delivered a cryptic account of "the boys' stupidity". Johnny's explanation of Isaac tripping in the snow, and Isaac's hilarious re-enactment of the absent Jason bounding around the shop like a dog with a shock collar, had Chet howling. It was all enhanced by Melissa's thin smile as she continued working like a Mona Lisa on Red Bull. Terry showed up at 4:15PM, and Chet called the six of them to take a seat at one of the tables. Melissa introduced Terry, who was gracious, and thanked them for their help and support.

"It was almost surreal, except for the horrible headache," Terry mused at the end of her story. "You only see this stuff in the movies – until it happens! Good thing for me the guys were such amateurs. They were obviously supposed to get rid of me. Maybe they're good at it wherever they worked before, but they sure didn't know much about the north.

"I mean, the lake they were going to drown me in was probably only a couple feet deep by the shore." She shivered, remembering the tape, cold metal sockets, and concrete block. "I've never been to that lake, but I could see reeds or some sort of plants sticking up through the ice—idiots! Who would try to drown someone at a boat launch?"

They were all serious as they listened, and the silence after Terry stopped talking became uncomfortable. Melissa patted her arm, saying, "Tell us what the RCMP have found out."

"Well, they found the stolen truck burning at a hotel in Jasper, too bad for the guy they stole it from. He wasn't hurt though. They just pushed him over the edge of the road, it was steep there, and took off in the truck. Those guys didn't know anything about commercial vehicles. Both of them tried to use first gear to start off." She shrugged. "I think if I hadn't been so disoriented from being knocked out with starting fluid, I could have got away a lot sooner."

As more details came out, they began to ask questions, and by the time Terry had told them the whole story, Jason and his date had returned with the food, though they had forgotten the sour cream and steak spice from Melissa' list.

The potatoes went on the grill, and Melissa made do with the steak spice she had, and asked politely if Jason would go to town for sour cream and a few more things. Jason, happy to oblige, was in another world and had no idea he had forgotten anything.

CHAPTER 19

The short version of Terry's story proved to be a catalyst for the most open and comfortable conversation the Banks Mountain crew had experienced together. Seeing Pete looking better, showing the kids his stitches while enjoying lobster tails, was good for morale.

The meal in the huge building was memorable, big grill smoking, tended by Johnny and Isaac who were glad to stand under the exhaust fan near the grill, as yes indeed, the three-bean salad was back as promised. Crimson lobsters came steaming from giant propane-fired pots, and as Melissa had planned, there was no shortage of food.

Melissa banged on a table until everyone was seated, and then asked if someone would say grace. Johnny was surprised when Frank stood up and said he would be glad to, removing his hat.

"God, we thank you for this day, and for keeping Pete and Terry from serious harm. Thank you for the feast the Banks have provided, and please bless them for their generosity. We pray this in your name, amen." There were a few scattered amens as Frank sat down, and Chet waved a soft drink around and told them all to dig in.

While serving up the thick, juicy steaks, Johnny watched Melissa sitting with a bunch of small kids at a low table, teaching them how to extract lobster meat out of the shell and dip it in garlic butter. A little girl held up a large piece she had successfully extricated by herself. Face shiny with butter, she declared, "Lobthter ith even better than ham!" and with a big smile, double dipped the morsel and shoved it in her mouth.

Johnny noticed Mary watching him, and grinned at her, nodding toward the little kids and offering her a choice piece, "You just shut up and eat some lobthter too", he said.

When everyone was full, Melissa recruited Jason, date in tow, to start a movie for the excited younger kids to watch. The troop of children followed them, crowding into the lunchroom to watch a cartoon on the media equipment normally used for safety demonstrations.

When they were happily engaged, and Jason back with another loaded plate, Chet asked Terry to share the full story of her experience. She spoke well and had everyone's undivided attention as she relayed the story. Isaac interrupted a few times with questions that highlighted the details of bravery that Terry's short version hadn't covered.

When Terry had finished, and received a lot of hugs from the women, Chet rattled off a short, heartfelt speech about the Banks Mountain crew being like a family, and how he was proud to see them caring about each other. He congratulated Terry on her quick thinking and made a few comments on using initiative in emergency situations.

Chet now turned his attention to the older kids still in the room.

"You kids have heard something important today. I hope you will never be in such a position where you need to defend yourself like Terry did, but," here he paused, "if you ever do, remember to use whatever is at hand. And", he stabbed a thick finger at them, "I hope you have learned something about helping those who need help. Like the lady who stopped to give Terry a ride."

He pointed again at the attentive audience. "And I know you can imagine how safe Terry felt sitting in that warm pickup with a kind person. You kids need to grow up to be people who help other people when they can't help themselves."

Mary started clapping, and the rest joined her. Chet was flushed by the effort of speaking in front of the whole crew, but when the applause was over, soldiered on.

"I'm going to donate a load of logs for firewood." He named a group in their community who helped the elderly. "I'll be bringing a load to the yard real soon, and next time a processor is in the yard "I'll cut it into stove lengths. He jabbed his finger at the dozen kids in the audience. "And I'd like you guys to give me a hand, and any of your parents who want to help, and we will deliver pickup loads of firewood to some of the older people living out in the boonies who could use a little help before Christmas. What do you say, I got some helpers?"

There was a tentative nod or two, and Jason burst out with, "Well I'll sure give a hand!" caught up in the moment. A girl in her early teens, who thought Jason was cute and appeared jealous that he seemed to have a girlfriend, raised her hand and said she would like to help, and then there was a flood of positive response from the rest, including many of the adults.

Chet raised a hand and went on. "I know it might seem we are, well," he paused, searching for the words, "sort of in a feel-good situation, relieved Terry and Pete are okay, but I think it's time we pay it forward, so how does next Saturday sound?" There were a few more cheers.

"Wow," Johnny said quietly to his wife, "he doesn't waste any time, does he?" He leaned closer to her ear. "What do you say, shall we get right in there too?"

She squeezed his big arm. "Absolutely, sounds like a date!"

The younger kids were still engrossed and the giggles from the lunchroom brought smiles to their mothers' faces. The older kids headed outside to look at a new snowmobile on the back of someone's pickup, and the adults tackled the issue on everyone's mind.

Terry started. "I really don't know if this is over or not. The RCMP haven't found anything yet, like why these people came after me. I recognized one of the guys as someone who was a friend of an acquaintance from Alberta." She cleared her throat, then said, "This acquaintance, Joseph, who said he was from Toronto, seemed to be friends with one of my attackers. I saw them together a few different times. Then, one night in a steakhouse, Joseph asked me to take some meat in a cooler down to his brother. Well, I assumed it was his brother, he actually said 'bro'". I didn't really want to do it, but he had given me Stampede tickets, so I told him to throw it in the truck. The problem was that when 'the bro' came to pick it up, he obviously wasn't related, and he had a cooler with some frozen geese in it that he wanted taken up to Joseph.

"I made that run, and even though Joseph acted surprised I brought him a cooler from his friend. He had his Jeep parked right in the loading docks where no one in their right mind would park their car, and pretty much grabbed the cooler and took off."

Isaac made a comment about truckers not being able to back up safely, but was ignored, and Terry continued.

"Everything seemed wrong. Joseph was more of a city guy, not a hunter, actually seems like he is from another country."

She was cut off when Isaac drawled, "Toronto *is* another country," scoring some laughter from the rural, western Canadians. They had their own opinions of Canada's largest city and the unfamiliar province of Ontario.

Terry smiled and kept talking. "The next morning when I headed south loaded, I called my boss and let him know I was quitting when I got back to Calgary."

She took a sip of coffee, then continued the story, everyone leaning forward to hear. "I figured, hey, I didn't need to get involved in something illegal, and just had a bad feeling about it. I planned to spend a couple weeks with my family, and then look for a job somewhere else."

Terry smiled at Chet, then Melissa. "Then I saw their ad, and I quote: 'Smart trucker needed right now to haul logs.' Figured this sounded like me, made a call, got hired, and here I am."

Isaac whistled, "Sounds like you made a good choice, but someone tracked you down pretty quick, eh? Think these guys are smuggling drugs or something?"

"I have no clue, but I do know that one or maybe two of them will have headaches worse than Pete's right now. The guy named Blake probably has a black eye, both probably needed some stitches," Terry said. "They would be easy for the police to spot, from the description I have given. Plus, the guy who they stole the truck from saw them pretty well in the headlights."

The furnace kicked on loudly as everyone waited for Terry to go on, and Isaac walked over and turned off the noisy exhaust fan above the grill.

"I would assume they were involved with this Joseph guy. The RCMP are looking for him, and they should be able to find him pretty easily."

Chet spoke up. "Terry doesn't want to hide. She wants to keep working, and I'm okay with that. But we don't want her to get hurt, or anyone else either, like Pete did."

Now Pete took a turn. "I'm plain old embarrassed. These guys up and whacked me on the head in my own shop, and I never seen them coming." His face reddened. "I feel real bad I was of no help to Terry. It's just not right."

"I don't blame you, Pete," Terry said. "In fact, I know it's actually my fault you got hurt. I sure am sorry."

A general hubbub broke out, as people reassured them both.

Melissa cleared her throat, and quiet ensued.

"The RCMP feel it's okay for Terry to keep working, and from the facts available, are confident there will be no immediate payback." Melissa cleared her throat again. "But we need to be careful and aware of what we see, like Jason did when he remembered details about the car the guys were driving, and like the woman from who reported the abandoned rental car, right? Like Chet said, we support Terry's decision to keep on working, but we want you all to think this through. We want you to feel safe."

"It's not Terry's fault that this happened." Chet spoke. "She has done the right things all along, shown good judgment. The people that grabbed her are the ones who are wrong, and a couple of them know right now how bad their judgment was!"

There were some chuckles, as Isaac mimed swinging a wrench.

"So, if you feel uncomfortable, please talk to us tonight or tomorrow. We want everything out on the table, no muttering around, etcetera. This company means a lot to Melissa and I, and I hope you all realize that it isn't just about making money," he paused and dropped his voice a register "although my name is 'Banks' and I do like money."

When the laughter ended, Chet said, "You all are important to us.

We want you to make a good living, have a good chance at family life, and feel part of something that is important."

There were nods, and Mary said, "And we really do appreciate it!"

"Thanks," Chet nodded at Mary. "So, here's what we're doing. We're going to continue working safely and watch out for each other. Descriptions of these two guys have already been posted on social media, and all along Highway 16 and various routes in Alberta. The RCMP have spoken with representatives from all the larger trucking companies servicing northern Alberta, and my guess is that coolers on Alberta highways will be treated suspiciously in the near future."

He grinned and hoisted a soft drink, tilting it toward Terry. "Here's to a brave trucker who put the hurt on the bad guys! I hope you feel welcome in the Banks Mountain family!"

Driving home late that night, Mary leaned across the center console, putting her head on Johnny's shoulder. While Johnny had spent an hour cleaning up the shop, Mary had helped Melissa drive a few people home. Melissa was strict about driving and alcohol, and Johnny and Isaac's earlier escapades hadn't helped the cause.

Now at midnight, Johnny started laughing at himself and Isaac. "Man, what a couple idiots we were today! It was a lot of fun though; did you see his face when he saw the shop?".

Mary got the giggles when he explained, and then giggled some more when Johnny began imitating how Jason was mooning over both his date and his multiple plates of food.

"Johnny, I am so glad we had this evening together, even though it was terrible what happened to Pete and Terry." She paused, collecting her thoughts, looking out the windshield at the heavy snowflakes that seemed to be rushing at their vehicle.

"I am actually jealous of you, working for the Banks. They really seem to care about us, like, how much did all the food cost tonight? And did you see Melissa making it fun for the little kids, making sure they all had lobster, like who does that?" She sighed. "It was just so nice. I felt like I was home. Not my home growing up, we were not that happy, but *home*, you know?"

Johnny knew.

CHAPTER 20

N ot only did Johnny understand, he had some ideas of his own. Early the next morning, while Mary was getting some much-needed sleep, Johnny went out to the workshop. He lit a fire in the ancient wood stove one of his uncles had installed many years before and started digging around in the long-untouched scraps of wood and boards stored in an overhead rack, dust filtering down through the horizontal rays of morning light.

He found what he was looking for and pulled down a fir board, the stain darker than he remembered. The wood was very dry, several cracks protruding into the grain of the wood on each end. He turned the rough-cut board over, and the skin around his eyes tightened when he saw the familiar letters burned into the wood.

The first line read in large capital letters: WELCOME TO THE AMUND HOME.

The second line was in smaller lettering, another language: BER ER HVER AÐ BAKI NEMA SÉR BRÓÐUR EIGI.

Johnny remembered asking his Uncle Lars what the strange words meant. The sign had been screwed to the front of the farmhouse, and the young Johnny reached up, tracing the dusty, indented letters with his finger. His uncle was sitting on the porch steps in the late summer evening, sharpening an axe, several more waiting their turn at his feet.

Uncle Lars had repeated the strange words to Johnny, unfamiliar cadence rolling off his tongue, his eyes on the horizon.

"But what does it mean?" young Johnny demanded.

Uncle Lars lowered the axe and file, and motioned Johnny closer. "In English, it would be, 'Bare is the back of the brother less man.'"

Seeing the question in the boy's face, he tried again. "If you have a brother, you will be taken care of. You have someone to help you get what you need, you have someone who has, how they say it, 'got your back.'"

The boy had processed this quietly, listening to the rasp of the file. Gray eyes serious, he said flatly. "But I don't have a brother."

His uncle nodded, holding out the axe in one hand, the file in the other. "You can always have a brother, Yonny," he said, "And you can always be a brother." He resumed skillfully sharpening the axe, using the flat file as he had taught Johnny many times; "respecting the metal".

"Show me the brother of this axe," he said. Johnny had indicated the axes on the ground, then nudged the one most similar with his foot.

"Yes, Yonny, but who is being the brother to the axe right now?"

Johnny remembered how he had thought before answering, familiar to Uncle Lars' manner of teaching. "The file?"

The older man nodded. "Even though the file and the axe are very different, they help each other. The axe needs the file to stay sharp, and the file would have nothing to do if it didn't help the axe."

"*You can always have a brother.*"

Although this lesson had begun years ago, Johnny felt he was understanding it for the first time. "You can always have a brother," he said aloud. The cat who had followed him into the workshop leaped onto the bench.

The pine kindling hissed and popped, and Johnny closed the stove vent and searched for a cloth with which to clean the board.

Lars and Nelsson Amund had been good friends, to each other and to Johnny. They had not gone out of their way to invite company to their home, but when someone stopped by, they were quick to make the visitors feel welcome. Johnny had learned much from the interesting discussions at the cluttered Amund kitchen table and had been welcome to join the adult conversation at any time.

"It's about time I started making this happen," Johnny said, surprising the cat. "Uncle Lars meant more than 'brother', he was talking about family, being there for others. And them being there for you." The cat jumped back to the floor, taking its place by the stove.

Johnny found a cloth and wiped dust off the board, an inner smile showing around his eyes. The fire was crackling now, warmth reaching into the cold.

The words were faded but legible. They appeared to be burned into the wood, or was that old paint? Johnny wondered who had made the sign.

He found a container of linseed oil, and using a clean, cotton rag, worked the pungent oil into the wood. The sign began to glow as he rubbed; the color variations in the grain coming back to life. He ran his hands over the wood, trying to read the words. Trying to remember how Uncle Lars pronounced them. *Ber er hver að baki nema sér bróður eigi. Bare is the back of the brother less man.*

The cat stood and stretched, the promised warmth not worth the noise, and disappeared through the pet door.

Leaving the sign propped up on the workbench, Johnny added

wood to the fire, and drove to town to pick up breakfast, light snow swirling and writhing in snakes on the road. He drank some coffee with the regulars at Charlie's, then ordered a bag of food to go.

Before entering the house, Johnny went to the workshop to check his project. The cat was in its place by the stove, tangy smell of linseed oil filling the room. The sign glowed warmly, reddish wood contrasting with the cool winter light outside the window.

Choosing several wood screws and a cordless drill, Johnny took his prize across the yard and up on the covered porch. Stepping back, he visualized where the sign would look best; from the driveway, from the lawn, from the graveled path. With the proper location chosen, he screwed the sign to the wall, using the holes already in the sign where it had been nailed to the wall of the farmhouse many years ago.

Returning his tools to the workshop and turning off the lights, he retrieved the keys and breakfast from the car and walked deliberately past the sign into his home to have breakfast with his family.

You can always have a brother. You can always be a brother.

CHAPTER 21

M ary came out to the kitchen to the smell of breakfast. Together they ate biscuit sandwiches and drank coffee from paper cups. They were comfortable together, enjoying the quiet morning.

"Come out on the porch. "Johnny gathered the half-eaten sandwiches and cooling coffee and put them on the counter. "Come see."

Always game, Mary wrapped herself in the jacket hanging on the back of Johnny's chair. She stepped out into the white winter morning, following Johnny down the steps and turning toward the house when he did.

"Oh!" Her voice was quiet. "Oh, Johnny." She had tears in her eyes, looking up at him. "Is it from the farm?" She ran lightly up the steps in her moccasins, stopping in front of the plank, and gently traced the letters spelling HOME.

"Johnny, it's perfect." He had never heard this tone in her voice, never felt so close to his wife, never felt so *right*.

She traced the smaller letters, disregarding the oil not yet dry. She wiped her cheeks with the back of her hand. "Johnny, what do they mean? What does it say?"

She wanted it to be important. She wanted fiercely to hear something meaningful in the strange words.

She looked up at Johnny and then took his hand as she turned back to the sign, *their* sign. Johnny read the words, "Ber er hver að baki nema sér bróður eigi." He said them slowly, the memory of the sound returning stronger.

He repeated slowly, "Bare is the back of the brother-less man."

Johnny watched her, *does she like it?* He hoped she also felt the deep emotions he didn't understand. He waited, remembering Uncle Lars explaining the words to him.

She hugged his arm, squeezing his hand. "I love it!" She stood still, in the manner one would watch a sunset. "Oh." She drew the word out. "It means more than *brother.* "After a time, she pressed her head into his chest, "I need you, Johnny Amund. I *want* to need you. And you need me."

And he did.

He told her the story of the axe and the file, his appreciation of Uncle Lars's wisdom increasing in graduating degrees. She listened quietly.

Mary was very, very happy.

"Johnny!" She spun away, moving into the kitchen, getting her own coat and boots, calling back through the open door. "Johnny, I want you to teach me how to sharpen an axe."

She handed him his own coat and dropped his boots in front of him, staring at their sign as he shut the door and got into his gear. On the way across the yard, she stepped in front of him, stopping him with both hands flat on his chest.

"What language is that? Could your uncles speak it?" She shook his coat, "Well?" He didn't know, but he told her it was probably

Scandinavian, and he had the impression it was a Norse proverb. Mary's eyes sparkled, she liked the answer; like the unfamiliar words it seemed wild, ageless, somehow magical.

In the shop, she watched intently as he chose an axe from its bracket on the wall and clamped it in a vise. Handing her a pair of old leather gloves, shiny from wear, he took down several files, arranging them on the bench.

"My uncles liked good tools; in fact, most of these tools were theirs." He pulled down a small box and handed it to her. It was heavy, the size of a match box, but longer. She pulled the top off, her hands clumsy in the gloves. The box contained a whetstone, worn thin in the middle, coarse on one side, fine on the other.

Johnny showed her how an axe blade needs a shoulder. "Never grind down the shoulder," Uncle Lars had said firmly, "then the blade is too thin and can break, in the cold especially. We must respect the metal."

Johnny demonstrated, imitating Uncle Lars' voice. "Yonny, take care to only file one way, only with the cutting ridges on the file, push, push, push, never push-pull, push-pull. That only dulls the file faster." He pulled out another file, holding it up for Mary to see. "This file, Yonny, is a 'bastard file' but in Canada you just call it a file, eh, because people do not like the word 'bastard', especially not at school."

He smiled, savoring the memory and Mary's laughing response.

"See, Yonny, how the cutting pattern is different on this file? If you have nicks in the axe, use the coarse side first. Save the fine one for touch-up." Johnny worked along the blade, precise in his movements, holding the same angle all across the cutting edge.

Johnny finished one side of the axe and turned it over in the vise. Now it was Mary's turn. She was surprised at the skill and attention needed to keep the file on a consistent angle, but with 'Yonny's' help, did a fine job finishing the axe.

Johnny took the whetstone, put a few drops of oil on it, and in a careful circular motion, spent several minutes finishing the axe. "Watch this." Shrugging off his coat, he smoothly shaved a wide swath of hair from his arm with the razor-sharp edge. Mary was impressed, and slightly alarmed. So was Johnny, who had never actually done it before, but had seen Uncle Nelsson do it once, maybe twenty years earlier.

She took the axe and hung it back in its place, wondering if it could be the same axe from the story. As she leaned forward, she noticed a picture hanging under the window. It was shiny under a layer of dust, and one side was uneven, obviously torn from a magazine. She worked the ancient tack out of the wall and brought the picture up to the light. It was a photo of a sword, dark with age, pitted and ragged. THE SAEBO SWORD was the simple heading on the top of the page. She read the short paragraph on the bottom of the page, informing her where the sword was found, and about the inscription on it. She hung the picture back in its place and turned back to her husband.

"You have real *history*! Your uncles wanted a good home. They wanted you to have a good home. They did their best for you!" Johnny felt a weight lift, *she understands*! No, he comprehended it was deeper than this. *He* was beginning to understand.

"Let's make a good home, together," he said, "a place where people feel safe. A good home for children." He reached out and took her hands.

And standing there in the workshop among the tools inherited from men without the proper skills to complete the difficult task of building a home, two lonely people began the process of truly finding each other, and the seeds of a real home, a family, began to grow.

CHAPTER 22

The Banks' house was still. Melissa, sipping coffee in her kitchen, enjoyed a moment of quiet in the eye of the storm. The boys had disappeared earlier, and through the window she could see Chet walking toward the house for breakfast and a second coffee. Daniel and Lance were planning a day with friends, snowmobiling or something, and Chet was getting ready to move a processor back to the yard. He said the machine needed the mechanics to look over a hydraulic pump that had been replaced recently, but Melissa knew an excuse when she heard it - Chet had a load of firewood he was itching to cut up.

"Chet, we need to talk. Take your boots off and sit. You've got a whole week to get the wood cut up, and you don't need to do it all yourself!"

He grunted and headed for the table, turning to discard his boots when his wife pointed at them. The house was warm, and his back was sore. Another coffee would be just fine. He caught the smell of something baking. She was right, one of the guys could cut up the wood as well as he could.

"Chet, I'm worried. We really have no clue what's up with Terry's situation. She got away, but was this just a stroke of luck? What if this is a lot bigger deal than we know?" She put her cup down, harder than necessary. "What if Terry is lying? What if she is, or used to be, involved in something illegal?"

Chet fidgeted; sitting still was difficult. He drank some coffee. "Look, we can only go on what we know, base our decisions on the information at hand. Worrying about it won't help. The RCMP say Terry has no criminal record or involvement to their knowledge, so, hey."

"I agree with you, but there is much we don't know. We are going to have to react to this situation as it unfolds."

He held up his hand. "Yes, I know, reacting to a situation is not as good as planning ahead of time, but heck, what can we do?"

Melissa needed to hear this. Chet was a rock. He was solid, worked hard, wasn't afraid of success or failure. She sipped more coffee, then reached across and patted his hand. "Thanks, I know you're right. But what if something happens, what if…"

He was grinning at her.

"Hey, you big jerk! I'm serious!" She was rising to stand and tried not to smile when he pulled her around the table. He tickled her until she giggled. "Okay, okay! I'll try to stop worrying." She went to the oven for a steaming breakfast casserole, setting it beside the coffee carafe on the table.

"Listen Melissa, our choices are simple: keep working as usual, or fire Terry right now." He took the steaming plate she offered and doused it with hot sauce. "I say we keep right on working. Terry is probably safer here than anywhere, and the whole crew, plus a hundred other guys in the bush will be looking out for her. She's a good worker too, and how could we just let her go after this whole thing?"

She nodded, waiting for him to burn his mouth on the first bite.

"Darn it!" He took a quick drink from his water glass, "That's hot!" Yes, Chet was nothing if he wasn't predictable.

"I like what I'm seeing in John Amund. He's a good guy," Melissa said. "You should have seen him and Isaac joking around yesterday. He and Mary are doing well. We talked some, Mary and I, while we set up the shop yesterday, and she is really happy. And did you see her looking at the little kids last night? She held Frank and Yvonne's baby for at least an hour." She took a bite herself, after blowing on the fluffy bread, egg, and bacon concoction.

"Mmm, that's good, one of Charlie's recipes." She watched him, blowing on each bite, eating hungrily. "We've talked about you slowing down a bit. You don't need to work seven days a week, and the boys are pretty much self-propelled. You and I could spend more time together. What I'm suggesting is that we consider having Johnny work with you, take over a lot of the low-bedding, pitch in at the shop when it's real busy, do some of the planning. Then see where it goes from there."

He smiled at her. She was quite the lady, and a good partner. It was smart to let her say the whole thing and ask questions later.

The kitchen door burst open, and startled, they both turned as their two sons stomped in together, shaking snow from their clothes, cheeks red.

"Dad! Is there some gas here somewhere?" Daniel, twenty-two, was home for the weekend from university. "We don't have enough fuel. You got some jerry cans?"

Lance was nineteen, employed part-time at a local sawmill and working to attain his Millwright certification. He worked in the bush for his dad during the week when he wasn't at the mill or school.

The boys meant business; the fuel shortage needed to be fixed now.

There were friends to meet, snowmobiles to be tuned, and the weekend was winding down. It was already 9AM on Sunday!

Chet turned to Melissa, bushy eyebrows arched. "Self-propelled?"

She laughed and scooped up two bowls full of breakfast, shook hot sauce on both, and put a spoon in each bowl. She handed them to her boys, her young men.

"Darn, that's hot!" Melissa rolled her eyes at her older son who laughed as the younger Lance took a drink from his dad's water glass, cooling his burnt mouth. Like father, like son.

"There's a whole row of jerry cans in the garage," Chet said, "use them."

"But they're empty!" was Lance's reply around a careful bite of casserole.

"Well, stop at the gas station and fill up there." Chet was done with the subject.

"Where are you guys going? Think there's enough snow?"

"This is good, Mom, new recipe?" Daniel took the travel mug she handed him.

"We're going up the Omineca Trail, taking saws and a chainsaw winch. We'll open the trail as far as we can, about ten of us going, and who knows who else will be up there." Lance held his bowl for another giant helping. "We're hoping to make it to the Fort, grab some early dinner up there."

With thousands of dead pine trees killed by the mountain pine beetle infestation, trails were constantly obstructed by fallen trees. The trail needed to be cleared for the first ride, and the regular users carried a saw or at least an axe.

He blew on his first bite, then spoke around it gingerly. "One of the guys needs to bring his dad's low-bed down from the Fort tonight. If we make it all the way up there, we will load all the machines on the empty deck for the trip home, save us a long ride."

Chet said, "And you boneheads will ride the sixty kilometers home where?"

"Yeah, that's what I said." Daniel grinned at his brother. "I have a ride back to Prince George with a buddy, and will leave my sled at his parent's house, but these guys, well, uh, they're out of luck!"

Lance spoke up. "Well, Mom's Caddy can haul six people, I thought, well, maybe..."

"No, I agree with your brother, who so politely said that you guys are out of luck. Your dad is taking me out to a movie tonight, no 'Mom's Taxi' available."

Amid the laughter and complaining, Chet remembered five full jerry cans of gasoline, a thermos of coffee was filled, the location of a chainsaw file and chain guard identified, and the whereabouts of a bag of ratchet straps confirmed.

"You spoil them, but I like it!" Melissa shook her head reproachfully at her husband. "You should have let them buy their own fuel, just for their own good." The kitchen eating area seemed empty with the boys gone, puddles of meltwater left on the floor, a glove deserted under the coat rack.

"They work hard around here. And what's this about a movie? This is the first I've heard about it." Chet scraped the crispy bread from the sides of the otherwise empty casserole dish, hoping for a snip of bacon.

The door opened, cold air rushing in with a hurried Lance.

"There it is!"

He pounced on the deserted glove, flashed a movie star smile at his parents, slammed the door, and the quiet resumed. Only to be broken as the window slid open.

"Wear your helmets!" Melissa yelled at his retreating back.

Aaah, life was good, Chet thought, as he sneaked noisily out the back. Time to round up some dry firewood. And he had already been thinking about John Amund. It was a good idea.

CHAPTER 23

Terry woke late, feeling good, happy for the extra sleep. She sat on the burgundy chair in her motel room making a mental list, then picked up her phone, checking her favorites screen, which now included several RCMP contact numbers and a few contacts relating to her new job. The simple act of changing names and numbers on a digital list seemed to change her from the person she had been several weeks before. She groaned as she stretched and contemplated getting ready for the day. She was going shopping and wanted to look good. Driving had its benefits; no makeup required, so the weekdays started much faster.

As she put on makeup, did her hair, and chose an outfit from the meager supply of clothing that wasn't packed in her stack of storage bins, she tried to contact her brother. No answer. Well, it was Sunday morning; she couldn't remember if he worked on weekends.

Before leaving the room, she checked the full-length mirror on the door. The cheap mirror had a curve, making her appear taller. Shaking her head, she went to the stack of storage bins and found her high heeled leather boots. She went back to the mirror. Now she really looked tall. She smiled, *Not bad Terry, not bad at all.* Her brother used to tell her, "You clean up real well, Terry, real well!"

She activated the remote starter and heard the Dodge engine rumble awake outside her room. It did not seem as cold here as in Alberta, but after shivering in the trunk of the car, Terry wanted her vehicle warm by the time she was ready to leave.

She said hello to the maid who was pushing a wheeled cart across the snowy courtyard and took the time to introduce herself and let the maid know her schedule for the week.

She ordered breakfast at a drive-through window and headed east toward Prince George.

Spanning Highway 16, the town of Vanderhoof seemed vibrant, busier than she expected. She had not yet driven through the whole town, but she liked the Hallmark-movie streetlights and young trees lining Burrard Avenue. Highway 16 served as 1st Street, and was industrial, not as friendly in appearance. She guessed many travelers passing through would have been surprised at the welcoming center of town between the highway and the Nechako River.

So far, though, she had not spent time in Vanderhoof during regular business hours and was now on the way to Prince George where she could purchase some new work gear. Driving log truck had many challenges that differed from her highway driving experience, and earlier in the eventful week she realized the need for some different work clothes.

She had learned some details about Vanderhoof at the party yesterday. The picture she had pieced together was of a small town which served a large rural area. It seemed that many people lived outside of the town limits in small communities, or on their own farms or ranches. She had been surprised to see so many fields, and the amount of farm-related business and equipment visible even in the early winter.

Terry had seen many young families, and due to the high proportion of jacked-up diesel pickups, she supposed the local bankers and vehicle dealerships believed in the economy as well. Her three-year-old pickup disappeared in local traffic like a family van at Disneyland.

The motel was busy, with high-school basketball, volleyball, and minor hockey teams filling all available rooms on the two weekends she had been in Vanderhoof. In fact, when she called from Alberta checking on accommodations, the helpful woman at the desk had recommended she book a whole month, as finding an apartment could take some time, and the local motels were generally booked all winter for sports and industry.

Besides the athletic tournaments happening, Terry had seen handmade signs for a Seniors Bazaar, a ski club fundraising outside a grocery store, and the local news sheet on the tables of the motel restaurant included notices of a farm association meeting, a fundraising banquet for a kid's camp, a Ducks Unlimited event, cattle auction, a local theater production, a snowmobile poker ride, a community Carol Sing, a barrel racing clinic, and more. A real variety for a small town.

It seemed like a nice place, but she wondered what the downsides were in a small northern community. Crime? Drugs? Racial issues? She wondered if she would like it here, if she stayed.

Outside town limits with coffee in hand, Terry accelerated to speed on the snow-covered highway. What a surreal week! She'd moved to Vanderhoof last Saturday and driven truck on unfamiliar roads for four days. After work on Thursday she'd been abducted and been to Jasper and back to Prince George on Friday. She'd spent Saturday morning with the RCMP, Saturday evening with a nice group of people, and now it was Sunday, and back to work tomorrow.

Well, she was glad to be safe, and suddenly wished for company on the quick trip to Prince George. It would be nice to spend the day with one of her brothers, or one of the cousins she had been close to as a kid. She sipped more coffee, blinking back tears. Sure, on the day she wore mascara! Just great.

The sun was bright, and a pair of sunglasses helped her eyes stop watering. Seeing several deer feeding in a field, she slowed back to speed limit, in case there were more.

There were snowmobile tracks in the wide cleared area between the highway and the trees. She passed several machines going west, a couple out with their children, the parents each with a small child riding double, little helmets bobbing, the swirl of snow behind the snowmobiles sparkling like diamond chips in the low morning sun.

Terry began looking for the side road leading to the lake where her captors had planned to drown her. She felt alone. For the first time she decided her upcoming meeting with a post-trauma counsellor was a good idea. "Get back on the horse, Terry!" she said aloud, and kept looking for a likely road to the south.

What she saw instead was a large cloud of snow, settling like dust, on the trail ahead. She was slowly catching up to a snowmobile. The guy was really moving! As she pulled alongside, she saw an older machine that had to be from the nineties with its vibrant purple and yellow graphics. The rider was wearing a matching jacket, and she could see it was as well worn as the machine, torn and grease-shiny. The rider glanced her way, then did a double take, lifting his left arm to wave.

She waved back. She saw the skis lift and heard the two-stroke motor wail as the rider pinned the throttle and left her behind. Within a minute, the sled was completely obscured by a cloud of snow, far ahead of her.

For sure it was a man, she smiled, or a large boy. She slowed. The snow machine was parked on a side road, steam rising from the tunnel, and the rider was waving her to stop, helmet in hand. She slowed, and as she passed the side road, she recognized Isaac La Crosse, the mechanic from work. She laughed out loud and reversed her pickup, then pulled forward off the highway.

He pulled a toque from his coat pocket and put it over his helmet hair.

"I thought it was your Dodge when I saw the license plate taped in the window. Figured I would flag you down." He was breathing hard, high on the speed.

"You are *crazy!*" she said. "How fast is that thing?" She got out of the pickup, walking over to the snowmobile, loud even at idle.

"These old triples are amazing, when they're not seized up," he said. "Speedometer doesn't work, no clue how fast she goes. Sure leaves the new mountain sleds in the dust though. Shorter track spins easy."

He was speaking another language, and she laughed at him.

"No clue what you're saying, but I know it's fast. How old is it?"

"Well, the motor's out of a '97 I got from…"

Oops. She realized she deserved the five-minute history lesson on the lineage of the machine and would be more careful in the future to avoid questions regarding snowmobiles or anything else the mechanic was passionate about.

"So, where are you going?" he asked her, switching off the noisy engine. The relative silence was a relief, and the two-stroke exhaust smell blew away in the slight breeze.

Terry waited for a string of traffic to pass and explained she was shopping for some work gear and wouldn't be in Prince George too long. She told Isaac she was also looking for the road to the lake.

"Want some company?" he said, tipping his head slightly.

"What about your snowmobile?" She nodded at the purple machine, strangely animal-like as it crouched on the side of the road.

"Let's load 'er up, follow me." Then he yanked the starter cord and disappeared around a corner in the road, the loud engine prompting Terry to cover her ears with gloved hands.

Shaking her head, she followed him up the side road. He was interesting, could be good-looking if he would lose the big metal-framed glasses and got a haircut. His intelligent gray eyes were magnified by his lenses. He looked like a... she thought about it... scientist? A doctor from an old movie? She giggled when she imagined him in a white lab coat.

Rounding a corner, she saw Isaac in a pullout next to half a dozen deserted pickups, some hitched to trailers, others with decks high above the ground. Isaac was pulling a loading ramp off one of the trailers and motioned for her to park.

She dropped the tailgate on her short box pickup as he walked across, dragging the aluminum ramp. Securing the straps, he loaded the purple beast, Terry cringing as the carbide runners on each ski scoured a furrow in the unblemished paint on the bed of her truck. Isaac returned the borrowed ramp.

"Guys park here all the time. If they have a security cam, all the better." He made an obscene gesture in the direction of the parked vehicles, then walked over to an old red Ford, and reaching under the bumper, came out with a magnetic key holder.

"What are you doing!" Terry looked around worriedly. What if there were cameras! "Are you nuts?"

He grinned as he unlocked the driver's door and reached behind the front seat, dragging out a tangle of ratchet straps.

"Just need to borrow something to tie down the sled. Can't have it sliding out the back."

"Whose truck is that? How did you know where the key is? You can't just steal stuff!"

"Don't worry about it, it's my ex's truck."

"What!" Terry was horrified. She wished she hadn't stopped. This guy *was* crazy. "Will she mind?"

"We won't tell her, she hates my guts."

Terry climbed back in the Dodge, and when Isaac had secured the machine with the straps and climbed in the cab, wiping his hands on his jacket, she beat a hasty retreat to the highway. *What the heck!*

CHAPTER 24

Back on the highway, Isaac was looking around the cab. "Nice ride. So, you want to find the boat launch? It's just a few klicks up the road."

Isaac soon directed her to turn right and follow a snowy road for several kilometers. The road literally ended on the lake shore, with spurs leading left and right. Leaving the Dodge idling, Terry got out and walked through the fresh snow, looking through a gap in the trees to see the snow-covered ice extending several hundred feet, ending in open water. Several swans were floating, silent on the dark water. Swans here?

Isaac was checking the straps securing his snowmobile, allowing Terry some time to herself. He stood by the pickup until she turned, motioning for him to join her.

"There are houses all along the lake." He motioned with his head, sandy hair flattened by his helmet, holding his knit cap in a balled fist. Dogs started barking, probably the same ones she had heard recently in the dark. Thursday to Sunday. She had been helpless, now she was in control, strong companion by her side. On Thursday there was no snow, still autumn. Today there was close to a foot, definitely winter.

On Thursday she had been fighting for her life, on Sunday she was going shopping.

The dogs came bursting through the trees, shouts from the house audible over their excited barking. A big shepherd cross and a pretty golden retriever bounded toward them, tails wagging, hanging back until they decided the intruders were safe. An ATV with a snowblade mounted on the front came down the road, and an older man in a thick plaid cloth coat and bright, red hat parked it in front of them.

He yelled at the dogs, who ignored him, sitting happily with Isaac. The retriever leaned on his leg, looking up adoringly.

"I was plowing my driveway when the mutts got away. Usually they are in the house. Always barking, drives a man around the bend. Then I looked over and I seen you down here, thought I'd come say hey."

He was dressed in older clothes, clothes that looked like they may have been used on weekends for many years. The new hat stood out, and on closer inspection, Terry could see it was emblazoned with a gold crest and the letters RCMP.

"Nice hat." she said.

The old guy grinned and took it off, looking at it under his glasses.

"Yep, she's a nice one." He put it back on his head.

"Always partying going on down here, summer for sure, sometimes in the fall too. Gets so loud down here we can't even hear our own music with the dogs barking, people yelling." He shook his head. "Just the other night they were yelling and screaming down here like you wouldn't believe, just ridiculous."

"That's what I told those officers, first when I called in, then when they came out. Legalize pot and it all goes to pot!" He nodded with a grin, tipping his hat to his own humor.

Out of view Isaac grinned too. Terry was worried he would say something to stoke the guy up even further.

"They gave me this hat though. Actually, they're doing a pretty good job, those cops. Maybe not wasting as much tax dollars as they used to. Got to crack down on the drug use, though."

He reversed his ATV, then spoke to the dogs. "Come on, mutts, let's get a snack."

At the word snack, the dogs froze, then tails began to wag.

"Let's go get a snack!"

The dogs leaped up, racing each other toward the house. They beat the old guy home, barking excitedly.

Terry smiled at the scene but was thinking about her close call. What if the lake had been deep, what if the dogs hadn't barked, what if the men had killed her and dumped her body?

She shivered and went back to the truck. Isaac followed, and when she reached for the shifter, he put his big hand over it, stopping her.

"Wait. Tell me what happened here."

She leaned back in the seat, hands in her lap, and told him what happened, and how it made her feel.

She was finished in several minutes, and he sat there nodding slightly.

"Well, you did everything right, didn't you?"

When she nodded, he said, "Say it. You did everything right."

"I did everything right."

"Come on, say it like you mean it."

"I did everything right!" she shouted.

"Heck, yeah! Say it again."

"I did everything right!"

"Again!"

"I did everything right, all I could do!" Terry yelled.

Terry started laughing, feeling a weight lift. Shaking her head, she rammed the truck in reverse and turned around.

Back on the highway she looked over at Isaac. "You are one strange guy! Are you all this eccentric out here? Steak and lobster served in an equipment shop, the boss getting the kids to help him with free firewood for people, just to teach them to care about others, huh?"

She paused and glanced over again. "But hey, look at me! *I* just stopped and picked up a guy who looks homeless, *and* his snowmobile which should be homeless, and one of them has actually made me feel better. Crazy!"

He grinned, pulling his hat back over his thick hair. "Don't worry about it. I'd do the same thing for a friend."

She looked at him again, holding his eyes for a moment, "Thanks. I appreciate it." She grinned at him. "Let's go shopping. I need some stuff and you, my friend, are buying a new jacket."

The day didn't get any less strange, but she had to admit, it was a lot of fun. Isaac was a good companion. He didn't hit on her and was easy to talk to. He was confident, Terry thought, and self-sufficient.

During her first stop, Terry looked out the workwear store window and saw another pickup backed up to hers, blocking all traffic in that aisle of the parking lot. Isaac and another guy dragged the purple snowmobile backwards into the other pickup, and a wad of cash changed hands. They talked some more, and Isaac removed his jacket and emptied the pockets, trading it for another bill.

Leaving her items, she hurried outside as the other truck pulled away, the purple beast regarding her reproachfully as it disappeared.

"You sold your snowmobile? And did you just sell your coat?"

"Sure did. You said I had to get a new jacket, and since it matched the machine, well, I sold them both."

He held up a bundle of bills. "Dinner is on me."

He headed into the store to buy a new jacket, Terry following along behind shaking her head. "Who just finds a buyer for a snowmobile in a parking lot, and sells a dirty old jacket to boot?"

He shrugged. "People like those old machines. Guy wanted to give me two grand, so away she went."

"But now you don't have a snowmobile. Will you buy another one?"

Looking through a sale rack, Isaac replied, "I have a few more at home, plus, that one was the wrong color. Had to get rid of it before Johnny saw it."

She didn't get it, so she left him to his sale rack and went back to the cart she had begun to fill.

In the early afternoon, Terry was surprised to meet Johnny and Mary in the Canadian Tire store and after a short chat, the four of them decided to meet for an early dinner.

Johnny was also surprised to see Isaac and Terry together, and chuckled, elbowing Mary.

"Mary, how did the two of them get together? I mean, they just met!"

Mary laughed, eyes sparkling.

"I can't wait for dinner. There must be a story here!"

Leaning against him, she shook his arm, a mannerism he treasured – unless he was holding a drink.

"Johnny, I wish we were not going to work tomorrow, this has turned into a great weekend."

She shook his arm again, shake-shake, the same squeeze and cadence hadn't changed since they met.

"I love the sign so much. It makes me shiver to think 'what if you forgot where it was stored' or 'what if it just got thrown away.' Now it's right where it belongs, and if we ever move, or build a new house, it goes with us."

"The Amund Home," Johnny said it aloud.

"I think it is more than just our house. Home, I mean." She squeezed his arm, "What I mean is, home is wherever we are, you and me."

"Like the atmosphere around us?"

"Yes, but it's *special* in our own home."

"You've got that right."

He closed an eye in a prolonged wink.

"Johnny!"

They ate at a steakhouse in the afternoon and discussed the coming week. The food and companionship created an atmosphere of warmth Terry hadn't experienced for a long time.

Terry watched the couple; they seemed close. Mary leaning against the big guy, touching his arm. She wondered how long they had been married.

She recounted details of her day, and soon had them laughing.

Johnny was asking questions.

"So, you're driving along, and you see Isaac here snowmobiling, and you pick him up?"

She nodded.

He narrowed his eyes.

"So where is his sled?"

"He sold it. He sold his old coat, too."

"What? "He turned to Isaac. "Isaac, did you sell your mountain sled? Are you going to buy a real machine?"

Isaac said, "Just eat your food, Clown."

Terry had to know; "Why does he call everybody 'clown?'"

They laughed, but Johnny wouldn't let the conversation get off track. "Terry, what did this snowmobile look like?"

"Well, it was purple, yellow decals too, looked real nineties. Why?

"Johnny burst out laughing, slapping the table.

"Isaac, you just sold the best machine you've ever owned!"

Isaac shook his head, "Nah, just an old junker." He took a large bite of his steak sandwich.

Johnny was still laughing, but Mary rolled her eyes, "These juveniles always argue about which snowmobile brand is better. Like it even matters." "Okay," Terry got their attention, "If I'm going to work with you guys, I want to know a few things. First of all," she indicated Isaac, as if he wasn't there, "why does he always call people *Clown?* And why does he say *clock* all the time?"

Johnny laughed some more.

Later over coffee, Johnny was delighted to hear details of the snowmobile sale. "I haven't laughed so much for years!" was his response when Terry told him about Isaac boosting the load straps from "his ex's" truck.

She punched Isaac in the shoulder, hard, when she found out the red truck belonged to a sledding buddy, and the straps belonged to Isaac, and that Isaac had planned to use the red truck to haul the old sled to Prince George for a pre-arranged sale.

"Free ride!" He snorted with a grin. "Why drive the old rust-bucket when I could get a free ride in a new truck, with a mighty nice lady, I might add."

When she set her alarm later that evening and slid into the motel bed, she was happy. She had three new friends and plans to attend a hockey game with them next weekend. But, if Isaac called her *Clown*, he was going to have a serious problem.

As she drifted off to sleep, she figured it out. She knew who Isaac reminded her of, and she looked forward to christening him with a nickname of his own, in the most public place possible.

CHAPTER 25

On Saturday, Chet's firewood operation was in full swing. He had been busy the previous Sunday, using the company's self-loading truck to collect a load of small, dry pine logs.

Chet had then moved a processor to the yard as well, to be used later in the week to cut the logs into short lengths of firewood. The load had been cut as planned by Chet and Lance and covered with an old hay tarp.

Many people in the Nechako Valley burned firewood, the newer wood-burning stoves were highly efficient, better than the crude appliances their grandparents had used. Natural gas was not available on the majority of back roads, and electricity was an expensive way to heat older homes, especially when the temperature dipped to minus twenty. Cutting firewood was a yearly tradition, enjoyed by some, dreaded by others. Often families worked together, pooling resources and abilities. While the tradition was declining, many children still grew up with the vicious howl of a chainsaw taken for granted, learning to stay well back from the spinning chain, and how to gather decent fuel and operate a wood-burning stove.

"Well, got some nice firewood, anyhow." was a common excuse

grunted by a disappointed, camo-clad hunter returning home midday on a Saturday.

Today, however, things were going much quicker than normal. All that was left to do was load the chunks of wood and deliver. The process was slowed slightly by Melissa and some of the kids Chet had enlisted. They had a table set up by the shop and were keeping another tradition alive.

They were filling paper lunch bags with an assortment of hard candy in wrappers, peanuts in the shell, cookies baked and wrapped by Melissa, candy canes; and of course, a mandarin orange. Melissa decided to send the treats along with each load of firewood. She guessed how many people were in each household, adding extra if the people had grandchildren.

This was a new idea to many of the kids, and Melissa made sure there would be a candy bag for each helper.

Pete stopped as he walked by the table. He was holding a chainsaw in each hand, on the way to put them in the service trucks. His weathered face crinkled into a smile as he looked at the row of finished bags, tops crumpled by little hands.

Melissa smiled at him. "Pete, did you ever get a candy bag when you were a kid?" She guessed him to be in his mid-sixties.

He nodded. "Yep, sure did. Every Christmas, Canadian tradition. My sister and I would each get our own bag. That was back in, well, back when we lived way north in Manitoba. We always went to the Christmas program at the little church, and after the singing and all, they gave out candy bags. When I seen you filling these bags, I had to come over and take a boo."

He dumped the chainsaws on the ground and turning away, wiped an eye with a rough hand. "Bump on the head making me soft," he apologized. "Still like those oranges, buy a couple boxes every year at Christmas, you betcha. Back then, well, that's the only orange I ever got. Up north you know, not much fresh fruit. And peanuts too, real tasty."

He looked at the kids, nodding a little, thinking of harder times.

"It sure is better now, lots to eat, nice clothes, hard not to spoil the grandkids. These little gifts you're sending out, they'll get a lot of people remembering, no doubt."

"Never will forget it. Always ate the orange on Christmas day, the peanuts during the holiday from school, and sometimes made that handful of candy last right 'til spring."

Melissa just smiled. She knew it had been a good idea, even if a couple loads were a few minutes later than Chet figured they should be. Good thing she bought that extra box of oranges.

When Pete disappeared into the shop, Melissa sent one of the kids to put several bulging candy bags in his pickup, extra oranges in each.

The mountain of firewood disappeared rapidly and by mid-afternoon everyone was back at the yard eating hot dogs from the grill, except Chet, who had decided to take a load to an old friend of his dad who lived several hours north of town. Just before Melissa and the kids gave everyone their own bag of goodies, Terry yelled for everyone to listen up.

"Thanks to you all for making me feel so welcome. You are a great bunch of people, and I'm glad to be working with you." She paused, sipping from her foam coffee cup. "But I have a few things to say. First of all, I hate clowns, and I refuse to be called a clown by our good friend over here."

There was some laughter. She really had their attention now. "And 'Lady Clown' doesn't work either," she shook a small fist at Isaac, "I've had enough. So, I have a deal for our mechanic." She paused, looking around. "Not you, Pete, you're sweet."

Pete blushed amid the hoots.

"If I get called *clown* one more time" she paused dramatically, "well, let's just say someone's life is going to get miserable. Just think about it," she paused again, "he has to fix what I drive."

More laughter – tempered somewhat by the fact that Terry had taken out two thugs with a torque wrench.

"So, no more *Clown* and by the way, I wouldn't answer to *Hoser* either, like some of you do."

More sheepish laughter.

"And then this 'clock' thing!"

More laughing.

"Yeah, seriously. So, I decided on a new name for Isaac here. I was thinking the other day about a picture book I had when I was a kid. Had this guy in it who looked a lot like Isaac, you know, dirt-colored hair..."She made scissors with her fingers, miming a needed haircut. "Mustache stolen from a spaghetti western, big glasses. And then there's the name, 'La Crosse.'"

Johnny and the other guys were enjoying Isaac's discomfort. Jason whooped, and then tried to hold it in when he remembered he worked for Isaac.

"So, the man in the kids' book was working over a workbench, fixing something, and it took me a few days, but I remembered. The man was a *clock maker*."

Even Melissa laughed aloud at this. *Clockmaker*. It was perfect!

Walking over to Isaac's service truck, Terry opened the door and pulled a roll of paper from behind the seat.

Johnny noticed the door had been cleaned. He was surprised to see

Mary help Terry apply a large decal on the blue door panel. Together they smoothed the paper with plastic scrapers, and then Terry carefully peeled off the translucent outer layer.

There on the door in graceful gold script, angling up toward the rear of the cab, were the words *The Clockmaker.*

It was perfect, without guile. A recognition of the man's skill, yet a flawless mockery of his own quirky humor. A complete christening, never to be undone.

CHAPTER 26

I saac's stories and running comments on Johnny's driving made for a boisterous drive to the hockey game later that afternoon. Johnny and Isaac filled the front seats, and the ladies shared the freshly-cleaned back seat. Terry opened several boxes of chocolate-covered almonds purchased from fundraising kids. These disappeared quickly, as she explained how the kids were shaping up to be successful extortionists.

Terry noticed how Johnny drove confidently and quickly and from the back seat watched the road with which she was becoming more familiar.

The CN Centre was packed, though both goalies seemed to be absent. Terry surprised her companions when she removed her jacket, revealing a Red Deer Rebels jersey. Isaac promptly went to the gift shop, and came back wearing a Cougars jersey, with some noisemakers for Johnny and Mary and a "Welcome to Prince George" sticker for Terry. The high scoring game ending in a Cougars' win.

Later, over pizza in a noisy restaurant, surrounded by other celebrating fans, Johnny leaned forward and made himself heard over the noise.

"You know, in the bush we don't get to pick our nicknames. Most guys don't even like the names they get, and the guys who try to pick their own? Well, they end up with really bad ones. But Isaac here, he scored a good one, and actually likes it!"

They laughed.

Terry asked, "What do they call you?"

"Well, I don't really have a nickname, but I know people refer to me as *The Big Guy*."

"That's right, ya big lout," Isaac said.

"Johnny doesn't have a regular nickname, but 'The Big Guy' works, I mean, I'm two inches over six feet, and you're a lot taller than me. How tall are you, anyway?"

Johnny just shrugged.

Mary spoke, "I buy him triple extra large shirts..." but Johnny interrupted,

"So I guess I should lose some weight. Pass the pizza," he deadpanned.

They laughed again.

"You don't need to lose weight," Mary responded. "You're just a big, solid guy. Eat up!"

They all laughed as Mary stabbed her fork at a large hand reaching for her food, causing it to retreat with a yelp.

"Actually, is your name John or Johnny?" Terry asked. "I mean, you sort of have a nickname, right?"

The three looked at each other.

"You've got us there." Isaac acted like he was impressed.

Mary laughed too. "I guess you do have a nickname."

"He may have a nickname, but mine's better." Isaac swigged his beer, "And no one can take it back, 'cuz it's on the door of my truck! Ha!"

A waiter appeared, holding a mug of tap beer.

"Some guys sent this over for the, for uh, the *Clockmaker*?" the young man said hesitantly, thinking maybe he was the butt of a joke. Isaac grabbed the drink and stood, then raised it in a toast to a couple of truckers sitting at the bar who were watching them, laughing, raising their own glasses.

"Mazeltov!" he shouted over the din. Looking at Terry, he quipped, "Kind of nice, coming from a couple of," he paused as Terry frowned, "truckers".

Terry raised a finger to her lips, then drew a point on an imaginary scoreboard. Mary changed the subject, "Johnny and I are going to Mexico for a week during breakup, the two of you should come too, we think it would be fun."

"What are you doing there?" The Clockmaker was buying time to think. Johnny could see his analytical mind at work, weighing the potential problems, risks, pros and cons.

Johnny and Mary had already discussed the invitation and thought it would be a good time.

"Well, we are for sure going to spend time fishing. I've already been looking up charters." Mary knew how to set the hook for Isaac; she wasn't sure about Terry. "We're going to do some tours as well and spend some serious hours on the beach."

"The beach! Where's the dessert menu?" Johnny said, drawing a jab from Mary, and a smile from Terry.

"I'm in," Isaac said. "Sounds great. I've never been to Mexico."

"Me too," Terry said. "I can sunburn like a pro."

Phones came out, destinations were looked up and argued over, predictions of when spring breakup would happen were discussed with people at the next table. Their excitement was infectious, the group next to them relating merits of different vacation spots and giving too much beery advice.

Their excited talk continued on the drive home. When Johnny slammed on the brakes to avoid a moose, the conversation changed direction briefly, and then snapped away from the dark winter night with its chilly hazards, to beaches, sun, and relaxation.

Nearing Vanderhoof, Mary raised an important issue.

"Terry, have you heard anything from the RCMP? Have they gotten any closer to finding this Joseph guy, or the men who kidnapped you?"

There had been nothing new, and this worried Terry. It irritated her, and she said so.

"I thought it would be easy to find this guy. I have even thought of trying to go find him myself. Closure would be nice."

The cab was silent.

Johnny shook his head. "I think you met the 'B Team'. Some guys sent out to fix a problem quick. If this is actually some sort of smuggling ring, or a gang-related deal, then the next people you meet might be more dangerous. "He paused, "I think we just keep working, make some money, enjoy Christmas, put some miles on the sleds, and go to Mexico. Let's leave the bad guys alone."

"Unless they come here," Isaac finished the unspoken thought.

"Unless they come here." Johnny echoed.

In the back seat, Mary grabbed Terry's hand, giving it a squeeze.

"I don't know about you, Terry, but with these big lugs around, I feel pretty safe!"

And watching the two big men filling the front seats, Terry agreed.

CHAPTER 27

The Banks Mountain crew worked steadily through the winter. Pete had reoccurring headaches, and although he did his best, loud noises, such as the air-powered impact wrenches, and hammering stubborn steel parts, were almost unbearable. Along with this, he had dizzy spells, and when he slipped while working on a trailer, falling onto the snow-packed yard, Melissa made some quick changes.

She took Pete to the hospital and marched him into the emergency room, ignoring his protestations of feeling just fine. She waited with him, realizing how traumatic this could be for the older man. While waiting for the doctor, Pete admitted he had only been to the hospital a few times in his life, recently for stitches, and once to see his daughter's newborn.

Melissa was a veteran, trips to labor and delivery, then the many return trips with the two boys for what Chet called "warranty work." Daniel and Lance had broken, sprained, and cut just about everything on their bodies in their eventful young lives.

Pete and the others in the waiting room were distracted from their pain when Melissa related how one day when the kids were in school, she had taken a big wheel loader, with which she was unfamiliar, and destroyed the dirt bike track Chet had built for the kids on the property. The young Lance had broken his arm the previous weekend on one of the jumps, and she was sick of what she considered a clear and present danger lurking behind their house. By the time the destruction was complete an hour later, Melissa assured her wide-eyed audience she was a much better operator.

A young man in greasy coveralls, holding a bundle of bloody shop towels to his left arm, wanted to know what the boys' reaction was.

"Well, they came home from school and after a snack, the boys went out to ride their dirt bikes. Well, Daniel was going to ride. Lance had his arm in a cast and was going to 'just watch'. They came running back in the house, eyes wide. 'Mom!' they yelled, 'some bonehead backed the loader over the garden shed!'"

She smiled ruefully and went on.

"The boys ran back out, and soon came back yelling! 'Someone wrecked our dirt bike course, and that's bad, but know what's worse? Dad is going to *kill* whoever did this!' Chet used to have a pretty bad temper."

"The boys went on, 'You're going to have to do something, Mom! When Dad sees what someone ran over.' At this point the boys started crying, and I won't lie, I was getting pretty worried!"

She went on. Her audience, now including a nurse, was attentive.

"'Mom, someone drove over Dad's Harley! It was parked by the lilac bush! It's wrecked!'"

Pete swore aloud, then covered his mouth, embarrassed.

The young man was not so polite. "Lady, you wrecked your husband's Hog? What happened next?"

"Well, the boys took their pedal bikes and disappeared. They didn't want to be around when their dad came home. That motorcycle was the first toy Chet had ever bought for himself, and he just loved it, found it in Nevada. He'd only had it for a few months. I just didn't see it parked in the shade where he had cleaned it and thought I had just backed over this big lilac bush."

"Like, what kind of Harley was it?" The young guy looked sick, from more than his injury.

She told him, and as the nurse led him away, they heard him muttering sadly. "She crushed a 1945 Knucklehead. She crushed a '45 Knucklehead ...'"

"Was Chet mad?"

"No, Pete, he didn't even get mad. He looked at the mess and just started laughing. He said, 'I saved up for my dream bike once, I guess I can do it again. And we need some more pasture space anyhow. Too bad about the garden shed though.' Then as he left, he told me he needed help loading trucks the next day, and I spent a lot of days that summer driving that loader. The guys driving the gravel trucks were scared as heck though, and always had some excuse to be out of the cab while I loaded."

The upshot of the visit to emergency was that Pete needed to take some time off, at least six weeks without loud noises, sudden movement, and climbing up on machinery. The young doctor happened to have paid for much of his degree by pulling wrenches in his family's heavy-duty equipment shop and was firm in his plan to help Pete recover fully from his concussion.

Johnny was surprised to see Mary's car in the shop driveway when he wheeled in at the end of his last run. He parked next to a few other rigs, and she walked over while he did his post-run checks, much more thorough than previous winters.

"Johnny, Melissa called me and wants us to come for supper. Chet wants to talk with you. I think it's about your job."

He raised his eyebrows in question.

"She said Pete needs to take time off. They must need some help in the shop."

Johnny had chained up multiple times that day and his clothes were filthy. He grabbed a duffle bag from the back seat of his pickup, and Mary followed him into the shop where he took a quick shower. She talked through the curtain as he lathered up and pulled his clean clothes out of the duffle so they could warm. She tossed his dirty work clothes in the coin-operated washer.

Through the clouds of steam rising to the vent fan, Johnny told her about the road conditions, and about the wildlife he had seen that day. Using a clean towel from the cabinet, he dried off and dressed, not seeming to mind the fact that the folded clothes were still cold.

They drove the several hundred meters to the Banks home in Mary's car. Johnny might not be bothered by cold clothing or vehicles, but Mary preferred them warm.

When they sat at the table, Johnny was surprised when Melissa asked Chet to say grace, which he did without eye-rolling or a cynical comment. Dinner was a delicious cut of moose roasted with potatoes, carrots, onions, celery and much to Johnny's delight, turnips. Turnips had been a staple when Johnny was a child, and the familiar taste brought back memories on which Johnny mused.

During the meal, Chet's phone continually received calls and text messages. He ignored it, but was distracted from the conversation whenever it rang, and though he seemed to be enjoying the food and company, it was obvious he wanted to deal with whatever communication was coming in. Melissa relayed details of the visit to the hospital with Pete, mentioning the young guy who was impressed with the Harley Davidson story. When Johnny heard, he reacted much like the young man.

"You weren't even mad?" He looked at Chet incredulously.

"Nope. Usually I would have been, but there I stood, looking at the couple acres of ground, a lawnmower, wheelbarrow, my outboard motor – all crushed accidentally, because my wife wanted our kids to be safe. I realized I really didn't want a Harley, especially one so valuable I didn't like to ride it on gravel roads. And it was really funny! She had never been on a big loader, and here she took that old 966 on a rampage, just like a movie!"

Melissa shook her head with a small smile.

"Plus, she loaded trucks for the next two summers. We were running gravel trucks then, and more than paid for the Harley in saved wages, she didn't dare ask to be paid. It was perfect!" He grinned. "But when our gravel truck drivers heard what happened, and some of them saw the mess, they were really scared, both of her driving, and just Melissa herself. Ever since, if she asks someone to do something, well, they up and do it! And the new guys see the older guys snap to it and follow their lead. I figure Melissa's rampage was just her way of buying a lifetime reputation, and you know what's the kicker? She wasn't even mad; she was just taking care of business!"

"Chet, stop!"

Johnny grinned at Mary, knowing something good was coming next.

"For the next couple seasons our boys played hockey, every time that song was played, friends would point at Melissa, it was hilarious!"

When Melissa derailed the subject matter by serving up seconds, Chet folded his napkin and got down to business.

"Okay, Johnny, we have a problem. Pete is out for at least six weeks. I'm too busy to work in the shop until he's back, my phone is ringing constantly, and I can't answer all the questions efficiently enough, and we have a whole bunch of meetings coming up with the mill and the Forest Service. And of course, we only have a few months before breakup.

"Melissa figures I need to quit taking on more new things if I keep doing everything I'm doing now, and she's right."

Chet paused for coffee, and Johnny let out his breath. He tried to relax.

"Johnny, I would like if you would jump in and help me do my job. I would like you to be free to do whatever needs to be done; help Isaac in the shop for the next month or so while Pete's out, run the low-bed, coordinate schedules, and go to meetings with me whenever possible."

He drank another quick sip of coffee.

"I need a good man like you, Johnny, to just jump in and make things happen. The guys in the bush respect you, and so do the truckers. You get along well with Isaac, and not everyone does. What do you think?"

Johnny analyzed quickly, weighing pros and cons.

"And Johnny, this is not because we are unhappy with what you're doing now. You are doing a great job, and your positive attitude has affected the whole crew," Melissa added.

Johnny cleared his throat, sliding his chair back a few inches. "Chet, I appreciate your offer. It sounds like a good job. And I have an idea; one that might make even more sense."

All three looked at him in surprise, his tone even, exuding confidence.

"Since we sat down for this delicious meal," he nodded toward

Melissa, "your phone has rang or beeped fourteen times." He nodded his head. "I know because it bugs me, not the sound or interruption, but because I know that some evenings it's me who is dialing that number and disturbing you. I usually feel bad about bugging you, but I need to know what's going on the next day and can't really plan unless I find out."

Johnny went on smoothly.

"There is a lot of frustration out there, especially on Sunday afternoons, when we don't know for sure what we are doing the next day, when to go to bed, all that. Mary is pretty good about it, but for the guys with families, well, I have heard some complaining."

Chet nodded. "You're right. I'm not always on the ball about letting everyone know my plans." Melissa did a dramatic eye-roll.

Johnny continued. "So, I have some ideas, but I am not the right person to make all of it happen." He smiled, the three were listening carefully. He pointed at Chet's phone. "That beep makes fifteen. I am good at getting things done. Working in the shop and getting the machines in the right places will be something I'm good at. But I have an idea for how the scheduling could work even better. What I think you are saying you need is someone to collect information from you and Melissa, such as; where we are hauling, when the first trucks go out, any info from the mill or scale, etc., and then make a schedule and communicate it to everyone."

Melissa nodded. "Exactly. Right now, Chet will be out on Saturday or Sunday moving machines. This is right when people want information about the week. On one hand we have the guys, or their wives, who want to know their schedule weeks in advance. Then we have the guys who get home from snowmobiling at 10 PM on a Sunday night and they get a message that we want them to go to work at midnight."

Johnny nodded. He had seen the extremes, had even been the guy who slept an hour after a long day snowmobiling before getting up for a full day of hauling logs. It wasn't responsible but happened more often than it should.

Chet wanted to hear The Big Guy's plan.

CHAPTER 28

Johnny's plan was simple. Neither the dessert Melissa served, nor the continued demands of Chet's phone distracted him as he laid it out.

"We have some catching up to do. Pete is gone for a while, so I will need to spend a lot of time in the shop. I'm pretty handy, but not a mechanic, not nearly as experienced as Pete. If Isaac does the specialty stuff, I can for sure get a lot of the grunt work done. But between that and hauling equipment around, my schedule will be full. Why don't you hire Mary here to work weekends and a few hours in the evening? She's really good at scheduling, making plans, and contacting people. Many times, when I'm busy, she takes extra overtime at the store – no reason she couldn't put that time into working for us."

Mary was surprised. She hadn't seen this coming and appreciated the compliments from her husband.

Johnny continued. "She is going to be quitting her job in the next year or so anyway, because we want to have kids."

Mary's eyes widened, and she stared at Johnny. It was so sudden she wasn't even embarrassed, at first, that is.

"Well, we'll start with one baby I guess." Johnny grinned. He liked a good reaction and had been thinking for hours in the truck. He had been hoping an opportunity like this would come along.

Chet took the news in his matter-of-fact way. Starting a family was just what people did, no surprise there. But Melissa reacted properly, jumping up and hugging Mary, who was beaming, happy tears now brimming, momentary embarrassment forgotten.

"So, Mary should be available to help us get started, giving us time to get Pete back in the shop, and then if she is coordinating the schedule, she can show me what she has done, and teach me how to do it too, or just keep coordinating herself. She can email the stuff to the four of us, and you can make any tweaks needed before she sends it out to everybody. If anyone has questions, they call Mary. She is used to this. She's coordinated the staff at the grocery store for what, five years?"

Johnny sat back, looking satisfied with his quick presentation of ideas.

While Melissa was congratulating Mary, she was seeing Johnny in a new way. He looked like the big quarterback on the poster in Lance's room, what was his name?

Yes, Johnny might make a pretty good quarterback for their team, calling plays, directing traffic, calming people down. And he was big and confident enough to direct a team, and with Mary helping coordinate…

Melissa looked at Chet, nodding her head. "I like it, Chet, what do you think?"

He looked at Mary. "Well, young lady, does this sound like a possibility?" Without waiting for her reply, he nodded, answering for himself.

"Yes, sir, I like it. It's a good plan."

And that was how a new and rewarding chapter in the history of the Amund family began, a familiar pattern in the human story of supply and demand. The Banks' extension of trust gained a little brother, a rather large little brother, and the talented woman who was his wife.

The Amunds were given that wonderful commodity, *opportunity*. A place to exercise their skills, talents, and experience; a place to be pushed into new trials, stretched in their thinking, taxed to the very core as they began to deeply care for the interests of their benefactors.

And Johnny was not so young as to have no experience. The story of Melissa and the loader impressed Johnny deeply, and he inwardly vowed never to begin big changes without getting advice from the boss. And as Johnny had planned, involving Mary was pure genius, She proved to be a gem, especially over the winter season when nerves were stretched, and workers were known to throw in the towel and quit on a whim.

On Christmas Eve, Chet and Melissa took a drive. It was a clear night, and the boys had driven to Prince George for some last-minute shopping. They dropped off cookies at the homes of several elderly couples, visiting for a few minutes in each place, spreading Christmas cheer and receiving some of their own.

Mary had called Melissa earlier and asked if she and Chet could stop in later, if they were not busy. Melissa was looking forward to the visit and said so to Chet, chatting as he drove.

"I am so glad we offered Johnny this new job. What a difference in our schedule, especially weekends." She laughed. "He's a lot sharper than I would have expected a year ago."

Chet nodded, watching the moon as it seemed to flit through the trees, remembering the same view when he was a kid.

"He's made a couple mistakes, but nothing compared to the load he has taken off your shoulders."

Chet cleared his throat. "You know what the best thing is? He hardly ever says no, always willing to get right in it. But he won't push safety limits. If he's too tired to do a good job, he will say no and mean it. The man has judgment, good judgment."

Chet was right. Johnny seemed to always be working, keeping them in the loop with concise texts, and earning respect as a capable foreman in the eyes of the other employees almost overnight. At the Christmas party Johnny had been commended. The occasion had been held in the Banks Mountain shop as an encore to the success of the November party.

Melissa had set up a speaker and microphone, squelching the festive din of the children playing with their gifts in the lunch room. A few men had thanked Johnny at the open mic, for kind things he had done in his several weeks of being foreman. One thanked him for driving his last load so that he could attend his daughter's Christmas play. Another recalled how Johnny had brought a shop truck and pulled him out of the ditch and quickly replaced several blown tires several days earlier, allowing the man to finish his day, the implication clear: no money lost on a paycheck at Christmastime.

Jason took the mic nervously and thanked Johnny for working with him in the shop, and clumsily explained how Johnny even made sure to find him a ride to work when his truck broke down.

Mary had also been thanked, and though all were gracious to Chet, the message was unmistakable, the new attention to communication was well received and greatly appreciated.

Johnny had thanked them for their kind words and went on to mention some of the highlights of the year. He had taken the time to express appreciation to the guys he worked with, and especially to Frank, for being a good example of a man he wanted to be like, surprising the quiet man, who gave him a thumbs-up, sleeping toddler in his arms.

A delighted buzz went through the forty or fifty people present when Johnny and Mary called up the Banks and presented them with two wrapped presents. They opened their gifts together and held them up for all to see. Each had received a beautiful die-cast model: a 1945 Harley Davidson Knucklehead for Chet and a Caterpillar 966 loader for Melissa. Chet grinned, hunching down, twisting an imaginary throttle and making the appropriate sounds. Melissa shook her fist at Johnny, and then gave Mary a big hug.

Now turning into the Amunds' driveway, they were surprised to see at least a dozen snowmobiles on the snow-covered lawn and a similar number of vehicles in the parking area. Some small children were tobogganing on the gentle slope along the driveway, but the yard was empty of adults. Walking up the steps to the house, Melissa stopped to read the sign.

"Look, Chet." She read the sign aloud, and then the translation Mary had typed on thick paper and tacked below the glowing wood. A few small spotlights had been carefully placed, flooding the thick plank with warm light so the sign seemed to be alive, separate from the wall on which it hung.

A little girl tugged her sleeve. "Hi, Mrs. Banks!"

She knew this nice lady. She was the one who had parties that kids could come to and always had fun games and treats. Her gift at the Christmas party had been a Banks Mountain toque, which was on her head at the moment, pink tassel caked with snow.

"All the grownups are around back at the fire. I had marthmallowth!"

She darted away, message delivered, tassel bouncing.

Chet stood stock-still, staring at the sign. "Well, I'll be! Wonder how long that's been up. Sure does explain some things."

Melissa took his arm, but he held still for a moment, captured by memories. "You know, I'm positive that was up on Lars' house, out on the farm. Johnny must have brought it down, probably years ago." He shook his head. "But I've never seen it here before."

They circled the house and followed the packed trail toward the glow behind some outbuildings where they soon could see a giant bonfire and heard laughter and happy voices.

Chet hefted the package of jerky he had smoked himself several days before, yep, should be enough.

He said it aloud again. "Bare is the back of the brotherless man." He reached out a warm, ungloved hand. "Come on, Melissa, let's give this jerky to our little brother."

CHAPTER 29

After conferring with Johnny, the Banks decided to shut down the whole operation for the week of Christmas. Several of the employees wanted to work through the holiday and Johnny coordinated a plan that would ensure a neat and tidy restart on January 2.

Mary had anticipated this and arranged vacation time for herself. This would be the first time in years they would have nine days free to spend together at Christmas, and they decided to make the best of it. Late on the 23rd they set off to visit her dad and Joanne.

Jason was house-sitting for them. He had no family west of the Rockies and wanted to spend Christmas in Vanderhoof with new friends and put in some extra hours of work. The horses would be fed, the antisocial cat would have company, and Jason would have a place to entertain, although Mary didn't want to think too much about that.

Mary had booked a hotel in Prince George. "We can keep our own special tradition, Johnny, and we will be an hour closer to Vernon!"

Johnny agreed and was happy to spend the extra time with Mary and to have a break from the daily stress of directing the logging operations.

They were in Johnny's Silverado, back seat crammed full of

presents, luggage, and their snowmobiling gear. Their machines were locked down, covers strapped on for the long trip.

When Al invited them for Christmas, he had suggested the four of them do some snowmobiling, and Johnny was excited to explore new country. Al arranged to use a friend's private cabin, and as he and Joanne had already enjoyed several trips in the area that season, was delighted his daughter and son-in-law were able to join them.

They would be riding an area suitable for the women's experience level, and for one day the men planned to take their more powerful machines to do some more serious riding and hill climbing and watch the professionals.

Johnny and Mary had chosen new snow gear for their Christmas presents to each other, and the smell of new winter clothing was an exciting aroma in the crowded cab. After talking with her dad, Mary had ordered Johnny an avalanche airbag to go with his new gear.

Each year there were stories of backcountry snowboarders or snowmobilers getting caught in unstable snow conditions in the mountains. Many were rescued, but sometimes the costly searches went on for weeks before the unfortunate individuals were dug from the snow. While many avalanches happened in the spring, when the snow was heavy, unstable from its own weight and repeated warmings from the sun, Mary was taking no chances. Though she didn't plan to be near avalanche areas, she wanted to know Johnny would be as safe as possible.

To keep things fair, she had ordered a heated vest and boots for herself and was looking forward to being warm this year while riding.

While Johnny checked and locked his workshop, Mary emptied the contents of the center console into a plastic container which she wedged into the pile in the rear seat and folded the console into the upright position. When Johnny arrived, she was perched in the center of the seat, ready for an hour of snuggling.

Johnny grinned, they didn't do this often enough. They both had enjoyed the bench seat in his '81 Chevy when they were first together.

They stopped for drive-through hot chocolates and the server smiled at them as she handed the drinks up into the truck window. "Merry Christmas! Have a nice evening."

An ancient Ramcharger, rear springs sagging, was turning into the restaurant as they waited to exit.

"It's Isaac!" Mary squealed. "*What* is he driving?"

Johnny chuckled, realizing this was the "Christmas present" Isaac had gone to Burns Lake to retrieve. Seeing Terry was behind him in her brown pickup, he turned the big Chevy and parked.

They climbed down to say hello, smiling at the unexpected meeting.

"We're going in for sandwiches, want to join us?" Terry's eyes sparkled.

"Sure. We can bring our drinks in for a few minutes," Johnny replied, turning to look at Isaac's latest project.

The women hurried away, Mary carrying their drinks. Johnny guessed Terry needed the restroom.

Isaac showed Johnny his purchase, lifting the hood to see the engine, acrid smoke rising from the oil leaking onto the exhaust.

"I'm starving, let's go in." He slammed the hood, cutting the tour short.

Johnny followed the Clockmaker into the restaurant and joined Mary at a table. Terry came out of the restroom and joined them after telling Isaac what she wanted.

They chatted until Isaac joined them with a tray piled with food.

"Here's a sandwich for you, little buddy." He pushed a wrapped package Johnny's way and a muffin toward Mary. "And something healthy for you, Mary."

He shivered. "Stupid heater doesn't work. I think I'm half-frozen."

"I wondered why you came in here so quick. Normally you would still be out there in the cold." Mary caught Terry's eye. "But I guess you've been apart for a whole two hours, just about a weekend record!

They both smiled, and Isaac put a long arm around Terry's shoulder.

"Meeting this lady here was almost as good as finding the deal on that old 4x4. Now I have to decide who to spend more time with."

Terry laughed.

The two had formed a real attachment, and Johnny and Mary figured it would get more serious quickly. After sharing vacation plans, and talking a few minutes about the upcoming Mexico trip, Johnny and Mary left the other couple and continued their journey.

The trip to Prince George seemed quick, their conversation centered on the last month and the changes in their lives. Mary was playing Christmas music and leaning on Johnny's shoulder, arm wrapped around his. She marvelled at the growth in herself and Johnny since last Christmas.

"Johnny, have I changed in the last year?"

He thought before responding. Mary had learned he was not ignoring her but was taking time to form his answer.

"You have, but it's not because you were so bad. I think you have been able to relax, now that I am being a better husband. And a better friend. I used to think you were a nag, but since I started acting more responsible, you haven't needed to get on my case, you know? Does that make sense?"

She sighed. "It does, but I think I have grown too. Now I *expect* you to do the right thing, where before I expected you to do things wrong."

He nodded. "I hate to admit it, but your mom was right about me more often than not. And she was right when she said you 'enabled my behavior.'" He growled out, "I can't believe I just said that, but it's true. Even though she was real mean about it, she was mostly right."

He drove for a while as she squeezed his arm tightly.

"You know, Mary, I'm really excited about spending time with your dad and Joanne. I think we will have a good time. But when we come back, I think we should try to spend some time with your mom, maybe a Sunday lunch or dinner out."

She looked at him and shook his arm in her peculiar way.

"That's an idea all right. But are you sure? What if she keeps insulting you?"

"A couple more jabs can't really hurt, can they? I won't be blindsided if it happens, and I think we should give her the chance to see us together now. She might even like what she sees."

Mary liked the idea. "Well, why not? Let's give it a try. I hope it works!"

Johnny pulled in to the brightly decorated mall. There were still a few gifts to pick up for Joanne. As they looked for a convenient parking place, Johnny changed the tone of the conversation.

"Imagine what it will be like at Christmas when we have a baby, our very own baby."

He parked crookedly, unable to see as Mary turned and wrapped her arms around him. A woman driving a minivan with three dented corners glared fiercely at the big 4x4 so rudely hogging several spaces, and swerved off to find another spot, almost denting the fourth corner on a security vehicle making its rounds.

Gifts purchased and wrapped, Mary pulled Johnny into a store filled with baby things. They were delighted and slightly awed by the choices ahead of them, and agreed their Christmas was off to a good start.

CHAPTER 30

Christmas Eve began with Johnny enjoying a quiet and early cup of coffee, looking out from their suite on the fifth floor. The little machine made a good brew, and he sat in the living area where he could see Mary still asleep through the open bedroom doorway and watch the weather outside, winter sky still dark, falling snow swirling through the headlights on the highway and visible in thick cones below the streetlights.

He felt refreshed and filled with anticipation. Not just for the holiday, but for life ahead. What would it be like to have a kid, to be a father? He sipped his coffee, thinking.

Johnny had very little experience with babies and small children. His uncles were his only relatives and had no children of their own, or friends with children. One day a girl in his elementary class had brought her baby brother for show and tell. The young Johnny absorbed the information his classmate shared and had been shocked to feel the soft spot on the baby's head. He was afraid she would drop the baby and hurt it.

Sometimes his friends would be charged with caring for their younger siblings, and the mothers soon learned that if Johnny was around, their little children would be well cared for. Johnny took the unwanted responsibility seriously; no baby or toddler was going to get hurt or deserted by their older siblings on his watch.

Johnny didn't want to admit it to Mary, but the thought of having their own child made him nervous. He had no clue how to care for one of his own. But Mary was confident, and he knew they could figure it out. He grinned. If his uncles could raise him, then he could raise a baby with Mary's help; or rather, Mary could raise a child with some help from him.

Johnny had been raised without the conflict or correction he had seen in his friends' homes. There was no arguing over things like food or bedtime in the Amund house; you ate, or you didn't. Not liking something wasn't a factor; food was food. If you missed supper, you ate more for breakfast. The salad he tried at the home of a complaining friend tasted good to Johnny, and when he had been old enough to help shop for groceries, he soon had his uncles eating lettuce salad and cucumber slaw, easy for a pre-teen to make.

This led to an extension of the potato and turnip patch, the three Amunds feeling adventurous as they planted an assortment of vegetables. Johnny had tended the large garden through his teen years. He smiled at the memory of a steaming bowl of over-boiled Brussels sprouts, the only time he remembered food going uneaten at the Amund table. The following February when the uncles sat down one evening to plan their mail-order seed list, Brussels sprouts were carefully crossed off, and Johnny had avoided the bitter little garden gremlins ever since.

From his chair he watched the snow through half closed eyes, hands clasped behind his head. The forgotten scenes from his childhood were comforting. His stomach growled, and he glanced across the dark room toward the kitchenette.

On the farm there was usually a pot of oatmeal ready on the stove each morning, cold cereal as an alternative. Fresh milk was delivered weekly by a neighbor who kept milk cows. Bread, mustard, and bologna were stocked in the refrigerator and canned goods in the cupboard.

The food selection grew when Johnny began doing most of the grocery shopping, and his teachers no longer needed to keep a can opener handy in their desk, in case the quiet boy showed up with a lunch consisting of a can of soup or mixed fruit.

When he was twelve, Johnny had been given an electric bread-maker, unsold at a neighbor's garage sale. Uncle Lars bought the supplies on the ingredient list, and after huddling together to carefully follow the directions and set the timer, the three woke early to the smell of fresh bread. Delighted with their success, from then on, they were well supplied with delicious, fresh bread from a succession of bread machines.

Lars and Nelsson Amund never asked him to do something that didn't make sense. He put himself to bed and got up in time for school. The brothers' rock-solid consistency was not something they could have explained, it was just the way they were.

The men were old enough to be great-uncles but had taken care to plan several events each year with the boy in mind. Summer was busy, but Johnny remembered several trips to Prince Rupert by train, where the three Amunds enjoyed a fishing charter, iced cooler containing their catch stowed in the baggage car on the return trip. Johnny remembered the view from the Via Rail dome car, and his uncles' silent appreciation of the scenery.

Several times during the winter Uncle Nelsson had taken time off from the insurance agency and the three of them had flown to Vancouver for a hockey game. They always spent a few extra days, touring a greenhouse, factory, or other business that seemed important to Johnny's development.

Johnny was taught to run equipment on the farm and when deemed responsible, was given his own snowmobile with which to check the cattle and run errands on the property north of town. This extension of trust had resonated deeply with Johnny, and he had cared for the little machine diligently, parking it the machine shed with the farm equipment after each use.

Johnny smiled at the memories and settled down to drink coffee and think. Yes, he had been lonely many times, but he had learned to find company in the hockey games on the radio and in the games he played alone while working on the farm.

When Mary came into his life, he had revelled in the way she held his arm, leaned on him, and looked into his eyes. He loved being near her, sitting together while driving or watching a game, or when she held his face in her hands. He did not take this for granted, even though he had never thought to express it. Now, he decided, he was going to try to explain his feelings. He wanted his kids to feel loved, to never be lonely, to have friends. He wanted to see Mary hold them, and love them, and he wanted his children to know he loved them, too.

His cup was empty again, and as he refilled it, he heard Mary stirring. She shuffled out warm and sleepy in one of his T-shirts. He handed her the cup of coffee and sat back in the chair near the window, pulling her onto his lap.

"Johnny, look! It snowed a foot, you can hardly see the truck!" When he didn't respond she pulled back to look at him. "What, Johnny?"

Mary listened enrapt as Johnny spoke. He took his time, carefully explaining his thoughts. Silently she watched his face, cup forgotten on the end table. Tears went unnoticed as he told her things she had ached to hear, intensity of his rich voice not lost in the quiet conveyance of his dreams and hopes and maybes.

They left the hotel room much later than intended, but as Mary said breathlessly in the elevator on the way down, "Now the roads should be plowed, and we can drive faster."

Her reasoning may have been flawed, but Johnny wasn't arguing. He was happy to spend the day with his wife and didn't care what time it was now, how hungry he was, or when they arrived. He knew one thing for sure; they were certainly closer in their quest of having a child of their own.

Watching the couple walk through the warm lobby and into the snowstorm, oblivious to all but themselves, one desk clerk nudged the other, "Look at her! She is actually glowing."

"You're just jealous, Mitch." was the catty reply. And he was.

The trip south was slow, hours spent in long strings of vehicles following plow trucks. The big pickup riding on winter tires and loaded with half a ton of cargo handled the snowy conditions well, but not all the travelers were as fortunate. They stopped several times as wreckers pulled vehicles from the ditch.

The snow let up south of Williams Lake, and by Clinton they were cruising at speed limit, surprised at the amount of traffic on the highway on Christmas Eve. They made one more stop at a big box store in Kamloops for fuel and to fill a cooler with snacks for the several days in the cabin after Christmas. Back on the road, Johnny let out a war cry that made Mary jump.

"Hey, what was that for? Crazy man!"

He did it again, and she joined in.

"You think that's how our children's ancestors ran into battles? Do you think we are going to be fierce parents?"

She just laughed. "I'm sure we will! They just better not be born wearing Viking helmets!"

Driving through the evening the trip seemed too short, and with half an hour left, Mary sighed.

"Johnny, this has been such a nice day." She felt dreamy in the warm cab. Snowflakes rushed into the headlights like moths in the summer. "And it's only the first day of a long break." She stretched her long legs and yawned luxuriously.

"I love you, Johnny Amund! That's my war cry." She said drowsily and dozed off.

"'Pass the eggnog' is going to be my war cry in an hour," Johnny replied, squinting through tired eyes into the snow, the final leg of the drive dotted with small communities along the winding highway.

But the eggnog had to wait, as his father-in-law had other plans. When they rolled in at 7 PM, Al and Joanne were glad they had arrived in time to attend an outdoor Christmas Eve service.

Standing in the calm winter night with one arm around Mary, the other hand holding a steaming cup of spicy apple cider, Johnny revelled in the warmth of being with family. While the small crowd sang Christmas carols, flakes of snow drifted down, adding a welcome serenity to the hillside, and through their veil, the city lights appeared warm and friendly below.

CHAPTER 31

Christmas with Al and Joanne was everything Johnny thought
Christmas should be. After a relaxed breakfast, they opened their
presents, the conversation flowing smoothly.

Later, while Al cooked a small turkey in his new outdoor fryer, the
skiff of new snow soaking up splatters of grease, Johnny made stuffing
from a box. Unimpressed with the amount, he made three more boxes
while Mary and Joanne were busy with a new dessert recipe.

The celebration continued while they ate the over-cooked turkey
and too much stuffing and all the other Christmas treats. Later, Joanne
read a familiar and hilarious Canadian Christmas story about some
guy cooking a turkey, as well as a few sobering classics.

In bed that night, Johnny thought about "The Gift of the Magi,"
a story he had never heard told. The story was depressing in a way,
the husband and wife each giving up their prized possession to buy
a gift rendered useless by their individual sacrifices. He thought of
the Christmas Eve drive, the sense of love he would treasure forever.
His thoughts had been on his wife, not on the pickup he had wanted
so badly and worked so hard to afford, or even the expensive snow

machines that in previous winters had probably captured his attention more than Mary.

He had to force himself to relax, as the regret and embarrassment of the wasted years filled him with an overwhelming sense of shame. He had never understood how close he had been to ruining his marriage, and the thought of not having what he now possessed was almost unbearable. He was grateful that he and Mary were not poor like the couple in the story and could give each other gifts that were enjoyed and useful. But he appreciated even more the way he was learning to love his wife, and she was learning to love him too.

They had discovered years ago that arguments were just part of the package of being together and worked hard to keep mean comments or name-calling out of their disagreements. This had been a good strategy and had helped them stay together. But when Johnny recalled all the weekends he had left to spend fishing, hunting, or snowmobiling with friends while Mary was at home working, he grew tense again.

Taking a deep breath, he disturbed the sleeping Mary, who turned over, throwing an arm across his chest. He gently squeezed her warm arm and vowed to love her like he'd promised in his hastily muttered wedding vows.

The next morning, Al and Johnny met accidentally at the refrigerator to graze on leftovers at 6AM and Joanne and Mary were up and around soon after, as they had made plans for a serious Boxing Day sale shopping trip. They found the men at the kitchen table watching snowmobiling videos and feasting on large plates loaded with Christmas leftovers.

The shoppers declined turkey for breakfast, eating bowls of cereal instead. They invited the guys to join them for a late lunch and Johnny was surprised how much he wanted this to happen.

Just after 7AM, the ladies disappeared; as Al said, "Like lady knights in search of the 'Holy Sale.' Stay out of their way, man!"

Johnny washed his truck and helped Al service his snowmobiles. They loaded all four machines, protected from road slush and salt in Al's enclosed trailer. They strapped down containers of fuel and returned to the house to load the coolers.

Both were veterans of many outdoor adventures and had learned to prepare ahead of time. In short order, steaks were marinating in freezer bags, deli salads were carefully packed, and loaves of bread were placed in coolers to prevent crushing. The Christmas leftovers were shovelled into microwave containers and almost filled a cooler of their own.

By mid-morning the trailer was loaded and ready to go and they hitched the loaded trailer to Al's SUV, tested the lights, and then piled their snow gear behind the rear seat.

Back in the house, Johnny asked about the cabin they would call home during their three days of riding. Al was pleased. "It's a nice place. A guy I work with on some surveying contracts owns it. It's fully equipped, even has a freezer full of food in case you forget something. Nice woodstoves and propane heat for when he isn't there. We should cut some dry wood while we're there, if you don't mind lending a hand. He has an old double-track snowmobile and a big sled. We can throw in a few old coats, so we don't have to use our riding gear."

Johnny was happy to cut some firewood. It was part of the experience and made such a trip even more fun.

"I've been going up to this place every year a few times for quite some time. We've got games, snowshoes, and lots of other stuff up there. If the weather goes bad, the trip is still just fine." "We cleared a place for choppers to land, and once last year a pilot buddy who was on the way to retrieve a broken snowmobile dropped off a bucket of fried chicken, still warm! That was cool."

Johnny could definitely understand how good the greasy food would taste during a day of riding. He was looking forward to the trip.

After a nap, they set off for some shopping of their own and to meet for a family lunch.

Boxing Day in Canada always involved huge sales and an amazing quantity of commerce. Johnny usually avoided shopping on that day, but this year he was content to go with Al and see the sights.

They were planning to meet Joanne and Mary in Kelowna and did a little shopping of their own on the way. A snowmobile dealer was blowing out old stock and they bought some discounted parts and accessories. Johnny found a two-up seat that fit Mary's Ski-Doo and would make doubling more comfortable. Al's big score was a spare hood for his Polaris, along with a windshield and graphics kit.

"Now I can roll my machine, and it won't hurt so bad!" he quipped.

They laughed at themselves, joking all the way to the restaurant, and Johnny wondered aloud if there were more snowmobile dealers in the area.

Lunch had an element of hurry to it, since the ladies had not made as much headway as planned through the sales. While waiting for their meals to arrive, the men proved to be just as excited about their morning's activities and were duly teased and congratulated on their purchases.

Both Al and Johnny were mildly concerned when the women's purchases filled the leftover space in the rear seat of Johnny's pickup, and they found the dusty snowmobile parts they had so carefully purchased relegated to the space under the snowmobile deck.

CHAPTER 32

While Johnny and Mary were spending Christmas in the Okanogan, Terry's holiday was becoming stressful and lonely. She had flown to Saskatchewan to be with her family, but it no longer felt like home. Terry was enjoying her work for the Banks in Vanderhoof and had rented an apartment near the river. Work kept her busy, and while thus occupied, she didn't spend as much time thinking back on her November ordeal. She had met with a psychologist as recommended by the RCMP, but she had not followed up with further counselling.

Now, in an unfamiliar, empty house while her mom was away on a Christmas cruise, the weight of loneliness and fear came crashing down, reality setting in. Her brothers were working, taking advantage of the holidays, their growing oilfield service company benefiting from the high fees charged during a time when so many employees wanted some time away from work. She missed their steady presence.

Christmas morning had been enjoyably chaotic, celebrating with cousins, aunts and uncles. The cousins near her age were all married and had small children. They had been delighted that Terry joined them for a Christmas brunch and gift exchange, but they had their own routines and holiday stresses, and by mid-afternoon on Christmas day had all disappeared. Terry helped her aunt clean the kitchen and vacuum the living room, and then she took a drive.

She missed Isaac La Crosse. He had quickly become a friend, and then more than a friend. He had invited her to live with him, and though she did spend many weekends at his house, she preferred to keep her own apartment. Isaac was sometimes cynical, but loyal and trustworthy. He listened, not speaking until she asked for a reply, then usually making her laugh with his perceptive and sometimes irreverent opinion. She thought of calling him but knew he would be spending the day with the complicated family he normally avoided in a good-natured but decisive way.

She also missed time with the Amunds who had become good friends. Johnny had a reassuring presence, and she had appreciated the work he had done in a few short weeks to help the company run more efficiently. Mary was kind and her inner strength and no-nonsense manner helped Terry feel secure.

Now, away from her friends and familiar work community, Terry felt her level of anxiety rising. Just the thought of connecting flights through Calgary made her nervous. What if Joseph was in the airport? What if her picture had been circulated to those Joseph worked with? If the RCMP could share information in their investigation, then why couldn't the criminals do the same?

Criminals. It was strange to even use the term. She hadn't done anything wrong. Why should she be wrapped up in this whole mess? The tears started, a mix of fear and anger in liquid form.

Terry had stopped at the liquor store on the way home, having noticed her mother didn't have much on hand. She poured a glass of wine, then funneled it back in the bottle and opened the Baileys.

Instead of feeling warmed and comforted as she sipped the sweet liqueur Terry was slammed with waves of depression and fear.

She remembered being homesick as a child when waking early at a birthday sleepover, a crushing, gray feeling of loneliness and abandonment. Looking around the unfamiliar house, Terry hadn't known how much worse this could feel as an adult.

"Come on, Terry!" she said, downing the small amount she had poured in a coffee cup. She looked through the cupboards and found a heavy tumbler. "That's better." she said, pouring a generous amount of the syrupy drink into the proper glassware.

She ran through the satellite programming on the television and watched the end of a Christmas movie. She cried, finding the conclusion to be consoling, no matter how predictable. Another Christmas movie was starting, so she ordered pizza and settled in for a marathon.

Hours later, she ordered another small pizza from a different company and tuned to another channel. She put on her comfy pajamas and brought a pillow and sleeping bag out to the living room.

"The Christmas Carol" would be playing in several minutes, and while she knew the story, she couldn't remember ever watching the movie. Before the movie began, there was an explanation of the history of the story and how it affected the world when it was written so many years ago. According to the well-spoken narrator, this 1951 version was considered to be the best movie produced of Dickens' story.

Terry was hooked, and it seemed the elderly announcer was looking right into Terry's eyes when she said in her perfectly modulated accent. "And just as Charles Dickens hoped would happen, his work began to turn the wheels of cultural understanding. We hope your life will be changed as you view this classic film and Charles Dickens' missive of hope will stimulate the Christmas message of love, forgiveness and change deep inside you."

Terry sat like a small child, cross-legged on the floor, riveted to the screen. Sipping red wine and nibbling pizza throughout, she sympathized with Ebenezer Scrooge and willed him to make the right decisions. She sobbed at the depiction of poverty and the Cratchit family's despair. She cursed Scrooge for his cold-hearted treatment of others, and then cried for him to change and become a whole person. She wanted wrongs to be made right, and for the pain to go away.

An hour and a half later, Terry was ready to hear the narrator's closing statements. She was emotionally spent but somehow clean inside. It seemed she was *so close* to a solution to her problems. Was this real, or just a result of the gripping story touching her in a state of emotional confusion?

While Terry was still alone, the fear was not so bad at the moment, and she felt a kinship to the old Scrooge and wished she could have joined him at his nephew's party. She turned the volume down but kept the same channel tuned, enjoying the now-familiar voice of the narrator as she introduced another classic. Terry curled up on the couch with a pillow and sleeping bag and fell asleep.

CHAPTER 33

The loaded SUV was on the road early for the seven-hour drive to Fernie, the multiple cup holders all in use.

Johnny was always amazed at the distances within his own province. "So, from Vanderhoof, which is the geographical center of British Columbia, Mary and I drove nine hours to your house. Now we're driving another seven hours toward the southeast corner of the province." He checked on his phone. "Okay, from Fernie in the lower east corner of BC to Atlin in the upper west corner is listed as over twenty-nine hours driving. And that's, uh, that's about the same distance as driving from Seattle to Chicago."

The conversation turned to travel and the location each would like to visit within the province. Al said, "For years I wanted to visit the Okanagan. Now that I live here, I want to visit Vancouver Island. BC has it all!"

After an hour of conversation and stories, they agreed that Vancouver Island was of common interest. They promised to consider a drive up the length of the huge island and maybe do a fishing trip out of Campbell River sometime in the near future.

The SUV was pulling its load without issue, Johnny noticed, which was reassuring as they had some hilly country to drive through. So far, the roads were well plowed, sanded and salted.

Mary and Joanne had been talking in the back seat, but they were napping now. Al looked over and grinned.

"I feel like a little kid!" His grin was contagious. "We are so excited to take you guys up here. I think you'll just love it."

"Thanks. It means a lot to us both." Johnny checked the back seat. The women were sleeping soundly, tired from a long day of shopping. They had been gone over fourteen hours and had come home happy, both with their purchases, and their growing appreciation for each other.

"Al, you're a good dad to Mary. Thanks, it really means a lot."

He was embarrassed, realizing he was repeating himself.

Al just nodded. "I know I can't make up for past wrongs. I pretty much deserted Mary and her mom, you know. But I am trying to do things differently now. Every day I wake up and think of Mary and I pray that she has a good day."

His eyes were on the road, on the line of traffic ahead of them.

"I have been praying for you, too, Johnny. Does that seem strange or weird?"

Johnny thought about it. It was out of his realm of experience, but not really weird. He knew people believed in God, and prayed, but had never really considered Al to be that kind of person.

"You know, Johnny, when I moved down here, I was really a mess. It wasn't just my partying, although that was pretty bad at the time. It was how I felt inside or tried not to feel, hard to explain. I just had no purpose at all, besides work and weekends. I had been pretty success-ful in business, but was so darn empty inside, I didn't even know who I was."

He grinned crookedly.

"Talking about serious stuff is tough, about snowmobiles we can chatter away like," he glanced guiltily in the rear-view mirror, "uh, squirrels!"

He went on. "You mind if I just try talking and not worry too much if it doesn't come out right?"

Johnny nodded. "Yep, you said it. It's hard to talk about important things."

"Okay, so I sold out and moved down here. I gave my ex-wife a big settlement," he grunted, shaking his head, "so I wouldn't have to worry about her anymore. My motive was selfish, but at least it was a good thing I did. I thought I'd party, do a little work, and that was all, I had no plans. Nothing. But then, living in a new place, a nice house, good weather, well, I realized I just had no clue what I was doing. Like, why buy furniture if you have no friends, and how do you party by yourself, you know?"

"So here I was, in the beautiful Okanagan, in an empty house. I started doing some odds and ends, some surveying contracts, seeing new country. And it's like I couldn't stop making money but had nothing or nobody to spend it on. I thought of traveling; but, a trip to Mongolia wouldn't make anything better."

He shook his head, freshly shaved that morning.

"So, I went to church. On a Sunday morning, I walked into the closest church and took a seat. A couple people said hello, they all sang some songs, an older guy preached for a while, and that was that. When the meeting was over, everyone just disappeared, no one looked happy, they just left. I don't know, I guess I was hoping for some encouragement, you know, like you see in the movies, the nice priest sits down, knows what to say, gives some hope.

"Well, that didn't work, so I went out and bought a boat. I mean right then. I just drove up the street and here was a guy putting a for sale sign on a little Glastron GT-150. I had always wanted one of those, so I paid the guy three grand and away I went, proud owner of a little speed boat with a big noisy outboard. I stopped at home for my fishing gear and a cooler of beer and went to the lake."

Johnny listened, staring through the window at the unfamiliar landscape.

"So, I was having a great time, even caught a few fish and then got pulled over by the RCMP. They do a pretty good job on the lakes here, lots of people on the water in the summer. Well, I was pretty well bombed when they pulled up. Needless to say, they gave me a free ride back. One of the officers even brought my boat in for me."

He glanced over at Johnny. "I had successfully hidden one cooler up under the front of the boat. Unfortunately, it was the one with the fish in it, and when I paid the fine and picked up my boat a few days later, the whole impound yard smelled bad. The boat was pretty much unusable for a couple of weeks."

"But going to church and buying a boat on a Sunday morning changed my life. When I paid my fine, guess who was working in the government office? Yep, Joanne, no ring on her left hand. A week later I asked her out."

He stabbed a thumb toward the back seat. "And then I started feeling like I had something to live for. But that's only the beginning. I want to tell the rest when Joanne is awake."

Johnny was curious. "Just keep going. I would like to hear more, and they might sleep for hours. You saw them drag themselves out of bed this morning!"

Al grinned. "Okay, but she will have details I forget, always helps me out. So, I met Joanne, and it's summer so we go to the lake and are hanging out by the water and these people come by handing out flyers for a concert that evening. I was too busy watching Joanne, who seemed interested, and said she liked music. I didn't pay attention to what the concert was but told the people we would be there.

"I dropped her off at her house so she could change and get ready. I drove home to get lawn chairs from my living room and a blanket and stuff. When I got back in the truck, I read the flyer. What I agreed to attend was a church concert of some sort. I had never been to any concert, sort of ambushed by the new experience, I guess. At first, I was mad and wanted to back out, but figured who cares, I'm going with someone, we can always leave."

"When we got there, it didn't sound like the church I had been to weeks before. The music was actually too loud. We found seats away from the speakers." He looked over at Johnny, "Oh, this was outdoors at a park. We got seats away from the speakers and settled in. I mostly listen to country music, and this rock and roll they were playing reminded me of high school. Joanne was enjoying it and said hello to a few people she knew from town."

Johnny saw Al check the mirror and guessed it was easier to talk without the women listening. Al saw Johnny watching him and smiled again.

"So, I sat there, basically thinking about Joanne and how I really liked her. The bands changed and wouldn't you know it, the next one was more my style of music. Up until then I hadn't even listened to the words, but they played this song that caught my attention. In fact, I'll play it for you pretty soon. I didn't understand all the words, you know how you hear a song for the first time, but I felt drawn to the song."

"Johnny, I think it was a combination of a beautiful evening, the excitement of meeting Joanne, the hope of being loved... I don't know. Whatever, it suddenly seemed like all the emptiness I had been feeling probably had a solution. I had hope for the first time in a long time."

Al drank from his coffee cup, then ran his hand over his smooth head.

Johnny was curious. The Al he had known years ago was a very different man than the one he was riding with today. The man he had known when he first met Mary was brash, smooth, seemed confident, and had no time for Johnny or even Mary. They had gone shopping together the day before, shopping! And it had been fun, relaxed.

"So, what happened?" Johnny nodded toward the back seat. "Obviously, you got together..."

"Well, remember that church service I went to the day I bought the boat? This seemed very different. The people at this concert seemed pretty normal, if my idea of normal is normal." He grinned at his own humor.

"So, the first thing we had in common as a couple was attending a concert put on by a church. So, the next week, I asked Joanne if she wanted to go to church with me. We attended the church that put on the concert, and it was different than the boat day church. Kids were running around, people talking in the lobby, the pastor had to ask people to come sit down, and then said it was a good thing everyone was enjoying each other, because that is what the church really is. That's all I remember from that Sunday, and still don't completely understand, but ever since, we go to the church meetings quite often, and we met many of our best friends there. Joanne went through a marriage breakup too and had only been in town for a year or so, so didn't know people here either. We gained a new set of friends together."

"What about the song?" Johnny was curious.

"Well, what's your favorite song?"

Johnny thought. "I don't really have one. Can't think of one anyway."

"Think back to when you were younger, what song has a really good memory?"

"Well, let's see." Johnny thought, and then he remembered a song that had been popular when he had bought his first car. He had a few CDs and played the song often, sometimes singing along as he drove.

He told Al the name of the song and what he remembered about it.

Al nodded, "That's sort of how this song hit me, but even as I heard it, I thought, 'Man, what is the matter with you?' because this song was more than just a sound or style of music."

He looked over at his son-in-law, looking for understanding.

"Okay." Johnny was nodding. "I think I get it. The message was as important as the band or sound, huh?"

"That's it, more than the music. It was if the song was written especially for me to hear. I wanted to hear it. I wanted to hear it again, to understand what it meant. And the guy singing it was really good, but was *telling* me the song, not trying to entertain." He paused, "Oh heck, I don't know. Here, I'll play it, see what you think."

And Johnny listened. Though unfamiliar, the tune was bright and the words he could understand were compelling. He understood the emptiness Al had explained, the longing for hope, and love, and a place to be. A home.

The men were quiet as the track ended, and Al touched the screen to play it again. The words touched Johnny deeply, speaking somehow of the love he shared with Mary, and the promise of better things to come.

It was really sinking in. Things were truly getting better and could stay better too. It was similar to unloading his snowmobile; the anticipation of a new ride, new country, new hills to challenge. He could feel a catch in his chest, the same as when he watched Mary sleeping or when he saw her unexpectedly in town.

Why did this song seem to so special? He didn't even understand the words, yet they pulled at his thoughts and made him feel like life was good and important and the future would be even better. "Turn it up!" Joanne was awake, smiling toward the front seat. She shook Mary. "Wake up, Mary, you've got to hear this!"

And Mary woke as the volume rose, the crisp high notes clear, and the rhythmic bass thumping, the rich vocals compelling her to listen.

Mary looked to the front. The important men in her life, husband and father, were listening, heads turned slightly to the side. From what she could see from the back seat, it appeared they might be trying to hide their eyes.

She smiled, contented. Her life was so good.

CHAPTER 34

Terry slept late on the day after Christmas and woke to a crisp, sunny day. She pulled the blinds open and looked outside as the coffee maker did its work. Frost was thick on the power lines and tree branches in her mother's neighborhood and a street hockey game was in full swing. Terry leaned on the counter, watching the game through the living room window. She sipped some coffee; the high-pitched shouts audible from the street.

A middle-sized boy scored and ran around with his stick in the air, celebrating. She grinned at his arrogance. The game looked like fun. The nets appeared new, and she guessed they were someone's Christmas present. The kids looked like they played a lot, the game fast with crisp passes and strong goaltending.

Her mom had left a note on the refrigerator and she turned to re-read it. It was sweet, directions to frozen food, a thank you for the ride to the airport, and some movie and restaurant coupons clipped on the bottom. Opening the cupboard, she pulled out a yellow container of hot chocolate mix. It was heavy, and when she pulled off the plastic lid, she saw the foil seal still intact. Perfect.

Terry took a large pot from another cupboard and set it on the stove. She checked the refrigerator. Yes, an unopened gallon of milk. She poured the milk in the stock pot, added some water, then turned on the heat. While the milk heated, she rummaged around in the pantry and found a plastic bag, partially filled with white Styrofoam cups.

She added chocolate mix to the warming liquid and shook in some cayenne pepper. Stirring with a whisk, she added vanilla and a touch of cinnamon. Terry next added unsweetened cocoa powder, the mixture darkening as she stirred. She tasted it. Pretty good. She sprinkled salt over the top and swirled it in vigorously.

There was a plastic tray standing against the wall on the end of the counter, a garish Santa and his reindeer emblazoned on its surface.

She did a quick count of the players and the little kids watching and started filling cups, standing them on the tray. A few parents were in their yards, one man cleaning out the trunk of his car, another struggling with a drooping string of Christmas lights. She added a few cups and headed outside to share some Christmas.

The hockey players responded to her cheerful "Merry Christmas" by stopping the play and watching her walk down the snowy sidewalk, their sticks resting on the frozen road. One of the goalies took off his mask and gloves and ran over to help. Grabbing a milk crate one of the little kids had been sitting on, he improvised a sturdy table, taking care to make it level. She had thought the players were all kids, but this guy was at least six feet tall.

"Thanks! That looks good!" He waved the others over. "Come on you guys, look what she made for us!"

He was a good-looking teen and was wearing a Prince George Cougars jersey. Terry was surprised. He was a junior hockey player who she recognized. She thanked him by name, and now he was surprised.

"Nice goal last week against the Rebels. I was there in Prince George, watched you beat my team."

He grinned. "Thanks, but that one was more about the assist."

This started an argument among the younger players, sure that their hero didn't need to share the credit. As eager hands reached for the hot chocolate, the argument continued, punctuated with a chorus of thank you's. Terry indicated the extras and the hockey player walked with her, carrying the tray while she handed out hot chocolate to the adults within view.

"That's really nice, you playing with these kids. Most of them are wearing Blades jerseys."

He laughed. "Some of these kids are probably better than me." He pointed to two boys, playing one-on-one. "My little brothers. Look how the smaller one holds his stick, beautiful hands."

Terry agreed. They did look very skilled, not yet teenagers.

He pointed down the street. "Our house is right down there, lived here all my life. We play hockey on this street all year. Lots of taillights broken over the years. "He sipped more chocolate. "This is really good. Is there hot pepper in it?"

She told him the ingredients.

"I'm going to make this for my host family," he said, sipping again. "I live with a great family in Prince George. Sure is good to be home for Christmas though."

They chatted about his upcoming games, and he invited her to watch a home game the following week if she was in town.

The kids were back at play, yelling for their hero to get back in net.

"Gotta go, today I'm a goalie. Thanks again."

She watched him trot off to grab a goalie stick and break into the play, stealing the ball, running up to score on a hapless twelve-year-old wearing an oversized Calgary Flames jersey.

Terry collected the empty cups and carried the tray back to the house. After cleaning up the hot chocolate mess, and the leftover pizza from the night before, she took the trash out to the garbage can in the garage.

A thin phone book, doing temporary duty holding up the Santa Clause tray, was resting on the counter. She pulled it over, flipping through the pages idly.

She thought back to the movies the night before. The day after Christmas, and here she was alone. Pulling out her phone, she sent a quick message to Mary Amund. She knew Mary had plans to go shopping on Boxing Day.

She received a reply immediately, followed by a selfie of a happy Mary in a tack shop, surrounded by leather horse stuff, not the kind of shopping Terry was familiar with.

She sent three question marks and a perplexed face emoji. Another selfie came right away. This time Mary was holding up a cute pair of blue and tan western boots.

Terry dialed Mary's number.

"Hi, Terry! Merry Christmas!" Mary's shopper's-high voice was rich and familiar.

"Do they have some good sales on boots?"

They did, and ten minutes later, after a flurry of photos and conversation, Terry's new pair of driving boots were safely tucked into Mary's cart, along with a cute western shirt with pearl snaps and a pair of jeans they were both sure would fit Terry perfectly. And she had saved seventy-five percent!

Unbeknownst to Terry, a similar shirt in extra large was also resting in the cart. Mary was sure Terry would like to give Isaac a post-Christmas gift, and they would look so *good* together.

Terry decided she wouldn't stay five more days in her mom's empty house and called the airline and paid to change her ticket. When this was complete, she opened the phone book and made a few more calls.

Her plane would leave in twenty-six hours, just enough time to take care of some business. An hour and a half later, she was driving her rental car into downtown Saskatoon.

Terry spent the afternoon helping three regular volunteers at a soup kitchen prepare place mats and fill small gift bags for a New Year's dinner that would be served in a week. They were happy for the help and enjoyed Terry's cheerful conversation. One of them was a counsellor, and Terry surprised herself by sharing her current struggle with fear and the story of her abduction.

The women listened and even cried with her when she broke down. As they tried to comfort her, Terry was struck with the realization they were lonely too. She suggested they each tell their story while they worked.

They finished the job faster than expected, and Terry treated her new friends to a nice meal at a nearby family restaurant. On a whim, she bought travel mugs while paying at the counter. In the parking lot, she presented them each with a mug, as a reminder of their time together on Boxing Day. The women responded with happy hugs.

When she dropped them off back at the soup kitchen, the counsellor pressed a card into Terry's hand. "If you ever need to talk to someone, please feel free to call." She indicated the door through which the other two women had gone. "And thanks again for helping us today, the dinner, and the mugs. I will be going home to my family, but those two really needed this unexpected blessing today. My kids wrapped gifts for them, and that's all the Christmas they really had. Your gift, out of the blue, really made their Christmas special!"

And with these words playing in her mind, Terry headed back toward the suburbs, fears diminished. When she got home, she was going to call Freda to thank her once more. And then she would call Isaac and see what he was doing tomorrow evening.

And maybe there would be more Christmas movies to enjoy this evening.

But when she pulled in the driveway and saw a note taped to her garage door, her plans changed. The note scrawled on wrapping paper read: Come on down to house number 2133. Hockey on the big screen, chili, and nachos! Game starts at 7:00, come whenever it suits. Go, Cougars!

CHAPTER 35

Terry was excited to get back to Vanderhoof. She realized that it was her new home; it truly felt like home. She had a growing network of friends, a good job, a relationship that could be the start of something special. And all in a place she knew nothing about before seeing the ad for employment.

But fear was a constant nagging presence, tempering her excitement of going home. Where were her captors, where were they *right now*? Were they looking for her, guessing she may be traveling at Christmastime, scouring airports? Her flight connected through Calgary, the city that could be the hub of operations for Joseph and his gang, or whatever it was.

Now, sitting in her seat on the plane at the gate, waiting for a few late passengers, she dialed her contact at the Prince George RCMP detachment. She wished him a Merry Christmas, and then explained where she was, her itinerary, arrival time in Prince George.

The officer was kind and supportive. He would be available during her flight and encouraged her to call at any time if she saw anything suspicious or just needed to talk. He gave her a different number and she guessed it was his cell phone. Hanging up before the steward asked people to stow their phones, Terry was glad she had called. She was not going to travel by herself again until this situation was dealt with, that was for sure.

Terry had enjoyed the previous evening with new friends. The teasing began when she arrived wearing a Red Deer Rebels jersey. The chili served in big mugs smelled good and the large nacho platters disappeared as if by magic.

She stayed late, enjoying the inside look at a hockey family. She had been surprised how young the parents were. The Cougars player was only seventeen, and the youngest child was a little girl Terry guessed to be six years old. The two younger brothers she had seen playing hockey had a small but wild horde of friends visiting for the game, and during commercials there was a lot of noisy horseplay going on in the back of the recreation room.

Now settled in her seat, Terry watched other passengers board the plane and tried to distract herself by guessing their stories. Were they returning home, going to work, visiting? Did they have problems like her own?

The flight and connections were uneventful. While waiting to change planes in Calgary, Terry was surprised to receive a call from the RCMP officer with whom she had spoken earlier. He was reassuring and let her know he had spoken with airport security, and they were on the alert for any suspicious behavior. He made sure they had the men's descriptions and sketches done by the RCMP artist.

Terry was relieved when her plane touched down in Prince George, and when she saw Isaac's smile in the warm reception area the sense of relief amazed her.

Isaac walked with her to her pickup and helped her clean the snow from her window. They drove in convoy to a new restaurant on the highway. Over dinner, they shared their Christmas experiences, and Terry looked forward to being home for a few days before going to work.

While Terry and Isaac were driving from Prince George to Vanderhoof, Johnny and Mary were washing dishes in the mountain cabin near Fernie. They had toured the Rolling Hills, meeting dozens of other riders on a Christmas break. Al and Johnny had challenged some rough and steep terrain, and the ladies had enjoyed the warm fire and the leisurely trail lunch.

"Mary, what was your favorite part of today?" Johnny was scrubbing the dishes industriously.

"Well, I liked the smells. The snow, the trees, and even the exhaust." She laughed. "I would rather not smell your gear though. You guys had steam coming off your heads when you took your helmets off at lunch time."

Al and Joanne were out filling the hot tub. They were all sore from the first day of riding and were not looking forward to getting up in the morning. The hose had been trickling into the hot tub all evening, and Al was tending the wood burner that heated the water. Joanne was keeping him company while the Amunds tidied the kitchen.

"What was your favorite thing today?" Mary blew a strand of hair out of her eyes.

"I liked riding with you. Just riding along with you." Johnny smiled at her. "I also liked seeing the other riders, the family with those kids."

Mary laughed. They had been picnicking beside the trail, feeding bread crusts to the jays, when they heard the drone of small engines. Three mini sleds were buzzing noisily up the trail, three little helmets bobbing. The leader slowed near their fire, was nearly rear-ended by machine number two, and machine number three peeled off the trail into the deep snow and tipped over, the diminutive rider disappearing helmet first.

Johnny rescued the little rider and brushed the goggles free of snow to reveal big, blue eyes and a high-octane smile. A quiet four-stroke machine was close behind, and seeing the tangle of small snowmobiles, the rider's helmet had quickly come off, exposing a mother's concerned face.

She had apologized for the interruption but stayed at the insistence of the party, drinking a cup of coffee and helping three small kids out of their snowsuits to pee, and then suiting them up again, one at a time. The process had been lengthy and looked difficult to Johnny. When the last helmet had been buckled on, the snarl of a modified hill climb machine grew louder, and the party was joined by a man on a custom machine that had Johnny and Al up and walking over before he turned off the engine.

Squeals of "Daddy" swirled out from three small helmets as the kids abandoned their sleds. The greeting from the busy mother was much cooler, though she was a good sport.

The man had a booming, infectious laugh, and the family was soon in harmony, the kids competing to show Mary and Joanne their prized machines, while Johnny and Al drooled over the modified Yamaha.

The little girl Johnny had rescued from her plunge into the powder wouldn't leave until he came and looked at all the special decals she had plastered on her little sled. One question from Johnny led to a torrent of information about cartoon characters and other subjects he couldn't understand. The conversation ended with the little girl peeling one of the prized stickers off her windshield, and carefully applying it to the windshield of Johnny's Ski-Doo.

Hello Kitty proved to be a conversation starter on the duration of the trip and was preserved that evening with some clear tape attaching it firmly to the window of Johnny's otherwise unblemished machine.

CHAPTER 36

The second morning started slowly for everyone but Mary, accustomed to riding her horses. Though she had been a little stiff the evening before, she woke refreshed and ready to go. The other three, however, were happy to sit in the hot tub and drink the mugs of coffee she brought them.

They ate the breakfast Mary prepared, sitting in the steaming water, enjoying the view from their vantage point, air fragrant with smoke from the fire of cured aspen.

After Mary had collected the dishes and refilled the mugs of coffee, she told them they had fifteen minutes to soak and then they had better get out and prepare for the day. When the allotted time had passed and there was no sign of movement from the trio, and their demands for more coffee grew too obnoxious, she left her magazine on the coffee table and went outside to assault them with shovelfuls of powdery snow. The exit was rapid and punctuated with groans and threats as her family slipped and staggered barefoot back into the cabin to dress.

The mood was light as they drove the sleds out of the trailer and checked them over before hitting the trail. The fleecy overcast was torn, revealing a few slivers of blue sky and they all checked for their sunglasses.

The riding was outstanding, and even though the sun was low in late December, the footage from Mary's camera would be treasured for years, the brilliance of blue sky, white snow and clouds, and rich green of the coniferous trees a perfect backdrop for a family adventure.

They ate lunch earlier than planned, taking a break as the boys tried to fix the damage Al's machine incurred when he miscalculated a jump and jammed a ski into a tree trunk, ten feet above the snow. Mary had caught the whole incident on her helmet-cam, and she and Joanne teased the men as the two huddled together to watch the footage. They watched and re-watched the video, hooting with laughter each time and using slow-motion to help identify where some of the missing pieces of the machine landed. Al was not hurt and kept reminding them about the spare cab for his machine, purchased on Boxing Day, waiting back at the trailer.

The front of the ski was broken off but using ingenuity and pieces of broken cab, they MacGyvered the big Polaris for the trip down the mountain. It was far too early to return home, and sore muscles had been forgotten. Johnny turned his Ski-Doo over to Al and doubled with Mary, the new tandem seat coming in handy. Adjusting the suspension to the highest setting, they spent the next few hours exploring trails, taking photos, and teaching the women how to set up for and land a jump.

Daylight and fuel were running low, and picking up Al's machine, they had an uneventful ride back down the mountain.

Before leaving in the morning, Mary had skillfully loaded a slow cooker and they feasted on barbeque ribs before spending a few hours under the stars in the hot tub, appreciating the clear sky, bright stars, whir of wind combing the pines, and the warmth that came from being a family.

"Dad, I bet I can run around the truck and trailer and back faster than you!"

Al began climbing out of the spa, and Mary launched over the side and sprinted barefoot through the snow, steam rising, shrieking. Al splashed back into the water, chuckling.

"Hey! No fair!" Mary picked up a handy shovel and flung an arc of loose snow over the group, catching Al and the others.

This led to more snow being dumped on those in the hot tub, and then Mary being tossed kicking and squealing into deep powder by her dad and husband. Sliding back into the tub shivering. Mary insisted they all climb out of the tub and make snow angels. Skin burning from the icy snow, they clumsily dropped back into the hot tub with yells or squeals.

When order was restored, and all were back in their places in the hot water, Johnny leaned back, eyes closed, and savored his good fortune.

Several bottles of wine had been chilling, forgotten in the snow, and Al leaned over to retrieve one. Mary refused a glass, opting for hot chocolate from the thermos. At the questioning look from her father, she explained. "Johnny and I want to start a family; no alcohol for me for a while."

"How exciting!" Joanne handed Al her glass, leaning over to hug Mary. "I'm so happy for you! And us!", she added.

Johnny laughed at Al, who threw his head back and howled like a wolf, "I'm gonna be a Grandpa, woo hoo!"

Four bottles of wine later, the toasts had turned from motherhood and grandchildren to the boys toasting the hot tub, free enterprise, and Al's broken ski. Mary and Joanne retreated to the house, disassociating themselves with the ridiculous celebrations, assuring their husbands they would bring more wine soon. The men spent twenty minutes discussing what kind of small snowmobile would be best for the Amund child, and they yelled for Mary to tell them whether the first child would be a boy or a girl, and where was the wine?

When they came dripping into the house much later, grinning sloppily, the women were already asleep, and they soon followed suit, leaving a trail of wet towels and empty bottles. Before retiring, they were careful to bring in the garbage can, which they placed on the kitchen table, reasoning that if a bear came out of hibernation several months early and figured out how to open the cabin door, he wouldn't be able to get into it and make a mess if the garbage was high on the table. Noticing all the water on the floor, they diligently put all the winter boots outside in the cold, as they had to be responsible for the huge mess no one had noticed earlier.

Joanne woke first the next morning, and her reaction to the dark shape hulking on the table woke the rest of the sleepers in the cabin immediately. Al mumbled something about bears, then thought about what he was saying and clammed up, starting the coffee pot without adding coffee.

Al and Johnny denied having headaches, refused the offered medication and an early breakfast, and at first chance headed outside coatless to get the sleds ready, cleaning up the empty beer cans scattered around the hot tub and sharing a handful of aspirin stashed in the SUV.

Later at breakfast, Mary noticed there were no boots by the door, and Al sheepishly brought them in and set them by the wood stove to warm. Laughter ensued, and by the time bellies were full, hearts had been lightened, and they all agreed the future Amund child had been duly celebrated. Mary had a brief chill when she thought of the celebration that may occur when the first child actually appeared, but she shrugged it off, guessing she would have much more to deal with than a husband with a hangover.

The men retreated as the breakfast dishes were washed with much banging, citing the need to finish replacing Al's broken ski. Quietly they replaced the aftermarket skis with the stock skis Al had stowed in the trailer. Replacing the tools carefully in their trays, they trooped back in to dress for the ride.

Joanne grinned at Mary as they joined their husbands outside, indicating the bright yellow earplugs protruding from their ears as they pulled their helmets on, red-rimmed eyes squinting in the bright morning light before dark glasses and hastily closed visors obscured them.

Mary was not surprised when Johnny motioned for her to take his sled, or when he climbed gratefully onto her smaller machine with the quiet stock exhaust.

Leading the way up the now-familiar trail, Mary smiled back at the friendly sticker on the windscreen and had to admit it would be fun to see their children riding little machines of their own. When Johnny pulled up beside her in a wide portion of trail, Mary smiled at him, then pinned the throttle. The skis lifted, the fighter-jet scream of the exhaust causing Johnny to wince and pull away, floundering through the deep snow and trees beside the trail as she disappeared up the mountain, Hello Kitty cheering her on.

CHAPTER 37

S everal weeks following the Christmas trip to Fernie, Mary wanted to do something special for Johnny. Ever since they had moved into their house, she'd noticed that Johnny had changed little in the workshop. It seemed to her that Johnny acted like he was borrowing the space, rather than treating it as something he owned. She respected his memory of his uncles but decided she would spend some time cleaning up clutter in the small building.

After work one afternoon, she changed into her chore clothes and sipped a cup of tea as she walked to the workshop, checking to make sure she had her Banks Mountain cell phone with her. Her horses were at the feeder, "burning hay" as Johnny put it, scruffy in their winter coats.

She found the attachments for the shop vacuum and began cleaning in one corner. The tools had their own places, several newer purchases leaning in a corner. She stacked small scraps of wood by the stove, and looked at the magazine photo of the sword, wondering what the significance was to the man who pinned it on the wall. Did he miss his homeland? Had his mother told him a bedtime story involving the weapon? Had a relative found the artifact on their property?

She smiled to herself and shivered, not wanting to start a fire in the unfamiliar stove.

She vacuumed the dust and sawdust from each wooden drawer under the work-bench. The third drawer stuck, wedged half open, and she knelt, using her phone's flashlight to investigate the deep drawer. Something was hanging down into the drawer, and reaching in, she felt a wooden box that had been taped to the underside of the workbench. The tape seemed to have loosened, blocking the drawer.

Curiosity aroused, she peeled off the tape and pulled the dusty box gingerly out of the drawer.

Placing the box on the workbench in front of the window, she wiped off the dust with a cloth. It was handmade, sanded smooth, complex joints not quite perfect. The box had been stained dark, the finely grained wood almost black. The lid didn't have a hinge. She looked closer and could see it was in a slot. Mary slid it carefully open and set the lid on the dust cloth. On a small sheet of lined paper was a note. In careful letters were the words, "For Johnny."

The contents were fascinating. There was a short stack of hockey cards, several little toy tractors, a few rubber balls, a small toy airplane. In the corner was a tiny red book, a Gideons Bible. There was a jack knife and a whet stone, far smaller than the one Johnny had used to sharpen the axe. Lifting out the Bible carefully, she saw it looked new, unused.

Something protruded from the pages, and careful to keep the place, she pulled it out. It was not a bookmark, but a photo of a stern yet handsome woman. She held the photo toward the light. The woman was not as old as her clothing and demeanor suggested. Turning the photo, she read the faint inscription. The first line simply said, "Mother, early

40s," followed by a question mark. The second line read "favorite verse, Psalm 46:1."

Mary's hands were shaking as she paged gingerly through the little Bible and read the first verse of the forty-sixth Psalm: "God is our refuge and strength, a very present help in trouble."

She turned to another bookmark, pulling out a photo of a big man of middle age, each arm on the shoulders of a boy. She was shocked at their resemblance to Johnny. This photo was in color, though very faded, the sober face of the man reflected in the expressions of the boys. The three were posed on the deck of a ship, harbor buildings behind them under overcast sky.

Turning the photo, she read, "Lars, Pa, Nelsson," and below these words were written "Psalm 40:1-3." Finding the place, Mary read: "I waited patiently for the Lord and he inclined unto me and heard my cry. He brought me up also out of an horrible pit, out of the miry clay, and set my feet upon a rock, and established my goings. And he hath put a new song in my mouth, even praise unto our God, many shall see it and fear, and shall trust in the Lord."

What terrible experiences had these people endured? Though the passages were comforting, what troubles or hardships would make them favorites? What was so terrible in their past that had inspired them to cry out to God for help? Mary hadn't read the Bible, but knew it was a source of strength for many.

Mary's thoughts moved on; there was another photo in the book. She pulled it out and was thrilled to find a picture of Johnny. He was young, staring seriously at the camera, shirt buttoned high on his throat, hair slicked down. Turning it over, she read, "Johnny 10 years. 5 grade."

She was disappointed there was no scripture reference; neither he nor his uncles had a chosen verse. She had hoped for something positive for them. Replacing the photo and the book in its corner, she noticed the box was deeper than the compartment she was exploring. There were several tiny, hand-carved pegs inserted through the bottom of the compartment. Carefully removing these, she slid the false floor out in the same manner as the lid had come off. In the shallow space at the bottom of the box was a folded piece of paper.

Mary knew she might be violating Johnny's privacy, and she took a breath before deciding to unfold the page. She saw it was a letter, handwritten in blue ink.

Dear Brothers,

I hope you are well, and that life is treating you fine. A great tragedy has come into my life, and I want you to know the true facts.

Thank you brothers, for sending me money for university. I also appreciated your hospitality when I came out there to live but simply was not happy there. I began to work in real estate when I came here and was off to a good start.

I received the same training from our parents as you. Father taught me that sometimes a man must do a thing he very much wants to avoid regardless of the cost. Mother taught me that troubles will come and we must make plans to overcome them. I have tried to live like this but may have failed.

Selling real estate was going well. I showed a farm property to a man and received a message that he wanted to purchase the land and wanted to meet me at the property the following morning to sign papers and conclude the deal. I was happy for a quick sale and met him at the time he requested. When

I arrived he was waiting at the table on the porch. While we were signing papers, I heard a noise inside. He told me I was hearing things, but then I heard it again. He tried to stop me from going inside, but I went in anyway and ran up the stairs. In one of the bedrooms I found a woman who was tied up. She had been beaten, and had a shirt tied over her mouth. I untied her and went back downstairs. The man tried to laugh it off. He said she was a prostitute he had brought out with him and had given him trouble. When she came down she confirmed this and said how when he was drunk the night before had bragged how he had killed at least six women like her and how would she like to be next?

He tried to leave but I made him sit down. I gave the woman his keys and she drove away. Then he said it was true he had killed other women but there was no proof and he would never get caught. He told me he would pay me a lot of money if I just forgot about it. Then he bragged how he wanted to get rid of as many as possible and make the world a better place. I told him he was crazy and he attacked me so I strangled him.

I would have got away with it probably, but after I had him partly buried I saw he was wearing a nice shirt. This man was a monster, he deserved no brothers, and therefore his back should be bare. So I took it off. I was shaking and crazy myself. Stupid, I know.

The woman went straight to the police, and they came. If I would have left sooner they wouldn't have caught me or found the body.

I am not sorry, it needed to be done. I will overcome this problem. Do not try to contact me. I will change my name. I wish I had known you better. I was always proud of you and the way you sent money to Mother after Father died. She was proud of you too.

Even though I will never see you again I will always know I had brothers, real brothers. I know you would have been proud of me soon if this hadn't happened, and I will regret it every day forward.

You have no children, and neither will I. I am sad the Amunds will be no more, we were a good family, strong brothers to many. Mother and Father did not deserve everything that happened.

With love, and for the last time,

Svend Amund, your brother.

Mary refolded the letter and reassembled the box and its contents. Returning to the house, she thought she was beginning to understand the story. She called Johnny and asked him to come home.

She brewed fresh coffee and sat in the living room, thinking while she waited, the wooden box alone on the kitchen table.

CHAPTER 38

Johnny was at the parts store, returning a starter core, when he received Mary's call. It was mid-afternoon, and he hadn't taken time to eat lunch. It would only take a few minutes and he knew there was leftover chicken casserole in the refrigerator, so after loading the parts in the bed of his pickup, he headed straight home.

He guessed the horses had escaped and Mary needed a hand. When he parked in the driveway, he noticed the door to his workshop was open and took the time to walk over and close it before going to the house.

He ran his hand across their sign as he passed it, a habit formed in recent weeks. He liked coming home.

Mary was waiting in the kitchen with two cups of coffee, and a wooden box. He stared at the box.

"Where did you get that?" his voice was flat. He walked forward, not seeming to want an answer, lifting the object from the table, turning it in his big hands, sliding the lid open.

He just stood there, looking at the box, rubbing the wood. He sat down, placing the box back on the table, sliding the lid in and out.

"Where's all the letters?" He looked more carefully at the contents.

"Hey, my tractors!" He pulled out the green one, rolling it on the table, rubber tires making no noise as he moved it back and forth. "Where did you find this? Uncle Lars kept family letters in this box. He kept it on his nightstand."

Mary could see Johnny was moved by the familiar object. She pushed his cup of coffee closer to him. He ignored it, setting the tractors in a neat row on the table: green, yellow, red, blue. She guessed it was some sort of familiar order.

"Johnny, today I decided to clean up your workshop." She paused at his look of alarm. "Don't worry, I didn't throw anything out. I took the tools and stuff out of the drawers, one at a time so nothing got mixed up, and vacuumed out the dust. When I got to the third drawer, the one with the container of big spikes in the front, it wouldn't open all the way."

She indicated the tacky residue on the sides and bottom of the box.

"This was taped up to the bottom of the workbench. The tape toward the back had come loose and the box had dropped down and was jamming the drawer. So, I pulled it out and brought it inside. Johnny, I looked at everything."

Mary was worried. She guessed Johnny had never seen the hidden letter, didn't know the details it shared. She had a terrible feeling it could set off a deep depression in her husband.

Johnny looked up as she paused and noticed she had tears in her eyes; her lower lip was trembling.

She rose and came to sit sideways on his lap, putting her arms around him, face pressed to the side of his neck.

"Johnny, I love you so much. I love who you are right now. I don't want you to change."

With her right arm still across his shoulders, she lifted the Gideons

Bible with her left hand and set it in front of him. Clumsy with his wife in his lap, Johnny reached around her and picked up the little book.

"A guy came to our school when we were in grade five and gave us each one of these Testaments." He corrected himself. "New Testaments. There was a big stink about it later. The school wasn't supposed to hand them out to the kids. Of course, that made us all want them even more. I brought mine home, and Uncle Lars told me I could keep it, and it might be useful some day."

He opened to the first marker, careful with the crisp pages.

"Uncle Lars told me to take care of it, so I never opened it all the way. It seemed like the binding might break."

He pulled out the photo, and Mary felt his body go still. She realized he was holding his breath. She watched the recognition in his eyes, his fingers holding the photo carefully. He exhaled.

"Every Easter we would look through the photo album Uncle Nelsson kept. This was one of their favorites of their mother, my grandmother. I never met her. I think she died when I was pretty young."

The next photo was also familiar. "Yep, here is my grandfather and uncles. They always liked this photo, too. I can't remember which harbor that is, but I think it was on a trip to the old country."

Johnny chuckled when he pulled out the photo of himself. "This picture I hated, I threw it out. Uncle Lars must have pulled it out of the garbage. I got that shirt from a neighbor boy. I didn't mind wearing hand-me-downs, but I didn't like that kid, even though his mom was nice."

Johnny looked at the front of the small book, reading the words. "New Testament and Psalms and Proverbs. Uncle Nelsson always said I should read these Proverbs, said any man could learn a lot from them, no matter what he believed."

Opening the back of the book, he cringed as the binding crackled. There was a slight bulge between several pages. Johnny pried the pages apart and grunted when a bill dropped out. The bill was folded over twice, an unfamiliar purplish color. Johnny moved stiffly and Mary stood, giving him room. He opened the flattened banknote, creases appearing to have been ironed. They looked at each other, surprised. On either side of the portrait of Queen Elizabeth were the numbers *1000.*

"Is it real?" Mary took the bill and slowly turned it, revealing a pair of birds on the back.

Johnny chuckled. "This had to be the work of Uncle Nelsson. I remember how proud he was when he paid for a new tractor with a handful of thousand-dollar bills. 'Cash is king, Yonny!' he always said."

They looked for a message, but finding none, Johnny continued looking through the box, setting the contents in a row on the table. He leaned back, taking a long drink of his coffee, eyes on Mary who had pulled a chair around to sit beside him.

"Is there something in the bottom?" he held her eyes.

She nodded.

"I was never supposed to look in the bottom, although they didn't mind if I read the letters in the top compartment. I figured they had private papers kept in there." He took a deep breath and pulled out the carved pegs, using a wood button Mary hadn't noticed to slide the flat piece of wood out.

"They said their grandfather made this box. Supposedly he built it from a shipwreck, wood washed up on the shore."

He read the letter, then stood up and walked to the window. He watched the birds in Mary's feeder, chickadees sharing the oily seeds with the finches whose normal food supply had been decimated by summer forest fires.

He walked to the refrigerator, then back to the table.

Mary put her hand on his shoulder. It was hard, the tension in his body a presence, filling the small room.

"Mary, do you still like the sign?"

She was alarmed. He hadn't called it "our sign" as he usually did. She wondered how he felt, wondered if this was all new information, hoped she had the strength and wisdom to help her husband stay on the plateau to which he had risen. She waited.

Johnny shrugged, rolling his shoulders back several times, and stood abruptly. He turned to face Mary. "Come with me."

He walked out onto the covered porch in his sock feet, mindless of the blown snow underfoot, and waited for Mary to join him before turning toward the sign that had become an important icon to them both. Mary shivered, and he picked her up, holding her as if she was a new bride ready to be carried across the threshold.

"Welcome to the Johnny and Mary Amund home." He said the words simply, as they should be said, then carried his wife into their home, set her down, and went to the refrigerator for some leftovers.

CHAPTER 39

Mary was surprised by Johnny's reaction, and waited, drinking her coffee while he warmed a plate of food in the microwave. He noticed his socks were wet and headed down the hall for dry ones, returning as the microwave chimed.

"I had never seen that letter before today, and I guess it will take a little time to get used to it. It seems so unnecessary, sad." He ate some chicken, looking out the window as he chewed.

"Now it makes some sort of sense why there was no contact. I always thought he must have been bad, a criminal, and the uncles had sort of disowned him. You think they were just honoring his wishes?"

He took another bite, looking at Mary as he chewed.

"Probably. They always gave you a lot of space, right?"

He nodded and took another bite. "This is really good, want some?" He held up an overloaded fork in Mary's direction. She shook her head.

She put her hand on his arm, shake-shake. "You know what's crazy? Your father probably doesn't even know you exist! Do you think he ever contacted your uncles?"

"I don't know. But I do know that you and I have made a new start, and we are going to build a good family starting right where we are. We can't do anything about the past, but we can work on the future, right? Let's just keep living. We don't need to worry about this, Mary. What he did, and took responsibility for, doesn't change who I am, right?"

Mary showed him the scripture references on the back of the photos and read them to him from the little red book. He nodded as he finished his food, showing that he remembered them, but made no comment.

"Do you know about your grandparents? Why they came to North America?"

He shook his head. "No, not much. I know my uncles sent money four times a year. I guess they must have done that until their parents were both gone. They did well out here. I always wondered why their mom, never thought of her as my grandmother, didn't come to live here. They lived in Minnesota maybe, or Michigan? Somewhere in the US, northern part somewhere. I guess she wanted to stay there. I don't know anything about the family, except what I read in the old letters. The letters were mostly about day to day stuff though, not about people. At least, that's how I remember it."

"Maybe she had friends there. Maybe she didn't want to leave her home, you think?" Mary looked at Johnny, remembering the photo of his grandfather and uncles, the similarity between him and them.

"Do you think you could find where she lived somehow? Do you have the old letters?"

Johnny stood and rinsed his plate at the sink, ignoring her question.

"That food was good. Look, Mary, I have a lot to think about. My family, which I have never really considered, well," He cleared his throat, "it seems real now, that I had more family than Uncle Nelsson and Uncle Lars."

He stretched, hands flat on the kitchen ceiling.

"The part about my father. I'm thinking this will probably bother me later, especially if I'm discouraged. Like, who knows where he would be now? Is he still in prison? How long would he serve time for what he did? Did he change his name? Which prison was he in?"

He cleared his throat. "And what about my mother?"

He paused, facing her. "There are just so many questions. I'm not going to rush them. Let's just see how it plays out. We've made a good start in the last six months, and this situation doesn't need to affect us, our home."

Mary was relieved and nodded.

"I was really worried. The letter is shocking to me, I mean, did he really have to kill that guy? Isn't that a little extreme? Did he have mental issues? I was so worried you would be different when you read it, or would want to distance yourself from everything…"

Johnny put his arms around her, lifting her off her feet. He held her that way until she relaxed, smiling at her. After a moment she sighed, returning his smile.

"Mary, I love how we are now. I don't want it to change. Our sign is our sign. Even if other people have used that message wrong, we can use it right." "Bare is the back of the brother-less man. He said the words. "but remember, that is just an old Norse proverb. The important part of the sign is the first line, *The Amund Home*. That's the part I care about, though I like the saying a lot."

He grinned. "And here we are, in our home, you and me. And with a sweet gift from my uncles! You ever seen a thousand-dollar bill?"

As he headed out the door, he stopped, turned back inside, closing the door behind him.

"We do have a problem to figure out."

Mary was alarmed. "Who? You and I?"

"No, Terry's issue hasn't been resolved. I think she cries a lot. I know she says she still has nightmares. I talked to her a few days ago, the day before she went to Prince George for 'an appointment with her shrink' is how she put it. She told me she could hardly sleep because the dreams were getting so bad again."

Mary nodded. "Yes, she has talked to me too. I can hardly imagine how it would be to live with those memories, especially because the guys have not been found. Northern Alberta doesn't have that many towns. You'd think they would have found the guys, or at least who they worked for."

"I don't think they were from Alberta. I think they came in from somewhere else, maybe not even Canada."

"I hadn't thought of that. What else are you thinking?"

"I would bet the guys that grabbed Terry were not from northern Canada, for sure. Look at all the mistakes they made, how unfamiliar they were with this area." He paused, big fingers carefully typing a message on his phone, and when the phone pinged, he sat down again at the table, reaching over to the drawer where they kept pens and a few notepads. He clicked the button on a ballpoint pen, motioning for her to sit.

"Tell me all the things they did wrong. I'll write them down."

"Okay, they planned to drown her in a lake that was partially frozen. I guess they didn't think to carry her out to the open water."

He nodded, not writing.

She frowned. "Why aren't you writing?"

He smiled. "Already have that one. I want to see if you can think of things I haven't."

In the next few minutes, Mary found her husband had already thought of everything she suggested, and she was impressed with his thought process.

"Here is the one that really gets me."

She put her hand over the pen he was clicking incessantly as he talked.

"Think of it like this: these guys were in a hurry, so they rented a car, planning to only use it several days, then fly away, probably to Alberta because that's where she met the one guy, but it could be anywhere. And why did they panic when the drowning plan didn't work? Why not just bash her over the head and toss her off a bridge? They had crossed the Fraser when they left the airport. Or, drag her into the bush; there was a whole lot of that on their drive."

"So, what you are saying is, when they couldn't just drown her, they had no other good ideas, sort of a one-trick pony kind of thing." She shivered, "Which was a good thing for Terry, but seems pretty stupid. It was night, their car wasn't easy to identify, except it was clean. Maybe they rented it in their real names?"

Johnny nodded in agreement. "I think they were brought in to quickly get rid of her, but were not experienced, maybe had never worked together before. I would guess that this 'Joseph' guy was probably involved, but Terry didn't see him. He wasn't in the car, anyway. The thing is, he was recognizable in Alberta, the northern part for sure. Didn't she say he worked in a warehouse there? Where has he been since? Did he skip the country? Why haven't they found him yet – or did they? We need to keep thinking about this, and you know, I'm going to call that cop, Barton. He seemed like a good guy. I wonder if they will tell me what is going on?"

"And I will keep spending time with Terry. She needs a friend."

Johnny was headed out the door again. "Let's invite her and," he paused dramatically, "the Clockmaker for dinner on Friday, maybe fire up the grill, watch a movie, what do you think?"

She liked the idea and said she would make the arrangements.

CHAPTER 40

It was mid-January and Joseph hadn't heard from his Alberta employer, hadn't been contacted by the RCMP; in short, there had been no repercussions from the issue in November. He hadn't heard a thing from any associates of the two men who had gone to deal with the woman, and of course, had heard nothing from them and never would.

He was sick of holing up in the apartment in Toronto and tired of the questions from his older brother's widow and children, though living with them meant his name was not associated with any address or location. They believed he was working online, his hours spent alone in his room with his laptop confirming this in their minds – as well his own mind at times. He never left the apartment during the day and only rarely after dark. "Why don't you go out with your friends? Why don't you come shopping with us? Why don't you have a girlfriend?"

A man could only do so much work without being face-to-face with your contacts, and Joseph had been severing one relationship after another, taking care that his mistakes were blamed on others, building a smokescreen between him and the botched abduction and failed elimination of the woman. The new associates he was cultivating had no connection to others he had worked with in the past. He spent hours making sure of this.

He guessed that the woman wasn't going to do anything about the issue, and if he laid low long enough, and changed his name and methods, the RCMP would give up too.

He cursed, mixing languages, the hours spent alone with his problems seeming to unravel him mentally. But Joseph, who was already disassociating himself from this name and the name his family called him, was nothing if not careful. Patience was an important code to live by, and when you started breaking rules, as he had when he botched his delivery method, bad things happened.

He cursed again, remembering his ill-advised idea to move more product which involved the woman, what had he been thinking?

He knew what it was. It was greed; also an important way to live, but *live* was the key word. Greed must be used as wisely as patience. Use it wrongly and you could die or worse, at least in his business. He had foolishly allowed greed to unbalance patience.

He pulled up a website and began another French lesson, the insistent rhythms and vocals of the music playing on the other side of his bolted door effectively covering his voice as *Francois,* yes, he thought, *Francois* worked diligently on the nuances and accents of Parisian French.

Joseph, now thinking of his name as Francois, wanted money, lots of money, and had tried with diligence and intention to get all he could. He had formed some careful opinions along the way. *Purpose* was a foundational value on which *Wealth* could be built. *Greed, Patience* and *Skill* were the three fundamentals needed to achieve wealth, and he worked daily to become better at these qualities. Wealth was important: a man could not accomplish important goals and tasks without it. He paused the tutorial and scrolled back. He had been distracted by his thoughts, missing important information and practice at his new language. Getting rich wasn't easy, but maybe someday he could even market his methods, become an international celebrity, change how business was conducted... he paused and tried again to find his place.

While Joseph was transforming himself into Francois, Terry was driving truck. She was on her second and final trip of the day, putting on the kilometers. The conditions were excellent, as she kept hearing on the radio, but she didn't really notice or care that the road was good, temperature right, equipment running well.

She had embarrassed herself earlier that day, chaining up her drive axles for a small hill that was well sanded, and chains hadn't been necessary. Her face had burned at the snide comments over the radio from passing drivers, taking the chains off at the top of the hill as quickly as possible before more truckers passed her parked rig.

She found herself double-checking everything, not quite sure if she had properly checked the first time, flustered when she reached for her log book and found she had already filled in the required information. She knew Isaac should be at the shop when she finished her day, and looked forward to seeing him, and talking for a few minutes, although she had learned he got impatient when she voiced the same concerns multiple times.

Her therapist had offered the opinion that this was because Isaac felt powerless to help her, and Terry agreed with this assessment. Her sessions had been helpful for coping, but had not yet helped her conquer the fear, and as Melissa Banks had offered in her practical way, "You *should* feel some fear, Terry, the bad guys are still out there. Don't feel bad for being afraid or having bad dreams, it's not your fault."

And this advice had probably been the best of all, even though it did nothing to help her sleep at night. Another piece of advice that offered comfort had come from Isaac, when he said in his emphatic way, "Whenever you're scared of these guys, just imagine what The Big Guy and I would do if we ever got our hands on them. You won't be scared no more if that ever happens."

Isaac was not bluffing, but was serious about his words. After working with Johnny several months, she realized the big quiet man, who she had seen toss a heavy truck tire up onto the deck of the service truck with ease, had brains as well as strength. But when he was riled, as she had seen him once when a trucker had run a car off the road, the big man could be very, very intimidating.

Pulling into the shop yard, home base, as she liked to call it, she decided to take up Melissa's offer, and join her for a late dinner. The woman made her feel safe. Terry hoped the boys would be there too. They were hilarious, especially when both were home.

As she parked her truck and did her post-trip check, she thought about the three offers of lodging from her closest friends in Vanderhoof. Isaac of course, but Mary Amund had also asked her to consider their spare room, and Chet Banks had urged her to live with them. "This house is huge, lots of room. We'd be honored to have you." And not only lodging, free lodging. She hit the remote start on her pickup as she walked to the shop to check in and ask someone to look at her malfunctioning trailer lights. It was good to have friends who had become her new family in a few short months.

Isaac was gone. "Somewhere up the Francis," Pete told her. The shop had an empty bay, and Pete headed out to bring in her truck, assuring her it was fine that she hadn't brought it in herself. "Shop's usually full this time of day. Don't worry about it. I need the fresh air anyway. Sure, is nice to be back at work, though, even if I'm doing a lighter shift."

The Banks' home was deserted when she arrived, but she saw a note on the door. She peeled the paper off the door, reading the terse message as she entered the warm house.

Dinner in the fridge, put in oven at 350 while you take a bubble bath. Back at 8:00

And she followed the directions, although she took the time to retrieve a bag with clean clothes from her pickup before going down the hall to the shower. She smiled again when she saw the note on the bathroom door.

Guys, if you get home before me, stay out!!! Use another bathroom, or the great outdoors like you always do. Love, Mom.

There was a scented candle burning. The bathroom was perfectly clean. Several fluffy towels and a basket of bath bombs were arranged on the counter, along with various shampoos and soaps. Several magazines were rolled up and tied with ribbons, beside a bowl of roses in gel beads. A number of tea lights were waiting to be lit.

Terry smiled and began to fill the large tub, looking forward to a relaxing bath and a hot meal. Turning off the main lights and basking in the glow of a dozen tiny candles, she was touched, understanding Melissa's desire for feminine contact in the mostly male world in which she lived.

Melissa had returned home in time to save the dozing Terry's meal. Now with the lights back on, eating chicken cordon bleu with a vegetable casserole on the side, Terry read through the fashion magazine, smiling at the contrast of the clothes to those she normally wore to work. She ran more hot water, steam curling visibly through the ceiling fan, warmth and humidity welcome after a winter day spent in the dry, cold winter air of central BC.

She dropped another bath bomb into the water, this one sizzling and bubbling, gold flakes floating in the water. Terry considered the difference between this and her first Vanderhoof accommodations at the motel. It certainly made her think of accepting the Banks's offer.

Later in her apartment, skin and soul glowing, Terry felt herself relaxing as she slid into bed. Even the warm-from-the-oven chocolate cake she had enjoyed with Melissa couldn't keep her from falling quickly asleep. Maybe there would be no bad dreams, at least for tonight.

CHAPTER 41

Toronto was one of the largest cities in North America with close to three million people crammed into its diverse metropolitan area, so when Joseph-Francois left his dead brother's apartment and braved the grit-filled gusts late one February afternoon, he expected to see many people, but none that he knew. He had spent hours each day in the last several months honing his French accent and needed to go out and practice, to compare his speech to the French-Canadian accent spoken in many places in Toronto.

His mind felt numb from the hours spent shut alone in his room, thin door unable to block the constant and raucous noise from his dead brother's four children and the corrections of their mother and countless aunts and cousins and others who came for regular visits.

To avoid suspicion, he had spent some time with the family, gaming with the older kids, paying for meals delivered by local restaurants, saying hello to the more important guests.

Some of his work was legitimate, the online trading he had begun out of abject boredom had augmented his sizable stash of funds, some through blind luck and other transactions through knowledge of the energy and mining sector.

On this evening, Francois left his temporary home for some contact with people, to practice his language skills, and to maybe meet a woman. This was a calculated risk, he knew, but in city of this size the chances of meeting a business acquaintance or former associate was millions to one. He had grown his hair longer and had it cut differently, and he wore glasses instead of contacts, the thick, multi-colored frames similar to a thousand other men in the city.

He practiced for hours in the mirror, watching his own eyes, preparing to ignore a greeting such as, "Hey, Joseph, how's it going'!" or worse yet, "Greetings, Tamaz!" preparing to ignore anyone he may have known before; an acquaintance from the oil patch, or heaven forbid, someone from his homeland.

"Francois, Francois, I am Francois." He repeated this in his mind, ready to use his new ID, newly arrived in the mail. He ran through scenarios; *Someone bumps into me on the bus, what will I say? How will I respond to "unfamiliar" words in English? What food will I order in a restaurant?*

The man was sick of restraint, disgusted with studying language, tired of being patient. He wanted to hang out with some good people, eat a delicious Canadian steak and watch a hockey game with friends. He wanted to relax and *live* for a while. The loud nephews were even louder hockey fans, and hearing the games blaring on the screen in the other room was torturous, especially when the game was happening only several kilometers away!

"Patience. Use greed wisely. What is the real goal?" His thoughts were mechanical, but the mantra repeated in his room seemed to lose its meaning in the real world.

"The heck with it!" Tamaz-Joseph-Francois thought in a very Albertan manner. "I'm going to the hockey game." And ditching all pretense of being anyone but exactly who he was, he caught a bus and lost himself in the crowd on the way to Air Canada Centre.

Johnny was quickly learning the complexities of a logging operation in the final months of the season. With the chance of an early spring breakup, and the mills predicting an early close to the scales, the Banks Mountain operation was in full swing but not as efficiently as Johnny had hoped. His admiration of Chet and Melissa Banks grew daily as he realized they had done the job on their own for many years.

The task itself seemed simple: harvest the timber allotted to their company, haul it to the scale yard where it was assigned value, and receive deposits in the company accounts with which to make payroll, payments, and necessary repairs and purchases.

Breakdowns, employee turnover, delayed arrival of replacement parts, and bad roads were just some of the variables Johnny was learning to deal with. While the personnel running the logging equipment had stayed constant during the winter months, the increased number of trucks and drivers needed to haul the felled trees was becoming a problem.

Banks Mountain had eleven trucks of their own and was currently short a driver. Chet had contracted much of the hauling out to another ten owner-operators, mostly from other parts of the province, and wanted a few more. Johnny was in charge of ensuring the subs drove to the safety standards of the company, and a few of the out-of-town drivers didn't feel the unfamiliar standards were necessary. This had the big man frustrated and he went to Melissa for advice.

"Just keep working on it, Johnny," Melissa had said when he showed up at her door. "The out-of-towners are unfamiliar with the roads, the mill, our standards, everything. Most of them were out of work in their home towns or lost their contracts. I would expect that they are nervous and worried they may not measure up. Just keep working on it." she repeated, "Expect them to listen, and feel free to fire anyone you think is unsafe. We trust your judgment."

She had walked with him out to his pickup. "I know you're concerned we won't get all the wood to the sawmill. Of course, we are worried, too. We all want things to run smoothly. But Chet and I have learned that things don't always go as planned. So, we just do the best we can and deal with the problems as they come."

Johnny felt better driving back to the shop, taking time to down a sandwich and a bottle of water. The short drive was even better when he took a call from Mary who was on her break. She told him excitedly about a new manager who had transferred in, "a super nice lady, and her husband is a trucker! He'll be moving here next week and looking for work!"

He asked Mary to give his contact info to the woman to pass on to her husband right away, and then they chatted for a few minutes about weekend plans.

When his phone chimed later, he saw a text from Isaac La Crosse, asking him to call as soon as possible. Dialing, he wondered how Isaac would answer the phone.

"Thanks for calling, I'm stuck in Prince George."

Isaac had driven one of the trucks to the dealership for warranty work, and the two-hour job had turned into something bigger.

"These guys are letting me use an empty shop bay to do some work myself, but they forgot to order the parts for the warranty job, so it won't get done 'til tomorrow. They're buying dinner, so if you boogie in real quick to pick me up, I'll make sure you get a free dinner, too."

Johnny smiled to himself. It sure was like Isaac. The guy had friends everywhere. Not every business would let someone else work on his own truck in their shop. Johnny had other business he could do in Prince George anyway, so he let Pete know what he was doing, put on his headset, and aimed the big Chevy east on Highway 16.

Johnny made a quick call to Chet. The boss was enjoying his new-found freedom from all the coordinating duties and was having some fun running equipment whenever he could, a big kid in a bigger sand-box. Johnny knew Chet had been talking about adding several new trucks and wanted to be prepared for a conversation with a sales rep at the dealership.

Mary was busy at the store and couldn't make the trip with him. On the weekend she was going to Edmonton for a "horse thing" with friends, driving Johnny's pickup so she could tow a trailer home for her friend. She was so excited for the trip Johnny couldn't help but be happy for her but was surprised to find how much he didn't like the idea of missing a weekend together.

Several weeks earlier he had been invited on a snowmobiling trip and had declined, simply to spend time with Mary. He hadn't men-tioned this to her and felt solid about his decision. But now, he called his buddy and let him know he could join him after all. He was happy with this decision too.

CHAPTER 42

At noon on Friday, Mary and her two friends who Johnny described as "certifiable horse people" left for Alberta, excited for their upcoming adventure. Mary accelerated up the road, knowing her husband would enjoy the sound of the loud exhaust and the turbo charger, as well as the satisfying cloud of black smoke that was slowly drifting across the road in her rear-view mirror. Johnny watched them leave, and then drove back to the shop in Mary's car, smiling as he thought of her departure.

She had hugged him, finishing with a devastating kiss. "See you next week." The simple sentence bolstered by a deliberate wink and a quick grab of his butt. Her friends had enjoyed the show, making inappropriate comments as they tossed their gear in the back seat.

Johnny's day got even better when he hired the new trucker. The man seemed dependable, had experience, and was eager to work. With enough drivers for the coming week, and anticipating a snowmobiling adventure, the afternoon went quickly as Johnny and Pete replaced a broken spring pack and replaced the fifth wheel assembly on Johnny's old Peterbilt.

Isaac had been out on a service call and stormed into the shop with news of "a major food shortage in my little world," inviting them to join him for "the biggest burger in town in half an hour" disappearing into the shower room where he was soon singing heartily, drowning out the radio.

Pete left for home early, pausing near the door, and with an uncharacteristic impish grin, he momentarily turned off the hot water supply. The brief lull in the singing was punctuated with several choice words aimed at Johnny and Jason. They met at Charlie's Bar and Grill, their favorite – albeit misnamed – family restaurant. While waiting for food to arrive, Johnny got a call from his snowmobiling buddy who now was unable to hit the mountains on Sunday. Johnny asked Isaac if he wanted to go, but the Clockmaker had previous plans. He turned to Jason, and to his surprise, Jason was glad for the invitation, just needed to be back at work by Monday.

"My dad and brother are riding in Wells this weekend, and they were hoping I could join them." Jason was excited. "But I told them Johnny was letting me work overtime on Saturday, and old Toyota doesn't want to make the trip for just one day."He looked at Johnny. "But dude, if I can ride down with you, it's all good!"

Johnny was amused, and winked at Isaac, who asked, "What are you going to ride? You have a sled?"

They guessed Jason didn't know what he was in for; riding in the high country was challenging even for experienced riders.

"Dad said he would let me use his old machine if I got down there. I'll just call him quick and ask him to bring the sled for me."

As the young guy leaned over his phone, thumbs busy, Johnny raised his eyebrows at Isaac, wishing he hadn't invited Jason. The thought of a novice on an old machine tackling the remote mountains at Wells was not pretty. Jason left when his phone rang.

As the food was set on the table, Isaac shook his head. "I don't know, dude," he said, mimicking Jason. "At least you don't have to babysit him. He will be with his dad and brother. You can go off and do your own thing, but take a tow rope; could be a long day."

Jason came back excited. Stuffing a fry in his mouth, he announced his good news. "Just caught them. They'll load up the extra sled and bring it for me. When we get there, we can stay in the camper, free night, dude!" He looked at Johnny. "Unless you wanted to stay somewhere else."

Isaac grinned at Johnny, who took a manly bite of the house burger and closed his eyes. Charlie may be missing a bar, but the grill made up for it! Johnny nodded. He already had arrangements, so if the camper looked bad, he could just drop off the apprentice and head to his pre-arranged accommodations.

"Sounds good. If we leave at three o'clock, we can be there by eight, easy."

Jason dug in to his meal, looking happy. Johnny didn't know for sure where Jason was from, the Calgary area somewhere. Jason hadn't talked much about his home, although they knew he liked fishing and four-wheeling, sports, and other outdoor pursuits.

Saturday was pure frustration. Parts didn't come in, Jason started removing the fuel tank on the wrong truck, and the half-ton Ford they were going to drive to Wells was nowhere to be found. At 2:00 pm Chet dropped off the half-ton, out of gas and with a flat tire. There was no spare.

Finding a loose tire behind the shop Johnny used an ancient set of tire irons to wrestle the old tire off and the "new" tire onto the rim. Seating the tire to the rim using a generous spray of starting fluid and a tossed match impressed Jason. "Nothing better than an explosion to get a job done, dude!" Transportation restored, they locked up the shop, Jason going to find a spare tire from the collection at Isaac's house and Johnny leaving to feed horses and get cleaned up at home. When Jason pulled in well after their planned departure time, Johnny had his Ski-Doo strapped into the pickup and his gear in a storage container.

Snow was falling heavily and the half-ton with its motley collection of old tires did not handle well on the winter road. Jason promptly went to sleep, and Johnny listened to the radio during the drive south, missing the comfort of his personal pickup.

Pulling into Quesnel, Johnny stopped for fuel and food, eyes sore from staring into the driving snow. Jason, who had woken on the downhill drive into the small city, was worried about the road conditions.

"That was some rough visibility. Want me to drive on to Wells?" Johnny was pumping gas.

"No, I'm good." He handed Jason a twenty. "You wanna grab me a bag of food?" He nodded toward the fast food restaurant across the lot.

Jason pushed the money away. "No, don't worry about it. I'm buying." He pulled a folded sheet of coupons from his back pocket. "Mrs. B gave these to me, said they came in the mail. She's one nice lady."

Johnny smiled to himself as the apprentice disappeared into the restaurant. You just couldn't help liking the kid, though he was about finished with being called "dude". Jason's smooth face and wiry frame made him look smaller and younger than he was. Johnny had watched him throwing a Frisbee in the yard with the Banks boys and saw that Jason could move like a cat. He finished fueling the tank and checked the air pressure in the pickup tires.

Jason came out with several bags of food while Johnny was adding air to the last tire.

"Now she's going to handle a little better. None of the tires had the same amount of air." Jason tossed him a bag and climbed in the truck.

"I thought truckers always checked their tires and crap before a trip, not almost at the end?" He stuffed half a burger into his mouth and spoke around it. "No wonder Isaac used to call you guys clowns!"

Johnny laughed. "Yeah, no kidding. I think I'm out of practice. My eyes are tired from just three hours or so with snow coming at us. Used to do it all day long. But, hey, we've got less than one hundred kilometers to go, should only take an hour and a half if the roads aren't too bad."

Two hours later, just minutes from their destination, the right front tire blew, pulling the pickup off the road. Johnny lost the battle with the steering wheel, and with sheets of snow flying, the Ford came to a sudden stop on the dense snow filling the ditch.

Jason looked across, laughing as Johnny turned on the windshield wipers, clearing the snow that had blown up from the bumper. Johnny joined him. "And we were so close!"

"Yeah, and what's Pete always saying about not putting good tires on the shop trucks!" Jason, relaxed by the slow ride for the last few hours, reached behind the seat for his high boots and pulled them on.

"No problem, we're almost there. Let's pull your sled off, and I'll go get us some help."

Johnny nodded and reached back for his snow pants. He mentally ordered a new set of winter tires. Pete knew what he was talking about.

Johnny watched the tail-light of his snow machine as Jason headed up the road, then reached in the pickup box for the snow shovel he had tossed in for an occasion such as this.

He then spent fifteen sweaty minutes clearing the snow away from the front of the Ford, peeling off layers until he was working in his

T-shirt, steam rising from his wet clothes. The snow had lightened, and then stopped falling altogether, and Johnny could see stars in one corner of the sky. Good news for tomorrow.

When Jason returned, he was in a lifted 4x4 with a snowmobile deck on the back. He introduced Johnny to his brother, who said little, tossing a tow-rope toward the Ford before turning his vehicle around to hook up to the hefty drop hitch. The rope stretched, loaded up, and the Ford popped out onto the road.

Jason's brother backed his pickup close to the Ford and Jason came around and held a flashlight. The tire change was a quick one as Jerry was equipped with an impact driver and a good jack, and kept them laughing with a few quiet jokes.

CHAPTER 43

There were clumps of vehicles and trailers parked around the perimeter of a large area cleared of snow, and Johnny followed and parked near an ancient camper trailer. A fire was blazing in a metal fire ring and several people were sitting around it on lawn chairs. Several old snowmobiles were parked nearby, one missing a windshield, another's seat so torn the damage was visible through a blanket of snow.

Johnny pulled on his sweatshirt and jacket and joined the group at the fire. More introductions followed, and Johnny soon felt comfortable with Jason's brothers Jerry and Max, and their father Bill. Jason's brothers pelted him with good-natured abuse, telling stories that had the "baby of the family" laughing helplessly and dealing out some effective punches to his older brothers.

Johnny was wet and a little cold from shoveling in the deep snow, and Jerry invited him to change clothes in the trailer. There was a bare mattress at each end, and Johnny guessed the table made into another bed. He didn't plan to stay overnight there, as it looked pretty crowded.

Although it was long past suppertime, sausage was soon roasting over the fire. They loaded soft rolls with sauerkraut, onions and mustard, and when the skin started popping on the steaming bratwurst, grease hissing on the coals, they wolfed down tasty sandwiches.

When they were finished eating, Jason's dad poured each a shot of cinnamon whiskey.

"Well, Jason, it looks like you're on camera tomorrow." The gray-haired man grinned, raising his drink. "To the Drone on the drone!"

Jason's face fell while his brothers cheered and held their plastic cups for another round.

"Ah, come on, you guys! I haven't even ridden this winter! Give me a break! Run your own cameras!" He accepted a refill, shaking his head sadly at Johnny.

"Now you see why I live up in Vanderhoof. Nothing but abuse from these guys, and even my own father." He looked woefully at his dad. "Even my own *father* picks on me."

They all laughed, but Johnny was confused.

"I don't know what the heck you all are talking about. What's this about a drone?" He looked at the group. "Are you photographers?"

All eyes turned to Jason, who shrugged. Shaking his head, Bill laughed. "Let's go watch some video. Let's show Johnny what we do."

Johnny turned toward the small trailer, but Jason motioned for him to follow. They walked past the decrepit little trailer into the dark. Johnny had assumed the little trailer near the fire was Jason's family's camp. He was mistaken.

Bill led the way to a gigantic triple-axle fifth-wheel trailer and opening the door, flipped on the light. Johnny's mouth dropped open as the four guys went up the steps into the warm interior of a luxurious motorhome.

They left their boots on the welcome mat inside the door and looked back at Johnny.

"Come on in, dude!" Jason said. "You're letting the warm air out! Where are you sleeping, Dad?" Jason tossed his bag up on a bunk above the kitchen. Johnny just stood and gaped, turning this way and that. He had seen big toy-haulers before, but never from the inside. This one had slide-outs on each side, making the living area at least fourteen feet wide. The furniture was leather, the appliances shiny.

Without thinking, he blurted out a few expressive words. Johnny stopped himself, cursing was not as much a part of his life anymore. He reverted to one of Isaac's favorite expressions, earning a laugh from Jason.

Bill showed Johnny his bunk, and then they joined the three young men who were looking at a drone at the table.

"Sweet! This is really cool, guys!" Jason was grinning. "You could have told me you got the new one." Jason switched the machine on, and Johnny stepped back quickly as the apprentice picked up the controller and with confident movements, lifted the machine off the table and swivelled it around in its own axis.

"What the heck?" They all looked at Johnny, whose eyes were still wide, uncharacteristic for the big man. "I thought you couldn't fly those inside?"

"You can't, or shouldn't, unless you are Jason." Max grinned. "The kid here's pretty much the best there is." Rising from the table, he slapped Johnny on the shoulder. "Come to the garage and see the way we haul this baby."

They crowded down a short hallway, and Bill led them into a heated garage where four gleaming snowmobiles were parked.

Johnny turned to Jason. "What the heck, man, I didn't know you were a sledder. I thought you were driving your dad's old machine, you said..." He stopped talking, looking at the men who were all smiling at him.

"Wow, Jason, Mom always said you were better than me at communicating." Jerry shoved his brother. "Looks like she was wrong about that."

Johnny started moving around the machines. "These are all brand new!" He stopped. "This one hasn't even been released yet... who are you guys?"

They enjoyed his confusion, but Max explained.

"Dad used to race years ago, then got us into it when we were little. We liked it so much we all started sledding. Then we got hooked on the mountains, hill-climbing, making our own videos, ya know. Then, well," he paused modestly, "then we got sponsored, and then, well here we are."

Johnny shook his head. "And here I thought Jason was going to be riding an old piece of junk. I thought I would have to babysit him in the hills."

Jason interrupted. "Ha! You saw the old sleds by Jerry's crappy trailer... oh, that's funny!" He looked at his dad and brothers. "Why are the oldies out here, are we doing something crazy?"

He gauged their grins and turned to Johnny. "Dude, you'd better get some sleep, tomorrow's gonna be a lot of fun!"

Warm from a hot shower, Johnny stretched out in a comfortable bed, unable to stop grinning. What a jackass he had been. His uncles had always said, "Never assume," and he wished he could share this situation with them. They would have enjoyed the humor of it very much indeed. He shifted in the bed - the mattress was long enough for him; never before had he slept comfortably in a camper. He thought of the mouse-chewed foamy on the cold cabin floor where he had planned to stay the night, and grinned ruefully in the darkness, the white noise from the furnace fan a welcome companion. His last conscious thoughts before falling asleep were worried. These guys were sponsored riders, what if he couldn't keep up?

As the noisy group of sleds neared the riding area Sunday morning, Johnny's fears proved to be true; he couldn't keep up with Jason and his family. These guys were ridiculous, confident and daring, never seeming to miss a trick and there was a lot of trick riding going on. Johnny's five-year-old Ski-Doo, with its custom sticker, was christened by Jerry the "Kitty-Doo-doo" and was no match for the special-order machines, tuned from the factory for professional riding. He spent much of the day parked, watching Jason set up shots while barking orders into his microphone, his brothers and father respecting his direction.

Johnny listened to the professionals' instructions through his newly installed headset. A few hours later Jason wedged his snowmobile firmly into a sidehill and directed Johnny through his intercom, filming some flattering footage, the zoom lens making Johnny more skilled than he was. As they wolfed down protein bars and energy drinks at around one o'clock, Johnny realized how tired he was and how much energy these guys were expending. Bill, who had to be in his fifties, showed no signs of slowing.

During the quick lunch there was more good-natured teasing about the sticker on Johnny's windshield and some bawdy names suggested for the video clip Jason promised to edit for Johnny. Johnny just grinned. These guys were the real deal. He had even watched some of their previous video releases without knowing who they were.

The topic turned to the plans for Monday, which involved towing the vintage machines high up into the hills, where they would try to stage some never-before-seen footage of forty-year-old machines doing what the engineers who built them would have never dreamed possible. Bill didn't seem sure the plan would work but was willing to help the younger guys try. He was chosen as the star rider, for, as Max quipped, "his gray beard would provide the crusty, vintage look we're going for, and there's no way I'm wearing that scabby seventies helmet."

At three o'clock, Jason said it was time to go, and they raced back to the vehicles, Johnny far behind even Jason, who was slowed by the expensive drone and other equipment mounted on the extended tunnel behind his seat. Back at camp, they annihilated several pans of lasagna, commenting constantly while they watched Jason edit some of the footage.

At 5:15PM, Jason stood up and said he and Johnny had to leave. Johnny felt like a little kid. He just wanted to keep watching the tape, enjoying the arguing and brotherly criticism that Jason ignored as he worked on a laptop connected to a wall-mounted screen.

The trip home on well-sanded roads went quickly, with Jason continuing to work over his laptop, absorbed in his work, occasionally leaning over to take the wheel so Johnny could watch a short clip.

Jason drove an hour, and Johnny took the time to check his messages and respond to several questions. Even though she was out of town, Mary was making the time to coordinate the Banks Mountain schedules for the coming week. He sent her a few still shots of himself from the day's ride, and she texted back some ego-friendly responses.

As he checked the horses and fed the cat in the dark while the house warmed, wood stove glowing in the basement, Johnny evaluated his trip. He had only been gone thirty hours. He found himself grinning – had he ever misjudged Jason! He was also glad he had kept his mouth shut and not made any patronizing comments on the trip down.

The weekend was over, like the closing of a door; hours of activity and travel and then suddenly sitting alone in a quiet house. It was empty without Mary. Johnny chuckled, breaking his momentary melancholy. What a great weekend, and Mary would be home soon.

CHAPTER 44

Joseph was near his breaking point. He was a social person and had completely cut himself off from friends and the business associates with whom he had enjoyed spending time. The hours alone in the room and proximity to his dead brother's family were making him crazy. They were ruining his mind, he could tell. He couldn't stay locked up anymore, even if it was self-imposed.

After the first hockey game he had attended several more, once even using his "Joseph" identification. Nothing happened. He had skillfully stalked the social media sites of his recent employer in Alberta, as well as anyone else he had connections to, and may have missed him or been contacted by the RCMP. Nothing. There were no comments, no search bulletins, nothing that he could find. The only thing out there was a description and names of his two associates, and he knew for a fact they would remain missing for several more months and wouldn't be talking then.

He quit studying French and spent more time out at night, choosing to sleep when the family was home. He was leery of returning to the West and enjoyed the city life as much as possible under the circumstances, but he wanted to get back in the action and had information that would provide the leverage to do so. He knew names, supply routes, and some of the methods used to transport the goods; how could they refuse him? Above all, he knew the plan, and had money in the game.

It was a bitter winter in Toronto, and Joseph, the name he was using again mentally, decided to find a warm place to hole up for a while. He had enough money to live comfortably for several years without working and began searching for somewhere warm. Somewhere to enjoy life as he devised his plan to ease back into the game. A place with sun and warm beaches would be a much better place to hide out, Joseph thought. How could Canadians stand this ridiculous cold? He chose to use a series of flights, and would purchase the tickets – first class, of course – from separate vendors.

A week later, in an office several thousand kilometers west, a man's solemn face split into an uncharacteristic grin. He typed a quick message. "It's working, the suspect is on the move." A man even further west opened the message, broad smile lighting the room. He leaped from his desk with a fervent exclamation, "Got you now, sucker!" Causing several coworkers to jump, wondering who had payback coming.

Johnny was driving north on the Francis, on the way to retrieve one of the D-6 dozers for use in another location. Several days of warm weather had not been kind to the road surface, and his empty trailer was skittering on the rutted, slippery surface, each corner a challenge.

Johnny was casually enjoying the challenge of keeping the trailer on the road. Driving the old Peterbilt brought back memories of a previous time.

The week hadn't been the best on the home front. When Mary returned from Edmonton several weeks ago, it wasn't the happy reunion Johnny had expected. First of all, after Sunday evening she had not answered his texts. This had been surprising, as had the message from his insurance company regarding an incident with the Silverado registered in his name.

He'd been wise enough not to call or text Mary immediately but took time to think about how to approach her. On one hand he was worried about the pickup, but he was much more concerned about his wife. He wanted to preserve their new-found happiness, not accidentally starting something negative with hasty words.

He was used to waiting, though in the past it often ended with a resentful tirade. Things didn't get any better when a guy from the tire shop flagged him down in the parking lot of a fast food restaurant.

"Too bad about your truck, man! I saw the pictures on Facebook. Wow, you must be hot! If my ol' lady did that..."

Johnny had been calm but this was too much. He was upset Mary hadn't called him and embarrassed to get the information second hand. He sent an angry text, and when there was no response, another.

His angry messages glared back at him from the screen, and with a sense of dread he realized he'd made the terrible mistake he wanted so badly to avoid.

When she had pulled in the yard late that Monday night, he waited until she came into the house. She was hot and defensive, keyed up to counterattack the anger she expected.

When she made eye contact, he was grinning nervously. "Want to see a cool video of your husband in the mountains?"

His timing was wrong.

He guessed she had appreciated not being questioned about the truck. But it was clear she wasn't yet ready for peace; the many years of conflict and uncertainty were not yet far enough behind them.

He rounded another corner, wide low-bed swinging, snow flying as the low tail carved a trough through the snowbank. He downshifted as he began to lose speed on the hill.

"Why would I want to watch a clip of you playing in the mountains?" Johnny had waited, not sure what to say. "You are just so wrapped up in your own things!"

This hadn't been right; he was trying to deflect the conversation away from his anger. He had tried once more, "Mary, I'm sorry about my texts."

What followed made Johnny think of pouring gasoline directly on a fire. After a few minutes, Johnny had simply walked over and held her. She had cried then, calming slowly.

In the past Johnny would have walked out, allowing time – or whatever – to make things better. This was more difficult by far.

"Well, I guess we should go see the truck." Her words had startled him, he hadn't known what to expect.

"Truck, what truck?" His unexpected reply caused her to laugh nervously against her will. She had taken him out to the truck and walking around the rear he was shocked at the amount of damage. The passenger side of the box was mangled, the large rear tire had been replaced with the smaller factory spare, causing the truck to list toward the ditch. The passenger door was badly dented, and the half-door to the rear seat was torn, duct tape patching the gaping opening. The mirror was gone, and the back half of the front fender flare had been cut off. The running board was broken, hanging dangerously. He had been surprised she had been able to drive the truck home while pulling a trailer, without being detained by highway patrol.

He quickly assessed the damage, realizing Mary had side-wiped something, probably after the rear tire blew, and just spun her way out of the jam in four-wheel drive.

"Johnny, it was terrible! I must have run over something under the snow, and then by the time we had hooked up the trailer I didn't notice the tire was flat." Johnny had kept his cool, until more details came out. Even then, he expressed anger only at the man who had sold her friend the trailer and left the women to navigate a snow-covered field and then attach the trailer surrounded by farm equipment.

When Mary handed Johnny her phone with the address and phone number of the farmer who had demanded she pay for damage to his baler, Johnny found an outlet for his frustration.

Johnny called the man immediately, even though it was late, and his volume and intensity changed the man's mind. After the now-contrite man had apologized to Mary and promised to pay for a new tire, all Johnny had been able to think of through the red haze, and to drop any expectation that Mary owed him, things began to calm down. Soon the neighbor's dogs had stopped barking and several lights went back off in the closest houses. A large man pacing under his yard light and bellowing into a phone held at arm's length had ruined the sleep of a few and provided juicy gossip the next morning in the coffee shops.

"Yep, that Amund boy, he sure takes care of his woman! I mean, did you see his truck? That jerk in Alberta better not ever show his face around here! Yeah, I heard it straight from Johnny. Well, no, he wasn't actually talking to me, but I could hear him from his yard, clear as could be, even over my dogs yapping."

Mary had sobbed openly as they looked at the truck together, shaken by her husband's tirade, impressed by the authority that had not been lessened in his anger and secure in the knowledge he was her protector. When Johnny started laughing, aiming the lights of Mary's car on the truck so he could take photos, she knew it was going to be okay.

"You're telling me the tire popped, so you just held 'er down and dragged that trailer out of the field?" He photographed the clumps of mud and grass, still frozen in the wheel wells after the nine-hour drive, chuckling the whole time, anger spent.

He smacked the cold metal. "So, my baby here hauled that trailer out of the snow, even with a flat tire?" He had moved to another angle, looking at the damage caused by the heavy rubber tire disintegrating, swinging off its rim like several forty-pound clubs.

"Was the trailer okay?"

"It had some scratches, kind of took off the fender."

She motioned to the front of the truck where the grill was marred by deep scratches that ran around both sides, continuing down the sheet metal.

"What happened here, did you drive through a fence?"

"Well, I didn't want to stop the truck, and he was just standing there, he could have opened the gate if he wanted. Jill was screaming, and Sandy was laughing like a maniac, and I just held it down and we kind of drove through his fence."

Johnny saw the signature of a fence post in the center of the front bumper and noticed the license plate was missing, bracket and all. He started laughing again.

"Where did you fix the flat tire? In his yard?"

She had looked at him, incredulous. "Are you kidding? He was real mean. We called him names all the way home. I drove up the road a kilometer and called BCAA. By the time they got there, we had all the barbed wire untangled and were just figuring out how to get at the spare tire. What a stupid place for a spare! It was all frozen in!"

She had taken a breath and continued. "I know I didn't do everything right, but at least he was too busy chasing his cows to bother us. In an hour or so, we were back on the road." She had leaned against him, shivering.

"Johnny, I wished you were there so bad, but I had to handle it myself. But I was so afraid you would be mad."

She started to cry again, and his first aid training had kicked in. He recognized her level of stress, knowing she needed to get in the house, warm up, relax.

While she stood in a hot shower, he emailed her boss, letting her know that Mary was not able to come to work in the morning. When Mary had protested, hair wrapped in a towel, sipping a variation of the potent drink Uncle Lars had called "glogg", he pulled her onto his lap in front of the computer. Johnny had finally gotten the chance to show her the photos and video footage from his trip to Wells.

As he slowed the Peterbilt to exit the main road, Johnny grinned, remembering Mary's reaction to the footage. Sitting on his lap, warm from her shower, and fuelled by substantial doses of relief and spiced apple juice he had substituted for wine, Mary's comments ended abruptly when she went to sleep.

Johnny drove on as he replayed the situation in his mind. The next morning had been fine until, disappointed with losing his truck, he had suggested how Mary could have handled the situation better. Mary reacted strongly, accusing him of being two-faced; and though not as severe as the initial conflict, he was still trying to figure out how to make peace, wondering if he would ever remember to keep his mouth shut. In desperation, the only idea he had was to call Al.

CHAPTER 45

Terry was sick of worrying and was excited about the fast-approaching Mexico trip. She felt when she left the country her fears would be put on hold, and she desperately needed some relief. She had learned some strategies from her counselor, and she did her best not to let the harmful actions of others stop her from being who she was. In short, she was learning to be herself. She was learning to stop giving power to others; allowing their actions to change who she was and who she wanted to be.

She thought this through as she dug in her storage bins for clothes appropriate for her upcoming vacation, the apartment suddenly feeling too small. While it had been a convenient place to live for the winter, she was sick of it now. She opened the door and stood in the cool air, absorbing the normality around her – traffic noise, kids playing nearby.

She could see a slice of the busy street and saw a Banks Mountain low-bed cruise slowly by, one of the shop pickups looking lonely on the big deck. She turned back to her quest; maybe her summer clothes were in the red bins.

As he drove through town, filling the entire right lane with the wide low-bed trailer, Johnny was also thinking of Mexico. Without saying anything, he had cut back on his favorite soft drinks as well as the donuts and chips that had been friendly companions while driving. This had resulted in a surprising change to the fit of Johnny's pants. He would either need to buy new jeans or eat more donuts.

Johnny hadn't weighed himself in years, but he knew he had dropped some pounds since Christmas. It was Mary who had unknowingly inspired him. She enjoyed an evening glass of wine almost as much as she craved her morning coffee, and since deciding they wanted a baby, had abandoned all alcohol.

He could tell she missed it, even though she never complained, so without saying anything, he stopped drinking beer on the weekends and soft drinks during the week. This was a decent start, although his loose pants prompted complaining by Isaac and Jason about "the plumber no one had called" and "the vertical smile no one wants to see."

Pulling to the side of the highway on the way out of town, he went into a feed and farm store to purchase some new work pants. He saw some brightly colored suspenders hanging on a rack, and smiled, remembering his uncles' Husqvarna suspenders they liked to wear. What the heck, he grabbed a set of CAT suspenders and tossed them on top of his new canvas pants, the sharp, unwashed colors sure to set off a comment or two in the shop.

Walking back to the low bed, he thought back to his conversation with Al several weeks earlier. Al had reminded Johnny that forgiveness was something offered, not something waited for. Johnny had never heard this approach before. What Al had explained was simple. You didn't need to wait for someone to *ask to be forgiven*; you could *choose to forgive* at any time. This made the power of forgiveness available to the offended party."

This concept occupied Johnny's mind for several days, and he began to recognize the logic in what Al was saying. He thought of Chet who was quick to apologize when he had wronged someone. But was an apology the same as forgiving? This was sort of different: even though Chet apologized, what if the guy he had yelled at didn't forgive? Chet didn't seem to care, as long as he took responsibility for his actions, but then Chet wasn't exactly a paragon of virtue, either; or was he?

Johnny had not figured it out completely, but he knew Mary had wronged him accidentally, if at all. On the other hand, he had wronged her intentionally with his words; or rather, the motivation to say what he did. And the yet-unknown monetary value of her accident with the truck was of much less concern to their future than his critical words, which cost nothing to say, yet made recovery so expensive.

He had leaned on a stall in the stable while Mary curried a horse, and apologized sincerely, explaining why he was wrong and admitting he understood the offense he had caused. He explained how he wanted so badly to never be mean and critical again, but that was afraid he would.

The horse had been well brushed by the time reconciliation finally took place, and they had both been shaken by the days they had wasted while floundering with their inability to handle the conflict. Mary cried when Johnny admitted he had asked Al for help, and they decided they needed to spend more time with her dad and Joanne.

After parking the low-bed and unloading the half-ton, he tossed his new clothes in the washer along with the suspenders and using the hottest setting, added detergent. As the tub filled, he mixed some bleach with water in a gallon bucket, pouring the diluted mixture into the machine. That would take care of some of the new look. It had worked before.

The door to the shop opened as Johnny hastily shoved the tags and wicked little plastic ties into a garbage can, and Lance Banks bounced in.

"Hey, Johnny! I wanted to see you." He grinned. "Man, do I ever appreciate the new tires you put on the company trucks! Now these old trucks rock! I was having a lot of trouble getting around, and now I can go anywhere in the snow. Even the old man is impressed, but I bet he didn't say so!"

Chet had a new pickup, but he chose to drive one of the older beaters in the fleet whenever possible, for reasons known only to him. With new tires installed, the pickup trucks were suddenly more popular, and there had been none of the lost time with the weekly flats that had been frustrating Pete, or the mileage being paid to the men who had to drive their own vehicles that had been frustrating Johnny.

"Why should three machines be sitting there losing thousands of dollars an hour, when their operators are fixing a flat on the way to work, or worse yet, calling me to bring them a spare tire!" Pete's lament had finally got through to Johnny, and changes were made.

Lance was right, Chet's only comment had been about changing back to summer tires in the spring. Johnny wasn't quite sure if he was grumbling or not. What no one knew yet was that Johnny had worked a deal with the tire shop and would be outfitting the company pickups with sets of discontinued, and therefore discounted, mud tires when the snow melted. The old pile of used tires had been hauled away, and no one could be tempted to install used tires that were barely legal.

While Chet didn't say much, Pete was a happy man, and would be even more so when Johnny had the commercial mud tires installed next spring. With their heavy sidewalls, the tires were notorious for a rough ride which would slow down the drivers. The safety bonus had

Johnny grinning; fewer flats, and not so many trips in and out of the ditch.

Johnny's thoughts were cut short by a call from Isaac, who needed parts. Johnny quickly assembled the supplies, loading them into the same pickup he had ditched with Jason not long ago.

Lance opened his lunch bag, and shared a big chunk of smoked fish, and they both chewed while admiring the grippy snow tires. Lance set his fish on the hood of the pickup, not seeming to mind it was crusted with road grime, while he struggled into a pair of coveralls without removing his boots.

"Chet just smoked this?" Johnny took another bite as Lance writhed against the dirty pickup, left boot refusing an easy descent through the leg of the formerly clean coveralls.

"Yeah, he said it was the last of the salmon in the freezer. I sure hope I get to go with him to Rupert next summer!"

Johnny knew Chet kept his boat in Prince Rupert and fished as often as he could, which had not been very much in the past five years. Lance won the battle with his boot and shrugged into a non-combative reflective vest.

"Hey, you going fishing when you're in Mexico this spring?" The Banks had taken their kids on a trip to Mexico seven or eight years earlier and had done some deep-sea fishing. Having all enjoyed the trip, Chet bought a boat the following summer, and the family used it several times each summer.

As Lance climbed in the pickup, Johnny told him a few details, then gave instructions on where to find Isaac. He watched the pickup leave the yard, thinking. Johnny was looking forward to the trip, but he was concerned for Terry. He was not sure it had been a good idea to invite her and Isaac to join them. She seemed fragile, like she was close to losing it. He had to admit she was doing a good job driving; her lack of experience on the snowy bush roads was more than compensated for by her dependability and eagerness to learn.

He sighed, understanding women was not easy. Mary was still edgy about the wrecked pickup, and it probably didn't help that he still had not replaced it, rather choosing to insure an old beater he had parked in the back of the property when he bought his Silverado. He was too busy to look for a new pickup, and wasn't sure he wanted to commit five years of payments for a new truck at the moment anyway. It was simply easier pull the old GMC out of the snow and make a few simple repairs, deferring the decision of fixing or scrapping the totalled Silverado.

CHAPTER 46

The logging season ended suddenly with an untimely rainstorm in March. Chet watched the weather forecast religiously, as did Pete, and they decided late one afternoon that the equipment had better come out of the bush immediately.

Johnny was parking in his driveway when he got the call.

"Johnny, it's going to rain." Chet's voice was excited. "You seen the forecast?"

Johnny hadn't, but he had heard Pete mention it a dozen times that afternoon and guessed what was coming.

"Let's keep the trucks hauling around the clock until we get shut down. I've got my brother's low-bed for a week, and I'll use it to haul the smaller machines while you and Isaac bring down the big iron. We're guessing they'll close the road."

Chet was excited, the challenge of what he was proposing and the risk that he could be wrong bringing a surge of adrenalin, on which Johnny knew the older man thrived.

"Johnny, get some sleep. I've already asked the machine operators to work as long as they can, and then get their machines ready to haul.

The processors and loaders can keep on working. We'll haul them last. The more wood we get out now, the easier we survive breakup."

Johnny was now in the kitchen and put Chet on speaker so Mary could hear too.

"Okay, Boss. I will make a schedule of who gets picked up first and let the guys know. Are your boys ready to pull some big shifts?"

Lance and Daniel were proficient on all the machines and when available, would substitute when a worker was sick.

"Yep, the boys are ready to go. They both went to bed to grab as much sleep as they can. Call Melissa whenever you need them, and she will get them moving.

Mary weighed in. "Okay, let's make it happen. If you think we need to do this, let's get right on it." The men both waited while she paused. "But we are not going to let anybody work too long, and we will even drive the guys home if they are too tired, right?"

While he ate a quick supper of leftovers, Johnny thought of the job they would soon undertake. They had two full operations going, and each round trip with the low-beds would take three to seven hours, depending on the location of each machine, road conditions, and how loading progressed. The biggest machines hung over the side of the low-bed trailers, and the high cabs needed to be tipped down hydraulically and secured, booms propped with supports, and everything chained down.

If indeed it did start raining, the frozen roads would quickly turn into a gigantic luge course, and chains on the trailers would be necessary to stay on the road.

Mary made Johnny take a hot shower before going to bed, and while he showered, she took notes of which machines needed to be hauled first, using several phones, conferring with Isaac and Pete.

Isaac voiced the concerns that were bothering them all. "If the roads get shut down while our equipment is out in the sticks, well, we can kiss a happy breakup goodbye! All that work will need to be done out in the weeds, or mud and ice, and the roads are going to be rough going with the pickups. Plus, we need to get a lot more loads out. All the timber sitting up there in bunches on the ground's not worth a cent until it's hauled!"

Within thirty minutes, they had a good plan, and Chet and Melissa helped make the calls.

Three hours later, four men drinking coffee at a window seat in Charlie's Bar and Grill on the highway noticed several Banks Mountain low-beds roll past, followed by another owned by Chet's brother.

"Hot darn!" A retired contractor grabbed his phone and called his son-in-law who was running his company. "Hey, Sam, the Banks's low-beds are all heading out. What does Chet know that we don't?"

Johnny called the mill, and after several conversations between five-minutes waits on hold, and a little pressure on the men who had grown to respect him in the last five months, they agreed to keep the scales open all night. Chet was happy. The company would not be paid until the wood was at the mill; each extra load made the financial situation during spring breakup a little more comfortable.

As Johnny made the turn north, his mind was busy. It was minus nine Celsius on a Thursday evening and the roads were perfect. He didn't know if he hoped Chet was wrong or right. Melissa Banks was riding with him so she could drive the big grader to a different location. If Chet was correct, they may need the big machine with its serrated ice blade to make several steep sections of road safer. Melissa had made it clear she would not be doing any grading, but she could drive the big beast home if needed.

Jason was following them with the sand truck, loaded far beyond legal weight. His brother, Jerry, was riding with him. Jerry had been on his way to spend a long weekend riding in Smithers, stopping for the night in Vanderhoof. When Isaac found Jerry had his Class 1 license, he had quickly notified Johnny who asked him to come along as a relief driver. Jerry agreed and was hired on the spot. The young guy was stoked. His normal job driving a fuel truck was boring compared to this.

Mary worked the phone until close to midnight and found four more drivers who were willing to work the weekend hauling logs.

In perfect conditions, the Banks Mountain trucks hauled all night, enjoying several hours of low traffic. Morale was high. Chet had rarely been wrong in this type of decision and pulling together for a final sprint was an adventure no one wanted to miss. Several of the wives disagreed.

As the sun came up on Friday morning, and the temperature stayed well below freezing, it appeared that Chet had made a very bad decision, and he took some ribbing over the radio from other contractors. But he was soon vindicated when a storm warning was issued just before noon, with snow and freezing rain expected to make life in the Central Interior very difficult.

Sand trucks were loaded, schools were emptied quickly, and generators were tested all around town. By three o'clock, rain began falling in the Nechako Valley, freezing on contact.

Hurrying down the North Road with a large loader chained to his deck, Johnny called Mary to check conditions. She was breathless, having just arrived home in the dark and was putting her horses into their stable. She told Johnny how she had driven into the driveway, and as she put her car in park, it began to slide sideways, ending up wedged against a snowbank. She warned him that the steps were coated with ice and to be careful when he got to lower elevations.

"Johnny, why don't we offer to park some of the equipment at the farm?"

He was quiet for a long time. The farm was a taboo subject. Johnny still owned much of the property his uncles had farmed. After their deaths, he had been surprised to discover they had transferred the various title deeds into his name many years before their accident. He seldom went to the farm, choosing to lease the land to a local farmer. Mary knew he didn't like to think of the farm, though wasn't sure why. She secretly hoped they could live there someday. She thought it would be a wonderful place to raise a family, the old farmhouse with its view over the valley, the rolling fields and stands of timber.

Johnny was thinking as he down-shifted carefully, keeping his speed low for the long descent. The farm was on the shoulder of the hill above the Nechako Valley, and the fields were accessible from the North Road. Chances were the rain in the valley would be snow at the higher elevation, possibly several hours or more before the warming temperatures forecasted would turn all precipitation into rain. At his present location, wet snow was falling heavily, and the unplowed road was becoming very rough.

Unloading the equipment at the farm would save at least forty minutes per trip, keeping the heavy trucks from traveling through the heart of Vanderhoof on icy streets. He made the decision.

"Okay, Mary, call Lance. He's about twenty minutes behind me in the grader. I'll open the east gate on the way by and he can plow a big area for us to unload. I will take this load through to the shop, but the rest of the equipment from the North Road can all go to the farm. Tell him to plow a really big area."

Then he was quiet for a moment, and Mary was silently thankful for his decision.

"We can do a lot of repairs right there if need be, and if the road bans are not slapped down right away, we can make a lot of short hauls at night and move the machines to the shop next week."

He felt better after the talk with Mary and keyed his mic to warn traffic he would be blocking the road for several minutes.

Climbing back in the cab, caked with snow and sweating from struggling with the wire gate that had been frozen into the plowed snowbank, Johnny left a message on the renter's answering service. The machines from the Francis would be coming to the shop from the west and would not need to travel through town. There were only four trips left up the Francis, but a lot of heavy iron to retrieve from locations on the North Road. Mary's idea was solid, and he felt lighter somehow, a sense of well-being that cut through his weariness.

The snow turned to rain just below the farm, and as he carefully navigated the icy streets, he was shocked at how quickly a town could be shut down by the forces of nature. He grinned when he saw a hockey game, and then another, enterprising kids skating on the glassy side streets, screen time set aside for some real adventure. Cars were abandoned on the icy streets, windows quickly glazing with ice. Several sand trucks were patrolling the highway through town, though the heavy freezing rain quickly encased the sand and salt.

CHAPTER 47

J ohnny unloaded the big loader in record time and aimed the Peterbilt back to town, stopping at the card-lock to fuel up. Leaving the fuel station, he drove a short distance up the highway to Charlie's. He had called ahead, and someone from the truck stop ran on cleated shoes through the rain to bring him a sandwich and a giant cup of coffee; they treated their regular customers well. The gang at Charlie's Bar and Grill were going to be very, very busy for the next few hours. Their lot was already jammed full, and people were gingerly walking from the vehicles toward the warm and friendly building, bright neon sign rotating high above the parking area. He poured the hot, black coffee into his thermos, saving several inches in the cup to drink right away, savoring the potent brew. Charlie knew his way around coffee beans, that was for sure.

The RCMP officers who had closed the highway allowed him to proceed when he explained his destination. They looked cold in the blowing rain, reflective slickers shiny in the headlights. Johnny climbed down from his cab and called the restaurant, asking that they send some hot coffee out and to put it on his tab. The officer who overheard his conversation grinned his thanks and told Johnny he "would catch him later!" The big trucker replied, "I sure hope not!" as he climbed back into his rig.

When the Forest Service Roads were shut down nine hours later, the Banks Mountain crew were exhausted, but happy. There were a few machines left in strategic locations, as Chet and Johnny hoped they would be able to haul more timber if the road was reopened.

The east field in the farm was littered with equipment. It could be organized later. Chet wasn't sure how Johnny had pulled this one off, but agreed it was an excellent idea. He knew the farmer was in Arizona or Florida, or somewhere warm, and hoped Johnny had taken care of the details.

More of the story came out the next morning at the Banks' kitchen table. The last several days had been a whirlwind of activity for the Banks family, and they had seldom seen each other, although there had been heated words and several miscommunications. Family tension was running high.

Melissa decided the bickering needed to stop and made a big breakfast when she heard the boys stirring in the basement. She called Chet to come home from the shop, and soon they were all sitting at the kitchen table.

Daniel, freshly showered, was upset. "Dad, listen. When I am doing something, you can't just tell me to do something else! Johnny had a good plan and you kept butting in and screwing everything up!"

Normally not one to confront, his words provoked a brief and surprised silence.

"Well, good thing you didn't listen to me then!" was Chet's hot reply, an instant before he burned his mouth on coffee fresh from the percolator. The choice words aimed at the coffee also applied to the argument.

Lance interrupted, and Melissa was grateful as she wiped up the coffee and handed Chet a glass of water.

"Hey, how come we parked all the equipment in that field north of town? Like, what's with that, anyway?"

Melissa shrugged. "Mary called me and told me Johnny had a plan to save some time. It worked, too. We got a couple more machines hauled, and all those trips through town and the roadblock were prevented. Good thinking as usual from our Big Guy."

Daniel, still grouchy, nodded toward his brother. "Yeah, but Bonehead here sure took a round out of that field. He plowed up a lot of dirt with the grader, we probably have machines over about three acres, at least."

Lance, unshaven and shirtless, was in no mood to be picked on. "Hey, the ground wasn't frozen under all the snow! Sure, I ripped up some dirt, but I had to hurry, Isaac was only about ten minutes out when I started, and I had to give him room to turn around. Then I had to pull him, and yeah, we made a mess, but come on. It's just a field!"

Chet intervened. "Guys, listen. We pulled off a pretty good bunch of work in two days. Let's knock off the arguing. If there's damage, we can pay for it; it's fine."

Lance wasn't finished. "Wait a minute, I want to know more about that farm, and why Johnny could get permission to use it."

He emptied a glass of milk. "About two in the morning, I rode down with Johnny to get the grader and bring it back up to clear some snow. We were tired, and Johnny said we should go up to the house for some coffee. "He shook his head, taking a bite of eggs, interrupting his own story. "That guy is pretty cool. Did you know on one of his back hauls he loaded up his Ski-Doo and dropped it off with all the equipment?"

They looked at him blankly.

"So?" was Daniel's reply.

"Well, we were tired, and Johnny said we should go up to the house, you know the one..."

"We know which house, so what about it?" Daniel was still angry.

"Really! Just listen! So, I doubled up behind him on his sled, that was quite the ride, and when we got to the house Johnny pulled out his keys, unlocked it, and in we went."

Now Melissa was curious. "No one was home?"

"No, we went inside, and I asked Johnny who lived there. He told me no one was there, and it was okay for us to use the house. He got some coffee out of the cupboard and put water in the pot and stuff, and then said he was going to take a shower! I was like, 'Dude, you can't just take a shower in some random house!' and he told me to relax, and don't touch anything."

The kitchen was silent. The youngest had their attention and liked it, taking time to stuff more food in his mouth.

"Well?" Daniel broke first.

Around his pancakes, Lance continued. "So, I turned on some lights and looked around. It was actually kind of creepy! It was clean, too clean, and the stuff was all wrong, somehow. There was a '55 Chevy on a calendar, but the calendar was from 2006! There were old Ritchie Brothers auction flyers on the table, no, I didn't actually move anything!" he said in response to Melissa's raised eyebrows.

"It was like a museum, like the people left years ago; everything was old! There were coats hanging on hooks in the entranceway, work boots, some fishing poles. There were cross-country skis in the living room, and like I said, it was kind of creepy. It was like going to the Hudson Bay Company museum in Ft. St. James, except the stuff was newer. There was no dust or anything and the can of coffee didn't look old, but the place looked, uh, deserted?"

"What the heck?" Chet was intrigued. "Melissa, do you think Johnny still owns that place? I assumed it had been sold, went to the bank, I don't know."

The boys looked puzzled. "What do you mean?"

"Johnny's uncles were both killed in an accident ten, twelve, maybe fifteen years ago. That had been their farm, and Lars lived there. That's where Johnny grew up." Chet looked at his wife. "He has never mentioned it. Are you telling me he still owns it?"

Lance swore, earning a quick reproof from his mom. "Well, that would explain a lot. There were pictures on the wall, you know, one of those frames that has space for a bunch of photos?" He pointed at a similar display on the wall in the hallway.

"Well, there was a baby, a little kid, and three more pictures of probably the same kid through school. In the last picture, he was for sure in high school, real tall, blonde hair. It looked a lot like Johnny. I thought maybe the house belonged to a relative. Then he came out of the bathroom, and I seen he had changed clothes."

"Saw!" Melissa corrected. They all looked at him, waiting.

"Oh, he got diesel all over himself. Well, I actually got diesel all over him when we refuelled up in the bush, that's why he wanted to shower. I asked him where he got the clothes and he said he borrowed some from the house. They fit him fine, but they were those gray work clothes, you know, like old guys wear. He had on orange suspenders, like the set you got from Grandpa, Dad, Husqvarna.

"I mean, what are the chances that Johnny would find clothes to fit him? Like, the guy that lives there must be one big dude!" He ate some more food.

"Well, Johnny seems to play his cards pretty close." Chet rubbed his unshaven face, "Worked for us all these years and never said a word." He chuckled, "There's enough land there he could probably work for himself, what a guy!"

"Oh, and you know something really weird?" Lance had more to say. "When we left, after we had some coffee, I pretended I was going to put on a little hat that was hanging in the entranceway. There were a bunch of old hats on a shelf, and a few hanging up on hooks, must have been at least ten or fifteen John Deere hats, but off to the side was a little straw hat, down lower than the rest, like for a kid. When I reached for it, Johnny told me not to touch it."

He looked at his parents and brother. "I said, 'Dude, okay, I'll leave it alone!' Like, come on, it's just an old hat. Why would he be so touchy? He kind of yelled at me."

Daniel raised his eyebrows. "I don't know about you, but I wouldn't want him mad at me. I mean, he's friendly and everything, but when he says to do something, you just want to do it."

"Yeah, that's how it was, except I was actually kind of scared. Or something. Whatever the case, I left the hat alone. He didn't actually even raise his voice, but I got the message loud and clear."

"Well, that's what you get when you mess around, kid." Melissa ruffled his hair, looking at Chet over the boys' heads.

Later, when the boys disappeared to the basement, Chet stretched out the footrest of his favorite recliner, turned on the television, and asked Melissa to wake him in half an hour. She paused by his chair, looking down at her husband.

"I'm proud of you, Chet. You did real good this week. We could have been caught off guard if you hadn't been willing to take a risk."

He reached up to take her hand and saw her eyes were wet. He squeezed her hand firmly. A minute later she set his hand down on the armrest. Her husband was fast asleep.

CHAPTER 48

Johnny ducked his head, shuffling sideways as he followed Mary down the narrow aisle. They were boarding the plane in Prince George that would take them to their connecting flight, which would fly straight through to Mexico.

He chuckled as he heard Isaac in the aisle behind him, accusing Terry of "grabbing my butt" and telling her to "keep your hands off," and her embarrassed laughter as she denied all contact, hands full with her carry-on bag and purse. Isaac shifted the blame to an older lady who enjoyed the attention and actually followed through with the action Isaac was protesting, to the delight of several other passengers.

The atmosphere in the front half of the small plane was almost riotous by the time they were seated, and the elderly woman was the star of the show. The flight attendants turned a blind eye when she shared a small flask with Isaac, seated directly behind her, and the flight she had been dreading became a highlight of her winter.

Mary had done her best to get seats with enough room for her husband, a rush of gratification when he noticed and thanked her warming her face. She knew he would be asleep long before they reached the

Rockies and had brought a book she planned to start on their flight and finish while she tanned on the beach.

They had been extremely busy for the last several weeks. The end of the season had come in several stages, none as convenient as the loggers hoped for each year. The mechanics had been busy with repairs and retrofits. Isaac and Chet preferred to wait until something was broken, while Pete, Jason and Johnny preferred to replace worn parts before it was necessary.

Chet had gotten it into his mind that they might go back to work early, and he and Johnny's stress while working with several manufactures on new equipment purchases concerned Mary. She knew Johnny realized he was somewhat idealistic, but he also wanted to do a good job during his first breakup season as foreman.

She could hear excited voices and good-natured teasing from several rows ahead. Isaac had something going with a white-haired lady, and the flight attendants were joining in. She stretched her legs as the plane taxied on the wet runway, smiling when she thought of her conversation with her dad the night before. He had teased her for her excitement, like he had when she was a little girl anticipating her birthday party. He also prayed with her before their call ended, something he had never done before, and after some thought, she decided that she liked it.

Johnny was already snoring softly in the window seat as the plane departed the northern capital, signature plumes of steam from the pulp mills rising in parallel, slanted salutes to the hopes, dreams, and sorrows of the individuals sharing the sturdy capsule climbing into the cold, gray sky.

Mary's novel slipped to the seat beside her before the drink cart came by, and the flight attendant smiled wistfully as she tucked a small blanket around the shoulders of the striking young woman, face relaxed in sleep. The attendant noticed she was holding the large hand of the sleeping man next to her and envied the aura around the couple. Someday, she thought, someday.

A larger aircraft was already at altitude, swiftly closing the distance between Toronto and its destination. The first-class section was dim, its westbound occupants on track to reach their destination within the four hours promised earlier that day. In a first-class window seat, a passenger lounged, face obscured by the hood of his immaculate track suit. A soccer match was ending on his small screen.

Johnny woke in time to see the Rocky Mountains, marveling at the huge expanse of rock and snow, the incredible cloud formations. Mary was leaning on his shoulder, a flimsy blanket tucked around her. The thrum of the engines was a sound Johnny enjoyed, the flexing of the wing outside his window pleasing to his machine-oriented eye.

Lift, gravity, thrust, and drag. His uncles had been fascinated with the principles of flight, and together the three Amunds had built several gas-powered remote-controlled airplanes. The construction had gone well on both occasions, the first as an exhibit for a science fair when Johnny was in elementary school, the second a few years later because they had enjoyed building the first.

Flying the airplanes had been a different story. Each plane had suffered a swift demise, the science project, piloted by Uncle Lars, bursting into spectacular flames on the roof of the tool shed. The second project had barely flown, smashing squarely into a tractor, young Johnny unable to handle the unfamiliar controls

The attendant came by, and seeing Johnny awake, asked if he

would like something to drink. She brought him a cup of coffee as requested and seeing the humor in his eyes when he took the small cup that looked miniature in his grasp, she returned quickly with a larger paper cup of airline brew. He thanked her for the coffee and for bringing Mary a blanket.

As they approached Calgary, Johnny thought back to the previous weeks. After the push to bring the logging equipment home, there had been some real problems to deal with. The heavy rain, following a winter of exceptionally high snowfall, had caused flooding unprecedented in the valley's recent history. The un-melted snow collected water and sponge-like, doubled and tripled in weight. Many buildings had been damaged severely, including the grocery store where Mary worked. Local building contractors worked together, combining their crews and resources, with an army of volunteers. The story of this community effort had been nationwide news, but more importantly, had saved many buildings and their contents from serious damage.

Students worked beside members of the town council to fill sandbags and pump water from basements. Churches set up stations for food and shelter. Coffee was free at Charlie's, for anyone who was helping, needed help, traveling through, or reporting. The complicated message on Charlie's sign on the highway once again brought a needed shot of compassionate humor to the community, and gallons of liquefied caffeine were dispensed freely.

Chet was seldom seen in town, spending his time, and a considerable amount of money, helping those he called "my favorites," the elderly people who lived out of town. Once again, Chet and Melissa were taking care of business. He had brazenly hauled his thirty-ton excavator through town despite the weight restrictions in place on the roads.

They had been pulled over by an angry commercial vehicle safety officer, who demanded Chet park his truck immediately and wrote up an excessive, if deserved, fine. Melissa had stormed down from her side of the cab, and through tears of anger and despair, explained the situation to which they were going. The ice-covered Nechako River had risen quickly, and large ice jams had scoured the trees, fences, and anything else off the lower deltas in the valley. At a farm down the river, a herd of cows had been trapped on the far side of a now-raging stream. The rancher had been unable to move hay across the water, and the cattle were starving. Worse yet, they were calving, and over twenty newborn calves had already died, either by drowning, trampling, or by wolves and grizzly bears preying on the herd.

Chet hoped to divert the floodwater from the trapped herd, and at least get some hay to the hungry animals. To the credit of the harried officer, he escorted Chet to the farm, and later when his shift was over, came out to the farm where he and his two teenage daughters spent six miserable hours helping Chet and the hastily assembled crew.

Johnny was glad the ordeal was over but knew that many good things had taken place because of the crisis. He settled against the side of the plane and thought about Mexico with Mary.

At thirty-thousand feet, Joseph was on his way out of Canada and was pleased to have encountered no difficulties. He would be landing in Calgary, waiting several hours, then planned to buy a ticket for the next stage of his trip. If anyone happened to see his name on the manifest, he reasoned, they would think he was staying in Canada, coming back to Calgary. In his mind, departing from Toronto or Vancouver to points south would cause more alarm than a simple flight within the country. Plus, there had been no interest showed in him at all. This was disconcerting, as his self-imposed exile may have been unnecessary.

A basketball game was now playing on the small screen and he ignored it, looking forward to warm weather. He smiled. Being smarter than the other guy had served him well, had always resulted in success-ful ventures. Who knows what sort of leverage he could build to get back into the scheme without being the grunt, the one who took the risks? He dozed, almost relaxing.

CHAPTER 49

Their exit from the connecting flight was almost as rowdy as the entrance. Isaac insisted on waiting to escort his elderly new friend from the plane, and enjoying the attention, she told everyone squeezing their way down the aisle. "thanks to my new boyfriend, I know how to Snap Chat and Twitter!"

Terry had changed places with the lady during half of the short flight, and Isaac had found her to be a fast learner on her new phone, purchased just before her trip.

In the terminal, Terry and Mary hurried directly to the ladies' room, while the men followed the signs to collect their luggage. A restless throng waited at the baggage carousel, a flight must have been late. After several minutes, Johnny's phone pinged in his shirt pocket, and he read a text from Mary aloud to Isaac.

We stepped outside for some fresh air its warm here lol and no snowbanks! Tell me when you get our bags. The words were followed by a string of heart emojis.

"Must be some delay on the tarmac." Isaac looked at his watch.

There were three tired suitcases making a continual circuit, but the luggage from Prince George had not yet appeared, and their fellow travelers were still waiting, some of them grumbling, checking the time.

"You sure made that older lady's day!" Johnny turned. A young woman holding the hand of a toddler was talking to Isaac. "It was so nice to see her have a good flight."

She paused, the toddler doing his best to pull her toward the vending machines nearby. She leaned back good-naturedly, smiling at her little boy. "I was talking to her in the Prince George airport. She was very nervous, I guess she doesn't like flying."

Johnny nodded toward the vending machine, pulling out some change. "I need to get rid of these Canadian coins. Could I buy your big guy here a drink?"

She nodded, releasing the toddler, the four of them following his haphazard trot and cries of "Appa joose! Appa joose!" Johnny had enough coins for two drinks, and he squatted down to open the matching bottles of apple juice with his new buddy.

The young woman said. "You know, if I hadn't seen the way you were so kind to the old lady, and the way you guys were so nice to your wives, well, I would have been afraid of you! It's too easy to simply look at someone and decide what they are like." She became flustered. "I mean, um, you guys just look tough, not bad, but..." She gave up, flushing.

Isaac fed some coins of his own into the machine, leaving Johnny to answer.

He just grinned. "We know what you mean, it's fine. We're a couple of big guys, and we don't mind if we look a little scary. Just don't tell our wives." He grinned over her shoulder at the look of genuine panic on Isaac's face. "They would tease us and probably make us cry."

She still looked embarrassed, so he went on. "We're on the way to Mexico for a couple weeks of vacation. We work for a timber harvesting company and have been going hair-straight-back for a few months, need a break. Where are you going?"

She lit up. "My brother's getting married. Tyson here is the ring bearer." She smiled at the little boy who was slurping his drink. "Our whole family is getting together!" Her phone rang, and excusing herself, they drifted apart, travelers enriched by the short connection.

An agent from the airline came over, apologizing for the delay. Johnny missed the reason but did hear "ten minutes." As they were in no hurry, it didn't really matter, so they chatted as they waited, discussing the fishing they hoped to do, and the weather forecast at their destination.

Isaac's phone rang. "Terry," he mouthed unnecessarily. He replied a few times and turning away, muttered something that sounded a lot like "love you too" eyebrows squeezing together at Johnny's snort.

"Shut up. They're hungry, so she said to meet them at the food area when we get the bags."

They were not in a hurry for the first time in months, but both men were impatient, not used to the slow pace over which they had no control.

"So, how's Terry doing, you know, with the whole thing?" Johnny asked, glad for the chance to talk with Isaac in private.

"I don't know, man. She goes up and down." He drank from his bottle of iced tea, grimaced, and tossed it in the nearby garbage can.

"You know, I've actually been *praying* for a quick conclusion. I mean, how much can a person take?" He shook his head, drawing attention to his Canucks hat. It had seen better days.

"How can people do stuff like that, and get away with it?"

"Isaac, do you know that my mom disappeared? No one knows what happened, where she went, nothing."

Isaac reached for a smoke and remembered he'd quit a long time ago. This was a conversation he had never wanted any part of. He'd heard the rumors of a disappearance, and also heard about what happened to a few guys who had made disparaging remarks about it in Johnny's presence.

He looked at Johnny, realizing they had become friends, the real deal. Johnny looked grim.

"You know, Terry could have disappeared just like that. But she didn't. And I think we are basically the only friends she's got. Besides her family, we're it, right?"

Isaac nodded, wanting to hear this out.

"She likes you, Isaac. And you need to make sure you don't get yourself or her hurt." He held up his hands, palms toward his friend.

"I'm not telling you what to do. It's just that I care for both of you, Mary does too, and we want things to work out, you know?"

His chest felt tight, throat dry, hoping Isaac understood.

"I get it, Big Guy. You are right, and you're not out of line. We've had this conversation and are trying to be careful. We think it will be okay."

"But how do you live with this unresolved problem? I grew up living with the fact that my mother is probably dead. But maybe she isn't. What if she hated my father for leaving, hated having a baby, whatever? She could've been a victim, or maybe she's a bad person and I'm the victim?"

They sat on a bench silently, watching the carousel turn, a variety of suitcases now sliding down the chute onto the belt, people collecting their luggage and leaving. Their own bags were coming by again.

Isaac stepped up to collect their bags, and rejoined Johnny on the bench.

"You know, Isaac, I will probably never know what happened to my mother. It's tough, man, and I didn't even know her. But I'll keep on waiting. I doubt if I will ever give up. I've been angry, sad, gotten into fights, was a jerk to my uncles and Mary sometimes. I have been mad at myself. I can't imagine the pain of losing a son or daughter, or someone you're close to."

He looked over at his friend, his face bleak.

"And none of it has helped. I used to make up stories when I was little, about who my parents were, and how our lives could have been perfect. I won't even get into what I know about my dad, although recently I found out it's maybe not as bad as I thought for years."

Isaac leaned forward slightly, eyebrows raised.

"I can tell you about that another time. But while we are in Mexico, why don't the four of us have a good talk about the whole thing? I think I'd like to tell you what I know of my background, and how I've been learning to live my life in the right way. I know Mary would like it if I did. We're sure a lot happier than we were a year ago."

Isaac nodded. "That's straight-up obvious and we all like it, I really mean it. Charlie has been bragging about you guys. He's always liked you, says he always knew you were a winner. Liked your uncles too, you know."

Johnny deeply appreciated the compliment from Charlie. When Johnny was young, the teenage Charlie had worked for Lars and Nelsson on the farm. He had always guessed they had financed Charlie when he started his restaurant. After the accident that claimed the lives of the Amund brothers, Charlie had been there for Johnny with kind words, many meals, and a few deserved reprimands.

He stood. "Let's go join the ladies. We'll talk more later. You and I are going to figure something out, and we need to plan to do it soon, for Terry's sake, and for yours too."

CHAPTER 50

Mary couldn't stop smiling. Her normally optimistic attitude was at its peak. She was so happy. The short flight from Prince George had gone by quickly. She felt rested after the brief nap on the plane. It had been a late night with the final preparations of leaving her horses in a friend's care. The unexpected fun on the first leg of the trip was a good omen, at least in her opinion.

The weather in Calgary was different from the winter landscape west of the mountains. A Chinook had blown down several days before, and the snow was almost completely gone, at least what she had seen from her brief walk into the bright sun outside.

Now, sitting in an airport cafe with her husband and friends, she only had a few nagging worries. There was that order at the store, but no, Justine would cover that... her horses, well, they would be taken care of... The only other thing was the underlying sadness Terry couldn't hide, the way she was always looking around, staying close to Mary while in the airport.

But they were sitting in a circular booth, the men in the middle, using Isaac's tablet to look at new pickups. "Mary Rip-n-tear" was Isaac's new nickname for Mary, and she was no longer bothered when they talked about Johnny's wrecked Silverado, although she had moved it behind the shed, so she didn't have to see it in the driveway.

She grinned across at Terry, who like herself, was leaning on her man's shoulder, not paying attention to the talk of aftermarket turbos and which exhaust system would be the best. She toyed with her sparkling water, a luxury she had discovered while avoiding liquor, and mouthed, "They're just little boys. When will they grow up?" her words just loud enough to penetrate the fog of guy talk and cause a few distracted protests.

"Used or new?" This was the discussion of the moment. She didn't care. Johnny would choose well, and as long as the new truck pulled her horse trailer better than the old GMC that Isaac had quipped "needed to go back to its 'rustful retirement'" she would be happy. They had several hours to kill before catching their next flight and relaxing in the unfamiliar atmosphere of a large airport was a treat.

She and Terry stirred from their relaxed state when the boys suggested catching a cab to go look at a used pickup near the airport, horrified at the possibility of missing their flight or having to leave the guys behind. Idea nixed, the online shopping and comparisons went on. The tablet disappeared magically, however, when the food arrived, and the conversation turned back toward their resort and activities of the week.

The quiet meal was interrupted as a large group of people flooded past the lounge; a large flight had arrived, and several hundred people were moving to their next gate.

"Terry, where did you say you've travelled before?" Mary looked over when her friend didn't answer, instantly alarmed when she saw Terry staring at the crowd, pale and drawn.

Mary unconsciously reached for Johnny's hand, watching Terry's pretty face turn fierce, nostrils white, lips parted slightly.

She was shivering. "Guys, I just saw Joseph." Her voice was strained, quiet.

"Where, what does he look like?" Johnny's voice was calm. He reached out and held Isaac from rising and blocking his view, motioning for Mary to move out of the booth.

"White coat with green stripes, Adidas shoes, too, I think. About five foot ten or so, slim, walking ahead of that group. Looks like a soccer player."

Johnny was standing, but Isaac was still seated, craning his neck around, trying to see. What the heck did a soccer player look like?

Johnny leaned down, hands on the table. "Terry, are you sure?"

She looked up, serious. "One hundred percent, absolutely sure."

"Okay, Terry, call your RCMP contact, right now. Isaac, let's get him."

Mary slapped his arm as he pushed by, realizing her gesture was identical to the way she sent her horses into the pasture. Terry fumbled for her phone. Mary sat and dialed 911, then motioned for Terry to stay in the booth, and followed the men, phone to her ear.

Joseph was hungry and decided to eat in the international departures area after he purchased his ticket. He was walking with the crowd into the familiar terminal, the exhilaration of success filling his thoughts, his whole person. He could see sunshine pouring into the huge building. There would be a lot more of that where he was going. He straightened his jacket; one sleeve had caught against his leather duffle bag. He loved expensive things, couldn't resist buying a new jacket and shoes to match, delivered to his apartment door.

The bag he had bought in the Toronto airport, overpriced for sure, but the smell of leather was worth it, and from the appreciative glances of a few business travelers he felt good about his purchase. A few more hours, then he would be out of Canada. Time to hit the reset button, make a plan.

The 911 dispatcher was patient, but it was difficult for Mary to explain the situation. She wished she hadn't called or could think what to say. "I will contact the airport police, or maybe you can call them." She was sure Johnny and Isaac could take care of the situation until Terry's contact arrived. She hung up and sprinted in the direction her husband had disappeared.

Johnny and Isaac soon could see the Adidas jacket on the slim man ahead of them. They drew a few reproachful looks as they hurried with the throng, moving faster than the flow. Johnny put his phone to his ear, chatting away, disappearing as best a big man could do. Isaac moved off to the right, looking for a clearer path.

Johnny was surprised to see Mary pass them without comment, walking quickly, her backpack bouncing rhythmically from side to side, a big golf umbrella in her hand. Umbrella? From a gift shop? She didn't acknowledge him, but kept going, passing the slim man in the white jacket. She pulled her phone from her hip pocket, looking at the screen, a worried traveler trying to make her connection.

Johnny glanced toward Isaac's position, he wasn't there. Looking back, he saw an airport cart with several elderly passengers had cut off the flow of foot traffic, and Isaac was at least twenty meters behind. He looked ahead. Mary had moved into the path of the man, and stopped, looking around. What was she doing?

Joseph looked up to see an attractive young woman in his path, scanning around for signs, looking at her phone. She was pretty and she needed help. He slowed, the crowd moving around him.

Johnny was stuck behind a group of foreign tourists. They were elderly, moving in a group, six wide, wielding carts and cameras. He would have to go around. He saw Mary stop in front of the man and watched him slow, looking at Mary and nodding.

Joseph was pleased. Maybe he would have a dinner companion after all, especially if she missed her flight. Maybe he could delay her. Here it was, opportunity. He grinned. Her serious profile was more than pretty. She turned.

Joseph had faced many problems in his life and had proved to be cool under pressure many times. But when the woman turned, he was not looking into the face of a beautiful, needy woman, but the fierce and dangerous eyes of a predator. He stopped, shocked, will to survive coming to life. The prey that was not prey at all. He tensed to bolt, and she dropped her umbrella. His hesitation sealed his fate as she stooped quickly in front of him, reaching down to pick it up. Her body and swinging backpack shielded her movement as she quickly straightened, the heavy wooden handle of the cheap umbrella slamming into his crotch.

A big man was kneeling beside him, comforting arm across his heaving shoulder.

"It's going to be okay, man. Here, let me help you to a seat." The big man lifted him, one huge hand gripping his wrist, the other a vise on his belt. He called to another man for help, and this one, also big, gripped his elbow with one hand, other arm wrapping around his ribs. The tourists pushed past, a few curious looks.

"Appendix?" The big man let go of Joseph's wrist and mimed a sick stomach with his free hand, and the elderly travelers moved on, unconcerned.

A woman pushing a cleaning cart walked over, asking if they

needed help. The big man with the beard shook his head. "No, my friend is sick from his flight. Is there a private restroom we can use?"

She pointed and headed back to her cart, happy she had been of service.

Johnny and Isaac quietly helped the ailing man into the nearby family restroom, Mary watched from across the passage, feeling a wave of remorse. She probably wouldn't have needed to swing the umbrella so hard. She looked at the thick, curved wooden handle, now cracked. Oh well, if it was the wrong guy, she would need to apologize for sure. Hopefully, she wouldn't get sued. She called Terry.

CHAPTER 51

A uniformed security officer had noticed the men and stopped to talk to the cleaner. He liked the middle-aged lady who had been working in this section for the last few months. She always had a kind smile, and her English was getting better by the week, but at first she had said very little. He asked her what was up with the sick man, and she explained how his nice friends were helping him because he "needed the help to be airsick".

He grinned and walked over to the washroom door. He grimaced and moved away. The sounds he could hear over the hum in the terminal were proof that she wasn't kidding, the guy was sick alright! He hoped he hadn't made a mess she would have to clean up later.

Walking away he repeated her words, hoping to relay them to his girlfriend that evening. "He needed the help to be airsick." Cute. Learning English had to be tough, eh?

Terry had the presence of mind to pay for their uneaten meal when a concerned waiter came by. She assured him the food was fine. She had just ended the call with the RCMP officer, who was on the way to the airport. She told him that the men traveling with her would try to watch Joseph until he arrived. He told her that an officer was near her in the airport, stressing that the woman was working under cover. He said her name was "Lucy" and she would recognize Terry from her photo.

When Lucy took a call on her cellphone, she caught on right away, and told her fellow officer she felt she knew where the Adidas-clad suspect was, and that yes, indeed, he was being watched. She wheeled her supply cart to the restroom and put an Out of Order sign on the wide door. She grinned. Her role at this point was to detain the man, and it seemed to her that he should be quite safe with his new friends, now that she knew who they were. She checked her phone again, and slid back into character, scanning the area for the woman named Terry.

Feeling very alone, Terry decided to leave the restaurant and follow the direction her friends had disappeared. She was loading all the deserted bags on an abandoned cart when Mary arrived, breathless, holding a cheap-looking umbrella. It was Terry's turn to be surprised at the expression on Mary's face, features made more striking by the look of pure, aggressive victory.

"We got him!" She held up the umbrella, then tossed it to Terry. "Look what took him down!"

Terry held the umbrella and looked back at Mary, an expression on her face that Mary later described as "dumb".

She fingered the cracked wooden handle, looking at her friend, not sure whether to laugh or cry.

"I wouldn't touch that," Mary smiled like a Valkyrie. "That wasn't cracked before it practically lifted Joseph off the ground. He won't be feeling frisky anytime soon, I guarantee that!" Her expression turned serious. "I sure hope it was Joseph though." She looked at Terry. "You're sure it was him, right?"

"Where is he?" They were standing outside a gift shop, and an employee walked over, seeing them discuss the umbrella.

"Johnny and Isaac took him into one of those small, family bathroom things. Then a cleaner walked over and put an out of order sign on the door. Strange, huh?"

The employee reached for the umbrella. "You don't want this one, it's cracked. How about this one here?"

"No thanks, maybe another time." Mary smiled, leaving the borrowed umbrella with him as they walked back the way she had come.

They were met by a woman in a cleaning uniform walking quickly toward them. Mary recognized her from the scene by the restroom.

She motioned them to the side, directing her attention to Terry. "Terry Mason?" When Terry nodded, she continued. "My name is Lucy, I am working here under cover." She showed them a badge, motioning randomly, as if giving directions.

"Oh, hi. I was expecting you to find me." Things were moving fast, but Terry was keeping up.

"Terry, are the two big men with you?" When Terry nodded, she turned to Mary. "And you must be Mrs. Amund?"

Mary was impressed, and slightly flustered. She had hung up on the 911 call and had just disabled and possibly injured the suspect. She chose to say nothing, nodding her head instead. Oh well, she inwardly shrugged it off; she was willing to take one for the team.

Terry's reply was brief. "Yes, they're with us." "We're on our way to Mexico."

"Okay, would the two of you come with me back toward the restroom? That way I can watch the door, and the two of you as well. I don't want to blow my cover, but I will if need be." She turned away, then back toward Mary. "You know, everything happened so fast, I couldn't see what happened!" She broke into a big grin, sliding back into her character, perfect English changing to that of a new immigrant. "And here I thought it was the airsick, who knew you could get umbrella-sick in Canada!"

In the spacious restroom, Joseph knew he was in serious trouble. First, he was trapped, in horrible pain, and didn't know what these guys had on him. Were they cops? They didn't look like cops. How did they find him so fast? How could they be watching the airport so closely? It didn't make sense.

His neck and throat ached. He heaved again, into the garbage can. The man with glasses had made him clean it up last time.

The big man's words had been simple, and he cringed inside when he replayed them in his mind. "Joseph" he'd said, "we know who you are, and you don't want to know who we are. You're going to give us some information while we, uh, help you get better."

Maybe that was it. Maybe they weren't cops but were the competition. Maybe he could buy them off? And so, he tried. They listened, and he could tell they were gauging his answers, amounts of money, how he could transfer it. He wished they would say something, but they just looked at him.

He talked some more, saying too much, pain clouding his judgment. How had she ambushed him with a stupid umbrella, right in the middle of the concourse, and no one even noticed! He didn't even put up a fight! He cursed himself silently, then cursed the woman, the men, and the stupid idiots he had trusted to fix the situation.

His brain was sabotaged by fear, and the pain. He was opening his phone, accessing information, showing amounts in his hidden accounts, telling how he could transfer money and close the account, and no one would know. At least he thought no one would know.

The man with glasses was working on his own phone, and activating the noisy electric hand dryer, he made a call in the far corner of the room. The big man just looked at him as he held himself shamelessly, rocking back and forth in agony.

"Tell me more, why did you do it? Why try to kill the woman?"

He was almost blubbering now, the pain and fear and shame of being caught had ruined his cool, his confidence. His track pants were stained with his own vomit. "She had to go, she knew how I was transporting the dust." He wasn't sure how much the man knew, and the more he talked, the more details rushed out. "I couldn't let her live, man, you should understand! She could have busted me at any time, she had to go."

He drank from the bottle of water the man had handed him earlier. "You know how it is, I can tell you're in the same line of work. I made a mistake, chose amateurs to get rid of her, they couldn't do it, so they had to go too."

The man with glasses came back, shoving Joseph's phone out toward him. "Okay, we're going to transfer all the money you have in this account," he shook Joseph's phone, "to another account."

A surge of hope flared through Joseph's distress. They weren't smart enough! He had only showed them his smallest accounts. He would only be giving up a few hundred thousand, a small price to pay to get away. He felt a little confidence returning through the pain.

Johnny wondered what Isaac was doing. Was he actually taking money from this guy? Was he setting him up? He was still shaken from his earlier actions, but his anger had receded. When Isaac had closed the door behind them, Johnny had released the man to the floor where he immediately vomited, angering Isaac, who told him to clean it up. When the groaning man cursed the woman who hit him,

Johnny's vision blurred and his pent-up anger found a mark. Though he couldn't hear the words coming from Isaac's mouth, the expression of both fascination and horror on his friend's face had penetrated Johnny's madness. He found himself pinning the man to the tiled wall by his throat, feet dangling. Thinking of his father, he had recoiled, dropping the man, who sprawled on the floor, gasping and retching.

He thought he should redirect the conversation and asked another question.

"So where are the guys who came out to get rid of the woman?"

Joseph didn't answer, busy working on the money transfer. He paused to clutch himself briefly, swearing softly, trying not to cry. He still wasn't sure how the woman with the umbrella was connected. Was she with them? But she had to be. He handed the phone back to the man with glasses, who entered a string of numbers and walked back to the corner, looking at both phones.

"Where are they?"

Joseph looked up and swallowed. "I sent them back to Alberta. I don't know where they are." It didn't sound convincing, even to himself.

"There are going to be more people coming to talk to you. I don't really care if you give me the information or not, but they will."

He broke, confidence oozing away again at the thought of more people coming. These two were just the hired guys sent to catch him? It made him feel even sicker than he already was.

"I met them in Jasper. I overheard some guys talking who were loading a shipping container with supplies for the next summer. I hid the men in the container, told them it was their escape route. I don't know where it went, but it was going be locked up way out in the hills, somewhere near the park."

He rubbed himself again, shifting position. "I needed to get them away, out of sight, everything was happening so fast. They were so dumb they would have ruined the whole thing." He spoke quickly, breathing shallowly through the waves of pain.

Johnny's face stayed calm, but inside he was angry. This was a sick man. It was bad enough to try to kill Terry, sending two thugs to do it. But to send them to their death too? The guy was selfish and deluded. Johnny was sick of talking with him. He was crouching beside the man kneeling on the floor, and when he shifted to stand, the smaller man flinched.

He looked toward Isaac, the large room suddenly feeling too small. He motioned his head toward the door. Isaac mouthed back, "Two minutes."

Johnny turned back, making eye contact with the groaning man who was still writhing on his knees.

"Why?"

Joseph thought about it. "I want to be rich," he hissed through clenched teeth, "I want to do what I want. Just like you, right?"

"What were you smuggling?"

Smuggling? The word seemed wrong, something wasn't right. Maybe these guys weren't players, maybe they would let him go. "Just goods, stuff, anything to make some coin." He lied, smoothly, he thought.

The man with glasses walked over. "It's done, let's let him go." He looked down at Joseph. "You stay in here for at least ten minutes, we're gone."

He walked out, the big man following, closing the door behind them.

Joseph counted to twenty, then relaxed, reaching over to lock the door. Ten minutes! He wasn't leaving even that soon!

Ha! He had done it, bought them off with only a portion of what he

MICHAEL SHENK

was willing to pay. They hadn't pressed him for details; his secret was still safe. Now, he'd wait until he could walk and go buy a ticket. His phone was gone, they must have taken it. He closed his eyes, leaning back on the door, wishing for a bag of ice. He hoped no one else was coming, slumping over on his side.

Chapter 52

L ucy saw the two men come out of the restroom, stepping around the cart, pushing it back in front of the door. She was cleaning a small kiosk close to the family restroom, watching closely, heart-rate accelerated. Her supervisor was happy to work with the RCMP, assigning Lucy a lenient and flexible schedule.

From a bench further up the concourse, Terry also saw the men exit the room. Johnny wasn't smiling, but Isaac had a look about him that made her nervous. His grin was hard, too cynical for her liking. Lucy was talking into her radio, moving back toward the cleaning cart. What was happening, was it over? Everything was moving so quickly, but slowly too.

Walking to meet the women, Johnny looked over at Isaac. "What the heck, man, did you actually transfer money from that guy?" Isaac didn't answer but frowned and shook his head at Johnny as the two women rushed up to them, faces tense.

"Where is he?" Terry demanded. "Is he still in the restroom? You didn't…?"

Isaac put an arm around her, grinning at the three of them, "Oh yeah, he's still alive in there!"

"Johnny, is he, uh, okay?" Mary looked contrite, shaken by her vicious attack.

Ignoring the question, Johnny asked one of his own. "Terry, how soon will the RCMP be here?" Johnny was scanning up and down the concourse.

"There's an undercover officer watching the door, the rest will be here soon." Terry looked at her phone. "Oh, they are in the building. That was a couple minutes ago."

They all turned, watching the restroom.

Johnny saw a cleaning woman walk over to the restroom, taking down the sign on the door. Two men with briefcases moved up behind her, pausing as she smiled apologetically and moved her cart away from the door.

Joseph had been watching the shadow of the cart from under the door, and when he saw it move, he opened the door and hobbled out into the concourse, his limp pronounced. He was shocked to see a man in his path. He was even more surprised when the man showed him a badge, and shoved him back in the restroom, followed by another who also flashed a badge.

The four friends watched, looking around an airport cart that was now blocking the door; the occupants in khakis and winter jackets sitting relaxed, one behind the other. Several minutes later the door opened, and Terry saw Joseph clearly across the concourse. She saw fear and anger in his features, and then he looked her way. With Isaac's arm around her she felt safe, and she simply looked at him. He stared back at her as the officer seated him. She was relieved he didn't yell threats or try to get to her. He just watched her until he was seated, and the cart disappeared silently in the foot traffic.

They stared after the people in the vehicle. They looked like anybody or everybody else in the airport. No uniforms, no sirens, no drama.

The cleaning lady pushed her cart past them, looking over momentarily. "I hear you are on the way to Mexico?"

Johnny shifted his feet, puzzled. How would she know that?

Terry broke away from Isaac and gave the woman a hug. "Thank you so much, Lucy! Thank you so much!"

The cleaning lady smiled broadly and pushed her cart back toward the restaurant, turning once more to wave a graceful hand. "Have a nice trip!" she called back, accent more pronounced.

The women had tears in their eyes but smiled at the confusion on the faces of the men.

"Are you telling me she's an undercover cop?" Isaac was incredulous, and the language that followed caught the attention of several people walking by, earning him a few scowls.

Johnny started to laugh. "Oh, man, am I ever glad we didn't rough him up! All she saw were a couple of nice guys helping a sick friend. That's righteous, dude!" His slip into Jason's slang made them all laugh.

"Now, what?" Mary was concerned. "Do we have to stay here, or can we go to Mexico?" They all looked at her, then at the time.

"We don't board for two hours, a little more if we push our luck." Isaac had the timing figured out, his internal clock and love of numbers still front and center. "If they need to talk to us, it shouldn't take long."

He looked in the direction the cart had disappeared, then at Terry. "Why don't you text the RCMP guy, what's his name?"

"It's Long."

Terry looked at her phone, "Oh, here is a message from him. "Wait for me, at your gate," she read, "We need to talk before you leave." She looked up, "Well, there we go. Hope we don't miss our flight." Johnny took Mary's hand, "You have a story to tell! Getting around us and stopping him in his tracks – what got into you?"

She interrupted him. "I'm starving. Let's go through security and then get some more food. They've thrown ours away by now." She smiled. "Do you realize we were all sitting at the table together less than half an hour ago?"

On the walk to their gate and security check, Isaac tried to keep the mood light. Johnny was brooding, and the women were close to tears.

Isaac caught their attention. "You know, I don't think I'll be able to lie on the beach at the resort."

Mary took the bait. "Why not? Scared of sunburn?"

"No, it's all the giant umbrellas, just standing there..." he paused dramatically, "waiting for scary Mary here." There were a few weak smiles as he continued, "Did you say she cracked it?" He stopped walking abruptly. "I need to go buy that, what a souvenir!"

He mimicked Jason. "Yo, Isaac, what'd ya bring me from Mexico, dude?" He switched to his own voice, emphasizing the unique accent. "Oh, here you go, Jason. This may look like an umbrella, eh, but you see, it's really a nutcracker. When I seen it, I just knew it was the gift for you!"

It wasn't really that funny, but they all laughed, tension having its effect.

"Why do you say I *seen it*? You should say, I *saw it*!" Terry had asked this before, and frustrated, she turned to the Amunds, hands outstretched. "What the heck! It drives me crazy!" They all laughed some more, unable to answer her question, or even try.

Seventy-five minutes later, they were free to board their airplane. Officer Long had interviewed them all, referring to Lucy's notes.

Who was Lucy? Mary wondered; what was her real name, why was she stationed in the airport? She looked around, wondering who else could be someone they did not appear to be – there was a lot of that going on.

Joseph had appeared to be Terry's friend – but wasn't. Johnny had appeared to be embittered for good – but wasn't. Terry had been fearful, depressed - and that too, would soon be changing. Mary wondered about herself, not recognizing the glow that set her apart from the woman she had been a year earlier. Being and feeling loved agreed with Mary Amund.

Officer Long was excited and easy to talk to. "You guys were really in the right place at the right time! We were tracking this guy. His real name is not Joseph, as you may have guessed."

He smiled at Terry. "We have had him under surveillance for a long time. He was living in Toronto." He rubbed his hands together. "This is a good day! And don't worry, we have a line on the other two. There's a chopper in the air as we speak. Hopefully, they'll be in custody this afternoon."

He watched the men closely as he said this, Johnny noticed. He was relieved Isaac didn't say anything, but it was obvious Long noticed his sardonic grin.

Officer Long knew Joseph had talked to them and Johnny wondered if there would be any follow-up questions for him and Isaac.

"Terry, we want you to know that to the very best of our knowledge there is no one else out there. From the emails and text messages we have intercepted, it seems, uh, Joseph was involved in a scheme to salt a gold mine."

They looked at him blankly.

"Our theory is, and we won't know for sure until spring, that they were taking small amounts of gold nuggets and gold dust up to mining claims in one of the Territories. It appears a consortium has slowly been buying a large number of claims across the North. We think they were planning to hire a prospector to test these claims, salted with all this gold they have been smuggling, and write up a report on 'the new bonanza!' Start a fake gold rush, so to speak. With a report such as this in hand, they could sell their pretty much worthless claims for a lot of money, especially to foreign investors who were looking for a quick buck in Canada."

"So, you're saying I hauled gold up to Joseph from his guy in Red Deer?" Terry was incredulous. "Gold? This just doesn't sound as dangerous as drugs, or guns, or whatever! And hey, what was I hauling on the trip south to Red Deer?"

"On the way down, you actually were transporting bags of pay dirt to be processed. From what we know at this point, some of the claims do have gold; just nothing special, nothing to make them valuable. They couldn't set up a processing operation on the claims without drawing unwanted attention. So, they sent the pay dirt south to be processed, and what gold they found could be sent north later with the gold from other sources."

Isaac interrupted, "This doesn't even sound smart, if there was already gold, why bring up more? And, I thought you could tell where gold is from, the chemical makeup… oh they probably mixed it with the dirt that they sent down, hoping they could get away with it." He nodded to himself, voice trailing off.

Long nodded, "These guys were in for the big score. We believe this was a long-term project. They probably were waiting until the price of gold went up again before selling."

"So, we had better be quiet about this?" Johnny smiled, but his tone was serious.

Long nodded, then raised an apologetic hand as he took a call. He walked away for less than a minute, rejoining them as he buttoned his phone back in his pocket.

"Weird, the guy chucked his phone in the toilet. The tech guy says it was wiped completely clean of fingerprints, he's checking it as they drive. Makes you wonder what Joseph was thinking." He shook his head again. "Smart guy though. He tried to blame you guys for taking the phone, took us extra time to find it. Tech says it was underwater too long, totally done."

Johnny was watching closely out of the corner of his eye, and he would have sworn Long winked at Isaac.

"So, you're telling us that Joseph was just one of the guys moving this gold into the north? Why wouldn't they just haul a truckload of the stuff up there?" Terry was harsh in her relief, tone more demanding than normal.

She continued, watching Long, who didn't reply, allowing her to continue.

"So, Joseph tried to kill me just to keep himself safe and hired the other guys to do it for him?"

Long kept nodding, mouth pursed.

"So, there is no one else out there looking for me, just Joseph and the two other guys?"

"Until we have confirmed the whereabouts of the other two men, we are not entirely sure. We hope to know in a few hours. But our best guess at this point is that no one else in the scheme even knows you exist, and no one has any reason to wish you harm. Except Joseph, of course. But he should be our special guest for a long time." He laughed – a man pleased with the situation.

"I wish I could tell you details about the team that has been working this case."

"But then you'd have to kill us." Isaac deadpanned, earning smiles from them all.

CHAPTER 53

When Long said goodbye, Johnny walked with him toward his exit.

"Is there anything else we need to do, uh, any follow-up?"

Long shook his head. "No, I don't think so." He glanced at Johnny, "So, that was your wife who stopped the guy, with an umbrella?"

Johnny just looked at him, waiting, no expression on his big face.

Long grinned. "You ever been told you're a poker player, son? No, the phone in the toilet, the umbrella, I don't think it will matter at all. He pretty much spilled his guts already. Living in hiding has him stretched near his breaking point. Our guys in Toronto didn't think he could make it much longer without a nervous breakdown."

He looked at Johnny closely. "I am guessing he said something to you about the other two guys. We sent a chopper out looking for them, and they already found a shipping container in the middle of nowhere in some sort of supply compound. It's near the National Park. The weather has been above freezing for a week, and they noticed this container with a lot of ravens circling. Some local guys are taking snowmobiles up there as we speak. I don't envy them at all.

"Maybe you shouldn't mention this to the women, could put a

damper on your trip. We will contact Terry when we have them in, uh, custody, and let her know we, uh, tracked them down."

He put out his hand, shaking Johnny's with a firm grip. "Terry has my contact info, and I have hers. If anything comes up, just give us a call. Enjoy your trip!"

Johnny walked back to the gate, smiling when he saw his wife and friends, thankful for the resolution. He knew he would do his part as Terry healed. He guessed there would be bumps in the road, but he was a trucker, a logger, and was learning to be a husband – and a brother. He had proven his ability to handle trouble in the past and knew that he would handle more in the future.

He knew it was time to talk with Mary about his past, and maybe a few close friends as well. It was now the time to face fear, reluctance, sorrow; whatever was holding him back. Maybe it was time to start farming, keeping the dream alive, the dream that had given hope and sustenance to his uncles, the dream that could become his own, and that of his children.

He thought of the forge he knew was stored safely in its box, hidden in a special place on the farm. He thought of the bar of ancient metal, greased and carefully wrapped in oilcloth, waiting for him or another Amund to replicate the work of an ancestor. He thought of tradition and honor and love and sacrifice. He thought about being a child and being a parent.

And settled comfortably next to Mary high above the earth, he thought about cool water and warm sand, and fighting mystical fish on the blue ocean swells. He thought about friends. He thought about loving his wife, holding her in his arms.

He was Johnny Amund. He could always have a brother, and he would always be a brother. He slept.

Later that afternoon: Calgary International Airport

The woman was exhausted, and while her husband went to order some fast food, she took the children into a family restroom she knew was always clean. She wasn't disappointed. The room smelled fresh, tile gleaming – the little joys. The baby was sleeping in his car-seat while she changed the three-year-old's diaper. It was time to finish potty training, but they had been so busy, so many trips. She pushed her hair back from tired eyes, and smiled at the baby, so small, so cute, so loved. She leaned down and kissed the toddler, making him giggle.

The four-year-old girl was bouncing, excited. She would have her birthday party soon after they got home.

"Mommy look!" she squealed, pointing at a cheerful poster on the wall.

"Shhh, don't wake the baby!" It was hard to be kind, but little Sarah had been so good, so patient.

"But Mommy, look! It's the hospital where we took Baby Stevie!" She wondered why her mommy started crying when she looked where Sarah pointed. The bright squares of color she saw on the sign at the hospital and now recognized on the big poster made her feel happy.

"It's okay, Mommy, Baby Stevie is getting better." She hugged her mommy's leg. "I'm going to share my birthday presents with him, that will make him better too!"

A little later that afternoon: Alberta Children's Hospital Accounting Department.

"But sir, really! It just came in this afternoon. How do I handle this so late in the day?" The weary manager sat up straight in his desk as he processed what he was hearing.

"Okay. What you're telling me is that a little earlier this afternoon we were given an anonymous donation of almost a quarter of a million dollars?"

He was standing now, his despondent search for good seats at the hockey game forgotten.

"That's right!" The breathless voice of an employee in the accounting office replied.

"It's anonymous, came in from an offshore account! We don't know what to do!"

"Well, that's just fine. We love donations! Just put it into our present drive. If something is fishy, well, we'll deal with it later."

Dinnertime: Calgary RCMP Forensic Unit

The technician smiled as he searched through recent activity on the phone. Someone had made a large deposit that afternoon, emptying an account, shifting the money to another. He entered the code into his computer.

"Hey, Boss, you've got to see this!" he yelled over his shoulder. "I think we've got the original jokester at work here."

A few minutes later, the boss chuckled. "I agree." He rubbed his thick hands together, now openly laughing. "Are you kidding me? They had him in the bathroom, and they transferred his money to a local charity?"

As he walked away, the tech called him back. "What do we do with it, let it go?"

"Well, why the heck not?" He shook his head and swore. "I like these guys' style; yes indeed, I truly do!"

He walked away, then stopped, and turned back, still grinning.

"Hey, listen, we got all we need. That phone was reported destroyed, so go ahead and destroy it now, stop digging. We really don't need to know any more."

Summer, 1991, Williams Lake, British Columbia

She moved slowly up the crowded street, enjoying the fit of her scarlet serge jacket and tall, black boots, mirrored columns in the sun. The summer heat was intense. She didn't mind. The parade would be starting soon at the Williams Lake Stampede. She had been chosen to represent the RCMP, riding at the head of the parade with her commanding officer, carrying the flag. Her new community was fascinating. She couldn't help responding to the excitement and traditions of the Stampede, and she looked forward to the rodeo dance that evening when she would be off duty.

From the saddle she scanned the crowd, recognizing several faces, a few friendly nods directed her way. Her posture was strong, her eyes were clear Her face did not convey the happiness she felt inside, the growing confidence, the relief of feeling useful and wanted.

Then her eyes narrowed, and she reined her horse to a halt. She sat very still, captivated by a scene directly in front of her.

Two big men were standing on the sidewalk and her attention was drawn to their strong, calm presence. One of the men bent down, holding a small, straw cowboy hat out to a young boy, whose shock of blonde hair was bright in the sun.

His little cheeks were flushed, and his sturdy chest was heaving, eyes shining. "Hello, Uncles, I was playing with..." His voice was excited but measured and trailed off when he saw the hat being offered.

"For me?"

He looked expectantly from sober face to sober face, taking measure of the gift.

"Thank you!" He took the hat with both hands, holding it out, turning it, looking inside, identifying the back. He put the hat on his head, tipping it back to look up at the men. He smiled.

"Thank you."

Her breath caught. The men looked strangely familiar, and then she knew exactly who they were – a hospital on a terrible winter day. She stared fiercely at the vignette playing out on the sidewalk, background noise fading, vision tunneling into a clarity she had never experienced.

One of the men stepped forward, calmly pushing a side-stepping Appaloosa firmly back onto the street, its young rider yelling her thanks.

The little boy's face was shining, quietly grateful, looking at the men soberly. But then his face fell.

"But what about Sammy?" He turned, indicating the dark-skinned boy behind him.

The men turned, looked, turned back to the boy.

"What about Sammy?"

"He doesn't have a hat." He took off his hat, holding it to his chest with both hands, looking up at the men.

Together, both men's stern faces creased into momentary smiles, and they nodded at each other.

"Vell what about dat!" The man in the Ritchie Brothers hat nudged the other, putting a large hand on the blonde boy's shoulder.

"Let's go find dat Sammy a hat." He stooped slightly and put the hat back on the blonde boy's head, and motioned kindly for the other boy to follow, stepping out to cross the street.

The little boy looked both ways as they began to cross, reaching protectively for the hand of his friend. He squinted up at the RCMP officer on her horse, face breaking into a grin. He stopped momentarily, looking straight into her eyes.

He was safe! The abandoned baby was loved and healthy and safe! The smile that both softened and strengthened her features was a promise fulfilled, a promise of healing to come.

"I got a new hat!"

He waved at her, then, checking both ways once again, he ran forward, pulling his friend with him.

"Come on, Sammy, let's get you a hat!"

The big men crossed the street at a more sedate pace in front of her. She saw one of the men nod at his brother and heard the quiet words he spoke.

"See? Dis is good. You can always have a brother, you can always be a brother."

www.ingramcontent.com/pod-product-compliance
Ingram Content Group UK Ltd.
Pitfield, Milton Keynes, MK11 3LW, UK
UKHW020837120325
456141UK00003B/187